A DOSE OF FEAR

Dianne Haley is the author of
The Resistance Girl Series:

The Watchmaker's Daughter
Under a Brighter Sky
A Light to Guide Us Home

DIANNE HALEY

A DOSE OF FEAR

A DOSE OF FEAR

www.diannehaley.com

ISBN: 978-1-0684408-0-9

Typeset in Adobe Garamond Pro
and Bebas Neue Pro.

For Martin

Chapter 1

Ella was putting her coat on when she heard glass shattering and a scream from the other side of the open-plan office.

She took a few steps towards the noise – her instinct to help uppermost – and saw a girl leaning over the pieces of a large, shattered, glass vase, blood pouring down her wrist and dripping on to the floor. Flowers and water were scattered over the desks and the brown carpet. Ella couldn't take her eyes away from the blood on the girl's arm or the piece of glass sticking out of her flesh. She felt her throat constrict, breath coming in gasps.

Some of her colleagues were trying to mop up the blood. It was as if Ella were all alone, set apart from the activity in front of her. All she could hear was the sound of her own breathing and she felt dizzy. Looking away from the girl's arm, she saw on the floor a pile of white tissues, stained deep red, snaking over the dark carpet.

All she could see was her sister's body in a pool of blood. She took a step back abruptly into Nicole, who was following closely behind her.

'What's the matter?' said Nicole. 'What's happened?'

'It's Ruth again,' Ella whispered, hardly able to speak. 'All the blood.' Her legs were suddenly unable to hold her up. She clutched the nearest chair to keep her balance. Nicole grasped Ella's arm in a painful grip, bringing her back to her senses and helping to steady her. Someone came running past them with a first aid kit.

'Are you all right?' asked Nicole, staring at Ella.

'I don't think so.' Her voice sounded strange, higher pitched than normal. 'I can't stay here any longer.' She lurched out of the room, walking quickly into reception and towards the door, nausea rising.

She waved a hand at the doorman and opened the glass door, moving to stand away from the people streaming out of the building. Gulping in huge breaths of air, she tried to push down the nausea and ignore the petrol fumes of the traffic in the street outside the South London office.

The normality of everything she could see calmed her down: people walking home from work, the road lit up with street lights and headlamps, the sound of London buses grinding along. The street was busier than usual, Christmas celebrations already started with December just around the corner.

After a few moments, she stood up straighter against the glass panel. There was someone crossing the street towards her. She blinked two or three times to clear her vision. It looked like Jamie Forrester. It couldn't be him. He was the last person she wanted to see. She could feel her heart beating and the nausea rose in her throat again. He couldn't be here. Frozen with dread and unable to move left or right, she looked wildly around for a way out.

The man stopped a few feet in front of her to look in a shop window and she saw that it wasn't Jamie. He turned and walked away without looking at her and she bent her head, knowing that her mind was playing tricks again. She hadn't seen him since his brother's trial and she'd sworn then that she would never encounter them again. Ben Forrester had ruined her world, had taken her sister's life away and all Jamie had done was support him, giving excuses for how he'd behaved. And now she was beginning to see Jamie everywhere.

Ella scrabbled sideways towards the door. It had opened and a group of people came outside. She took her chance and slipped in. So desperate to get out of the office only a few moments ago, now she wanted nothing more than to escape from the world outside. She ran past the doorman and through reception to the back, panting as if she really was being chased and couldn't get away.

Standing at the window in the corridor at the back of the office, she leaned against it and looked over the unkempt car park, taking a deep breath, the cold air from the open window flowing over her flushed cheeks. As the pain in her chest began to ease, she knew she had overreacted to the sight of blood, but thinking Jamie had been there made everything around her become a threat, a constant reminder of how she could never get free from the death of her sister or the man who had caused it.

She was aware of someone coming to stand next to her and heard the familiar voice of Mary, who ran the small homeless charity and worked tirelessly to keep it afloat.

'Are you all right?' asked Mary in her calm voice.

'Not really,' said Ella. 'All that blood…' She couldn't continue.

'I know what it looked like.' Mary shook her head and pursed her lips, watching Ella closely. 'It's been very difficult for you over the last few months. I know you refused it before, but I still think you should take some time off,' she went on. 'Your contract was coming to an end at Christmas anyway and I know you've already done the handover. I think a holiday would be good for you. You'll easily find another contract in the New Year when you're ready.'

Ella didn't reply, unsure if she could deal with the hours of empty time which would face her at home, she and her parents struggling with their memories of Ruth. She usually enjoyed looking for her next contract, found her freelance life exciting and challenging, but, now, any optimism for the future seemed hard to summon up.

'Nicole told me you think you're being followed,' Mary said.

'I keep thinking I'm seeing Jamie Forrester. I thought I saw him today but it was someone else. Other times I'm sure he's behind me, but when I turn around, he isn't there.'

'Are you sure? Why would he do that?'

'Because of his brother. It's Ben who's behind it,' replied Ella flatly. 'I know it's him.'

'But why?'

'He wants to scare me just like he scared Ruth.' Ruth, her big sister, who'd always looked after Ella, but was unable to protect herself when it really mattered. She looked up at her boss, who was frowning. There was nothing she could say to convince Mary when she herself didn't know whether she was imagining things.

When Mary had gone, Ella leaned her head back on the cold glass, seeing again the image of Jamie's face staring at her. She wondered whether she would ever be able to move on with her life when she was so consumed by hate for Ruth's killer, scared that his brother's obsessive presence would never leave her in peace.

*

Later that evening, Ella left Wimbledon Park tube station and walked towards her parents' house, trying to clear her head and calm her nerves. Although it wasn't that late, the street was dark and empty, with only one couple walking ahead of her. The sound of laughter came from a few blocks away, but it grew fainter as Ella walked along the pavement next to the park. All she could hear was the sound of her own footsteps and the noise of the wind in the trees, blowing the remaining leaves off the branches and swirling in the cold air of the winter evening. She walked faster, jumping when she saw moving shadows around her, even though she'd walked along this way hundreds of times before.

Her mobile phone rang and she stopped, fumbling in her pocket to find it.

'Hello.' Her voice sounded loud in the empty street. 'Who's there?'

There was no reply. Suddenly the wind rustled and fell silent. Ella heard the sound of a step behind her in the darkness. Pulling her bag closer, she whipped round towards the direction of the noise but could see no-one there.

The unmistakable smell of cigarette smoke reached her. Someone was in the park. She could feel their presence, waiting and watching.

'Who is it? Who's there?' Ella's voice sounded thin and frightened in the darkness. She could hardly breathe, her throat tightened, instinct telling her to run from the unseen threat, all the fear surrounding her from the trial bursting into life. Suddenly the wavering sigh of the wind blew across her face as if the figure in the shadows had flown into the sky. She ran towards the safety of her parents' house, careering across the road and colliding into a group of teenagers who were hanging around the pavement casually smoking.

'Oi, watch it.'

'Have you come from the park? Were you in the park?' She looked from one to the other, but they just laughed and wandered away.

'Crazy woman.'

She glanced behind her, but no-one else was there and she pushed open the iron front gate against the late autumn leaves that had fallen on the path, the rusty hinges protesting at the sudden movement. Breath coming in short gasps, Ella fumbled for her keys with shaking hands and flung open the door with a crash, then pulled it behind her and leaned back against the wall to try to calm her thumping heart.

The logical side of Ella's brain screamed that she was being paranoid, that she was imagining things, but someone had been there and whoever it was, they'd almost frightened her to death. She looked around the dark hall. This house was so familiar and yet now nothing was the same anymore. Every time she came home, she hated Ben Forrester all over again for ripping her family apart.

Chapter 2

'Ella, is that you?' Her father's voice came from the kitchen and she forced herself to move from her quiet, dark sanctuary in the hallway, putting a smile on her face.

She went into the kitchen and kissed her father, who was sitting at the table, surrounded by press cuttings of the trial. He was shuffling the newsprint into piles, moving the scraps of paper around as if, in an altered pattern, they might reveal something new, different from the reality they now had to live with.

His brow furrowed, and it struck Ella how much older and greyer he looked. The semi-retired lawyer, Ray Scott, was only in his early sixties, but, as he studied the cuttings, he looked like an old man.

Grief was an oddly individual thing. While her father read obsessively about Ruth's case even though it was now over, her mother could hardly bear to look at the newspapers. He seemed to devour information, while she couldn't see past the overwhelming truth that Ruth had gone. Ella was buffeted between them, compelled to discuss the minutiae of the case with one parent while trying to find small ways of comforting the other.

She grasped his hand, which was still sorting and resorting the piles of paper. 'Dad, let's put them away.' She tried to come up with something, anything, that would distract him, but could think of nothing to say, threading her arm through his and resting her head on his shoulder.

'I thought I heard the door slam,' he said. 'Are you all right? I heard some people in the street earlier. It wasn't any of these reporters wanting to speak to you again?'

She was hit by pity for him. He shouldn't have to deal with her fears as well. 'No, there was no-one there,' she replied.

'Maybe you should get out of London for a while,' he said. 'You could come back for Christmas, but go away for a few weeks first. There's bound to be another story to take up their attention by the time you get back.'

'I can't leave you and Mum,' said Ella, all the while thinking how tempting it would be to leave everything that reminded her of Ruth. It was exactly what Mary had suggested. Maybe she wouldn't jump at shadows somewhere else.

'Think about it. You know you're all we have—' He stopped suddenly, not able to finish the sentence.

Ella squeezed his arm. 'I will. You know I'm always careful.'

He snorted, sounding much more like his old self. 'Careful isn't the first word I'd use to describe you. You rush in just like me when you find a cause – up for action without thinking of the consequences.'

'Like father like daughter. Can't change it now.'

Pleased she'd got a proper smile out of him, not a distracted one, Ella went to look for her mother. She knew exactly where she'd find her, in the study at the back of the Victorian semi. It was her favourite room, with a door out into the large garden at the back of the house. As she walked in, Ella averted her eyes from the shelf of pictures, the graduation photos and the one of Ruth in her nursing uniform. Her mother stood up quickly to greet her, swaying slightly and catching the edge of her desk to regain her balance.

Ella frowned and grasped her hand, steadying her mother, who enveloped Ella into a warm embrace that smelt of her childhood.

'Has it got worse again?' Ella asked, guiding her back into the chair.

Her mother's multiple sclerosis, benign until Ruth's death, was now prone to deeper and longer relapses that seemed to leave her weaker each time. It was almost, Ella thought, as if her mother used up so much energy to keep her spirit strong that her body was suffering. She shook her head and pulled her mother a bit closer. Isobel Scott would be the first one to tell her not to dwell on the negatives. Up until now, her mother, an academic, who was happiest being surrounded by books, hadn't been much affected by her illness. Ella pushed away the thought that everything might be about to change.

'Yes. Feeling a bit slow. It'll pass.' She grasped Ella's arm more strongly. 'I'll be fine.'

Later that evening, after supper, Ella went into her childhood bedroom and pulled the curtains to shut out the darkness, the familiar wave of guilt and pain washing over her once again. She had not found the words to persuade Ruth of the danger she was in and would never be able to forgive herself. In a flash she was back in their Fulham flat, standing angrily in front of her sister.

You don't know what he's capable of, he could hurt you.

And Ruth's confidence that she could manage him.

I can help him... Ella's fear at the park caught at her throat again and she sat down suddenly on her bed. Was she really imagining dangers in London that would disappear somewhere else? Were they all in her mind? The most frightening thing of all was that she was no longer sure she could tell the difference.

Ella looked around her room, feeling like a prisoner. It was at this time of day that the loss of Ruth hurt the most. They'd shared a flat together and it was during the evenings that they'd talked about their days. Slowly but surely, Ben had started to control her sister, and latterly Ruth no longer seemed to trust or confide in Ella. She realised now that her sister had been taken away even before her death.

Restless and unable to settle, she looked at the picture of herself and Ruth when they were children, giggling together and sitting in the sun in their garden. A wave of pleasure welled up within her and then it faded as quickly as it had come. She went to pick up the picture. All the joy she had taken in the relationship with her sister was going to be spoiled, ruined by dark thoughts, fear and suspicion. She didn't want her memories to be tarnished. Trying to take her mind off the track her thoughts had gone down, she pulled out the top drawer of her bedroom cabinet.

Inside were jumbled all the small personal things that had been scattered on Ruth's dressing table at the flat they'd shared. Up to now, Ella hadn't been able to bring herself to look through them, but nor could she throw them away. Looking at them now might enable her to recapture some of the joy she'd felt.

With a deep sigh, she picked up old tickets for concerts they'd been to, hair bands, and the pens and pencils that Ruth always used. Smiling to herself, Ella remembered how Ruth wrote herself notes all the time. It was a habit she'd always had, scribbling down cryptic messages for things she might forget and leaving them around the flat.

Ella went through the items and picked up a small metal box that Ruth had kept on her dressing table. It was tightly shut and Ella tried to prise the lid open. She failed to open it so got a nail file from her bedside table and forced it apart, the small lid springing open, a folded-up note lying in the bottom of the box.

Ella unfolded the note and turned it over. There were only a few words written in Ruth's handwriting. *Is Muir Pharma behind it?? Talk to Laura.* She stared at the note. She hadn't ever seen it before but it must be important because it was the only one Ruth had kept.

The name was very familiar. It was where their friend Laura had gone to work a few years before, when she moved back to Scotland. Ella felt cold. It was like a message from Ruth. Ella's hand moved unconsciously towards her mobile, as if following the prompt in the note – as if she had to follow an instruction.

Ella went to sit on the bed and twisted her shoulder-length dark hair between her fingers, staring at her mobile phone. She pressed the number for Laura. It was late but her friend never went to bed early. If she could call anyone at this time of night it was Laura, her closest friend. They'd met at Edinburgh University in their first year and had remained close ever since. Even though Laura had been back in London a few times, she and Ella hadn't spoken properly since the funeral. Now, Ella gazed at the phone, willing her friend to answer.

After a couple of seconds, she heard the familiar voice.

'Ella, it's so good to hear from you. How are you?'

Laura's lilting tones filled the air and suddenly Ella felt a deep yearning to see her friend again. She knew that she'd been pushing away contact with people who were close to her, nervous of their reactions and afraid of the depth of her own emotions, but maybe it was now time to change that.

'I'm fine,' replied Ella, 'we're all right.' As was so often the case, Ella felt as if she should do the comforting rather than the other way round. 'We're coping, but it's difficult.'

'I'm sorry I haven't been able to support you more, work has been frantically busy,' said Laura. 'How are things down there?'

Ella didn't reply, glancing down at Ruth's note, the instruction she couldn't ignore. 'Did Ruth speak to you before she died?' asked Ella.

Laura sounded surprised and hesitated before she replied. 'Yes, the last time she called me she wanted to find out more about Muir Pharma, so I told her what I could. I'm on the marketing side so I couldn't say much about the science, but I think I told her what she wanted to know.' Laura's voice sounded worried. 'Is it important? I thought maybe she just wanted to look around for a new job or something.'

'No, no, it was nothing important. It doesn't matter now anyway.' Ella couldn't stop the hopeless note in her voice.

In the silence Laura said, 'My invitation to come and

stay still stands.' Her words tumbled out; the old enthusiasm unchanged. 'Come up and stay with us. We've moved north of Edinburgh and have lots of room. You could stay for as long as you like, get out of London for a bit. It must be so hard being there.'

'Who's we?'

'You'll never guess who I met,' said Laura with a self-conscious laugh. 'Do you remember Mitch? From Uni? I met him again when he joined Muir Pharma earlier this year and it's all been a bit of a whirlwind.'

'Didn't you two go out for a bit?'

'Yes, but the timing wasn't right. When we met again, it was as if we'd never been apart.'

Ella remembered how kind Mitch had been. It was always Mitch who had helped them move into new flats. He seemed so unassuming. She hadn't been surprised when she heard he'd secured a first-class degree. She'd always suspected that a sharp mind had been hidden behind his relaxed demeanour.

Ella took a deep breath, a glimpse of brightness coming from her friend's offer.

'Are you sure, Laura?' she said. 'If you're both busy and have moved outside Edinburgh, maybe it's not suitable. I don't even know where you're living.'

'Don't argue,' Laura replied. 'We're staying in a new company house up here. Muir Pharma opened a new research centre in the middle of Fife and we've got one of the houses on the site because there's been so much work since the facility opened a few months ago it's easier being on the spot. Once things settle down a bit, we'll have more time to look around for something else.'

'I thought Mitch went to work for the university in one of their research labs?' said Ella.

'Not any more,' replied her friend. 'Say you'll come. We'd both love to see you.' Laura's voice softened. 'It isn't far north of Edinburgh, just off the M90. You leave at junction 4, drive two or three miles and you'll see the research centre right in front of you. There are three new houses if you turn off to the right before you get there. Designed by an award-winning architect, no less. You can't miss them, three houses in a clump of trees. We're in the first one you get to. I'll text you the directions. Come this weekend, I'm working at home writing a marketing plan for one of our new drugs, so I'll be there whenever you arrive.'

'Are you sure, Laura?' Ella could feel any obstacles fading away. She knew suddenly that this was what she needed: to leave London and go back to a place where she'd been happy.

'Please come, Ella,' insisted Laura. 'I could do with your company too.' Laura's voice sounded different, suddenly clipped and hard.

Ella shook her head in surprise. 'What's the matter?' she asked.

'Oh, you know what Mitch is like. Withdraws into himself every so often. I'd forgotten that about him. And it's been getting a bit lonely up here. Some company would be good.'

'What's upset him?' asked Ella.

'No idea.' Laura's voice lifted as she changed the subject. 'Come up when you can,' she said briskly. 'You can just chill out when you get here, go for long walks around the area. Mitch goes for a walk every lunchtime, swears it does him good. To be fair, the scenery round here is lovely.'

'Even in winter?' asked Ella.

'Bring a few extra jumpers and some stout boots. The weather isn't too bad yet.'

When she put down her mobile, Ella thought about what Laura had said. Even at university, Mitch had always been the serious one, the deep thinker who needed his own space; while Laura was bright and extroverted, pulling along others with her energy and enthusiasm. She was pleased that her friends had reconnected, and a little surprised that they had run into problems so soon.

So much for being able to understand other people's relationships, she thought, hunching her shoulders. She couldn't even manage her own. Thanks to Ben Forrester and the intimidating behaviour of his brother, she was more likely to mistrust any man who came into her orbit. It was better protecting herself from heartbreak than risking getting into a close relationship with someone who might try to control her.

She read Ruth's words again. *Is Muir Pharma behind it?? Talk to Laura.* What could her sister have meant about Muir Pharma? Was she really looking to leave London for a new job? To leave Ben? Ella had to find out what Ruth had meant, but what could she discover that would change anything?

Chapter 3

Ella gazed out of the window at the houses and fields of East Lothian as they flashed past the train speeding towards Edinburgh. After the rush of packing, the busy underground station crammed with early December shoppers and the afternoon crowd at King's Cross Station, she hadn't had much time to focus on her destination.

She felt her spirits lift as she looked ahead towards Edinburgh and saw the unmistakable silhouette of Arthur's Seat, lit by a ray of sunlight just piercing through the grey sky. Even the dull weather couldn't dampen her excitement, a feeling still strange and clumsy. Despite the protestations that she couldn't leave her parents alone, they had insisted that she go. Laura had phoned to check she was on the train. For the first time since the trial, Ella could forget about her damaged family. She could escape from the London streets where she always expected to bump into Ruth around the next corner, and where she now avoided their favourite haunts.

The train careered out of the tunnel under Calton Hill and she felt a thrill of anticipation as she saw the tops of familiar Edinburgh buildings, their chimney pots laid out across the skyline. Maybe she should have come back to Edinburgh before – put a bit of distance between her life and Ruth's death. At least she was here now, and she had two weeks to sort herself out, not just brood about Ben Forrester and what he'd done to her family, or imagine that he was stalking her in some kind of crazy revenge. She didn't have to drag herself out of bed every morning and sit in front of the computer; struggling to find patterns in the numbers in her work, which had once come so easily.

She had enjoyed her work as a forensic accountant and knew she was good at it. The move from company to company, always seeking a new project and making new contacts, and the independence that she'd once valued so highly, now seemed to be draining. The choice she always made to alternate high-paying work with other projects gave her the opportunity to help people when they really needed it, and argue for them when they were at their lowest ebb. It was why she'd taken the job with the homeless charity. It wasn't a coincidence that she and Ruth both gravitated towards organisations that helped others. Neither of them could walk away from a cry for help or ignore the burning responsibility to help others whenever they could. It was why she still felt tormented for leaving Ruth alone to face her killer.

When the train came to a stop, Ella stepped onto the platform and followed the crowd walking towards the main concourse, the recognisable glass canopy over the station covering a mix of old and new shops and cafés since her last visit. She walked to the car hire counter at the side of the station and was soon emerging outside to collect a dark grey SUV. Ella shivered as she walked across the car park towards the row of identical cars, the bitter chill of the late November wind catching her breath, the few degrees' difference always making it feel so much colder in Scotland than in London.

Throwing her bag into the back seat of the car, she manoeuvred carefully out of her space and was soon driving through the well-known streets towards the Bridges. She caught glimpses of the medieval Old Town and the castle at the top of the Royal Mile looming over the city as it had done for centuries, before she swept through the elegant streets of the New Town and towards the outskirts.

An easy drive later, Ella left the motorway at the top of a sweeping ridge and turned onto a country road, surrounded by woods and fields. She followed Laura's instructions and drove further away from civilisation, only a few lonely farmhouses and barns dotting the landscape. The glimmer of sunlight that had promised a brighter day disappeared behind the clouds, and Ella could see that the dull afternoon would soon slip into the November dusk. She wanted to reach Laura's house before the late afternoon darkness forced her to drive more slowly through the twisting country roads, and she pressed her foot down on the accelerator, making the car bounce over the lip of a hill. Then she breathed a sigh of relief when she saw a low white modern building up ahead, and braked sharply, glad that the road was deserted and no-one was there to witness her rusty driving.

As she drove towards the research centre, she saw, with a jolt, a large Muir Pharma sign, and then, to her right, a new road leading up to some detached houses surrounded by tall fir trees. The first one was Laura's, which, like the others, was made of dark timber and stone with large glass panels to let light fill the space. Driving closer, Ella saw that the two houses at the furthest end of the small cul-de-sac, looked empty and stood in darkness but Laura's one was full of light and there was a car in the drive. She parked next to the car and looked up to see a familiar face beaming at her as Laura emerged from the house. Ella scrambled out of the car and almost threw herself into Laura's arms. She couldn't speak for a moment, just hugged her friend as if she couldn't let her go.

'Come inside, Ella,' said Laura, shakily. 'We'll look after you.'

Ella had recovered by the time she was sitting with a cup of coffee in the warm, modern kitchen. As the conversation began to flow, she was reminded how she and Laura used to talk for hours.

They heard the noise of the back door opening and Mitch came into the kitchen. He came up to Ella and hugged her.

'Hello stranger. I'm sorry about what happened to your sister,' he said, pulling away after a few moments to look at her face.

'Thanks,' she replied, glancing at Laura. 'I feel so much better now I'm away from London.'

Mitch went to put the kettle on without looking at Laura, and Ella glanced from one to the other, feeling a chill in the atmosphere.

Laura turned and switched the cooker on. 'We'd better get your bag in and you can settle into your room,' she said to Ella. 'We have people coming for supper tonight, so I need to get some food on.'

'Who's coming?' Mitch asked sharply.

Laura tossed her blonde hair and avoided his stare.

'It's only Sam and Robert. They're working late today so I offered to make them some food before they drive back to Edinburgh.' She turned to Ella. 'You've heard me speak about them. I report to Sam, the Chief Executive, and he's bringing Robert, the Chief Operating Officer with him. They won't stay for long, I promise.'

Ella tried not to react, torn between the desire not to see anybody and the chance of finding out more about Muir Pharma. She looked at her friend. It was something she'd forgotten about Laura, the fact that she was always working and seemed to mix her personal life with her work. It wasn't a surprise that her boss was coming to dinner, and that it hadn't occurred to her that Ella might not be so keen on this.

Mitch didn't even try to hide his irritation. 'Ella's just got here. Why do they have to come tonight? And I need to go out later to meet someone. I didn't know they were coming.'

By now, they were glaring at one another. It looked as if it was going to develop into a full-blown argument and Ella could feel herself withdrawing awkwardly. She didn't want to get involved, she didn't feel strong enough and wondered, with a pang, where the teasing camaraderie of her friends had gone.

*

Later that evening, Ella studied Sam Renwick as he sat at the table. He was in his early forties. She knew from Laura that he had started Muir Pharma over fifteen years before, and in that time had created one of the most successful pharmaceutical companies in Scotland. The company's leading drug, Evexitrol, a medication for epilepsy, was now sold all over the world. CEO Sam, whose charisma she mistrusted from the few articles she'd found, was the face of the business: a marketing whizz, speaking to government, the regulators and the press about their success. The man he'd brought with him, Robert Young, was the Chief Operating Officer. He was quieter and more serious, his bearded dark good looks a foil to Sam's fairness and charm.

Laura was complaining to both men about the animal rights demonstrators who haunted the site. She turned to Ella. 'You must have seen them when you arrived?'

'No,' replied Ella, but Laura wasn't listening and appealed to Sam.

'It isn't good for our image. We've always used animals but we'd only opened the new lab for two weeks before the demonstrators arrived. I know this is a difficult issue for a lot of people but they never protested at the old place.'

'See it as a sign of success,' replied Sam. 'Anyway, they don't cause any trouble.' He glanced at Robert, who nodded his agreement.

When Ella looked across the table, she would hardly have recognised Mitch, who had stayed quiet throughout the noisy discussion. He seemed much thinner than he had been even a few moments before, sitting awkwardly at one end of the table. She watched Laura's colleagues as they talked and laughed together, voices growing louder as the good food and wine flowed. Sam told another story, effortlessly monopolising the conversation. Only Mitch seemed not to be enjoying himself – back ramrod straight and expression serious.

Suddenly Mitch stood up, mumbled an apology and walked towards the door. Robert got up after him and Ella saw him grab Mitch's arm in the foyer before he could open the door. She glanced back at the table but realised that no-one else could see the entranceway to the house, and Laura and Sam had just continued their conversation, their blond heads close together. She turned back and saw that Mitch and Robert were arguing about something. Ella watched Mitch throw off the other man's hand, grab his coat and catch Laura's ski jacket before it fell to the ground. He hung it back up again, fussing around the pockets, before going out and slamming the door behind him.

Ella looked away from the door and blinked a couple of times, processing what she'd seen. Robert had come back to the table and Ella was sure he'd said something to Sam as he sat down. She stared back at the foyer.

Nobody seemed worried that Mitch had gone, apart from Ella. As time passed, she tried to relax in the warmth. Despite their promise that they wouldn't stay long, Sam and Robert lingered around the table over coffee, and Laura poured more wine before getting up to clear the plates. Sam jumped up and followed her. She waved to Ella to stay seated, and Robert slid round the table to sit next to her. The noise of Sam and Laura arguing over who was going to do the dishes made her smile and she looked at Robert, who was watching the other two. She couldn't help but compare him to Sam, who always seemed to want to be the centre of attention.

Robert turned to her and spoke in a soft voice. 'I've heard you've had a very difficult time. Laura told me what happened to your sister. It sounded awful.'

Disarmed by the wine and the laughter in the background, she felt tears prick her eyes and blinked them away.

To her relief, he wasn't looking for a response. Robert carried on talking in his quiet way about her trip. She was grateful for his lack of inquisitiveness. So many people wanted to discuss what had happened to Ruth. It brought all her emotions back every time.

'So, what plans have you got for your trip?' he asked. 'Have you got anything particular in mind you want to do up here, or places you want to go?'

'Not really,' she replied. 'I'm just going to stay around here, walk a bit, drink wine and coffee.' She lifted her glass of wine in a toast.

'Sounds like it's going to be wet for the next few days. Before we get the snow, there'll be lots of rain. I'm not sure how much walking you'll be able to get in.'

'It doesn't matter.' She looked around the comfortable room. 'Even if I just stay in here, it will be fine. Laura has some good books she can lend me and there are some films I've missed that I want to watch.'

'If you walk, I'd keep to the fields. These country roads can be a bit hairy with the local farmers and their jeeps. If you don't mind my advice.'

'I'll be careful,' she answered absentmindedly, watching Laura flirting with Sam as they both sashayed back to the table. She felt Robert's intense gaze.

'And you'd be better to keep away from the plant,' he added. 'We've increased security today because of the animal rights activists, so you might get questioned if you come too close to the fence.'

'I thought you weren't worried about them,' she said.

'We're getting a few who are becoming aggressive. If you see anybody on your walks I would avoid them if you can.'

'Come on, we need to go,' said Sam, breaking into their conversation. Immediately Robert got up to follow him, and Ella watched him go.

'I'll take the cups and glasses over,' said Ella, clearing the rest of the table. Laura nodded and finished loading the dishwasher. As Ella handed the last few cups to Laura, she looked at the photographs pinned on the board next to the door, a recent photo of Mitch and Laura smiling at the camera, others from a party where Sam was dancing with Laura. Ella stared at the photograph of her friends. They were very different people: Laura outgoing and bubbly, Mitch quieter and needing time on his own, but he was always there and always reliable. Even the photographs Laura had pinned up made Ella think that something, or rather someone, had come between them.

'I'm going to bed now,' said Laura. 'I need to be out early tomorrow morning. I'm afraid we're all working this weekend. Mitch will be in soon; he's probably walking further than he'd planned. He's always doing that on his lunchtime walks, losing track of time.' She gave Ella a hug. 'You should explore some of the walks around here, get some fresh air into your lungs. Just avoid the protesters if you meet them – some of them can be quite belligerent. They seem to think they can go everywhere here.'

In her room, Ella threw her bag onto the bed and stood at the window looking out into the darkness, only a few glimpses of light from the lab facility shining through the trees shrouding the house. At that moment she felt very isolated and was sorry not to look out onto the well-known Edinburgh streets. In the darkness she heard the hoot of a solitary owl and shivered, pulling the curtains shut and turning towards the bright modern bedroom. She opened the suitcase purposefully, reminding herself that she had two important goals here: to rest, and also to find out just what her sister had wanted to ask Laura. What did Ruth think Muir Pharma was doing? What could Ella hope to find out? As she unpacked, she tried not to feel guilty that she hadn't been entirely honest about her reasons for staying with Laura. She didn't want to burden her friend or let her paranoia cast a shadow on Laura's life too.

Chapter 4

Ella slept late the next morning. She woke up slowly, for once rested after a deep night's sleep undisturbed by dreams or visions of the past. She snuggled down under the cosy duvet, listening to the heavy rain falling, and looked around the modern furniture in the bedroom and the crisp lines of the blind over the window looking out onto the trees behind the house. Apart from the sound of the rain, there was silence – a far cry from London. She was hardly awake, but Ella was impatient to do something to answer her questions about Muir Pharma. Although the rain meant that her plan to walk round the plant and have a look at the outside of the lab would have to wait, her research into the company could start.

She got out of bed and put on a soft sweatshirt over her cotton pyjamas, then sat down and pulled on warm slipper boots. She had heard sounds earlier when Laura and Mitch had left, and knew she now had the house to herself. She felt hungry and pushed open the bedroom door, intending to go down the stairs to the large kitchen-diner. Laura had taken her upstairs the evening before to show her around; a rapid tour to show her their bedroom, which looked out onto the field in front of the house, and the spare bedrooms at the back next to a bathroom. The high ceilings and clever use of glass in the modern house pulled her in the opposite direction and she turned away from the stairs, despite the hunger pangs, and walked to the end of the corridor. The tall picture window at the end of the hall stretched down to the ground floor. Through this window she could see the other two houses, set apart, but still quite close. Both were in darkness.

The new road leading to the houses snaked along the front and came to an end in the woods behind the third house. Laura had said that the medical director, Martin Fraser, lived in the middle house when he was up from Edinburgh. As she gazed out of the window, the sky grew even darker and larger raindrops started to hit the ground. There hadn't been any landscaping attempted around the houses, the surrounding carpet of pine needles stretching into the woods, and only a few shrubs had been planted between the houses to separate them.

Ella turned from the window to run lightly down the wooden stairs towards the kitchen. She stopped on the bottom step and looked around the space. Another large picture window dominated the room, the view of the fields seemed so close that Ella could almost touch them. After a few moments she went to the dining table and noticed a note next to a setting for one. It was from Laura.

> *Good morning, sleepyhead. Help yourself to breakfast. There's fresh bread and lots of goodies in the fridge for lunch. Mitch and I will be back later. Feel free to use the computer in the snug. Also, could you watch the lunchtime news for me because there might be an item*

mentioning Muir Pharma on it.
See you later, Laura x
P.S. Don't be surprised if you get a four-legged visitor. A local cat has adopted us and may appear.

Ella made herself a cup of coffee, munched a corner of the Danish pastry they'd left for her and went to explore the rest of the ground-floor level. The main door she'd arrived at the night before opened into a small entrance hall at the side of the open-plan living space, so she went towards the door at the end of the kitchen. There was a well-equipped utility room and, beyond that, a boot room, wellingtons arranged against the wall; and a small toilet and shower tucked at the other side. This house was designed for the country and for people following country pursuits.

The use of glass at the back had also been clever. A tall pane next to the back door faced directly onto the wood behind the house. At the bottom of the glass panel there was a cat flap and Ella smiled at this sign of domesticity. At the corner of the bench, she saw a small bowl of water and a half-finished saucer of food.

The boot room led onto another smaller sitting room at the back of the house. This room was like a snug, with comfortable chairs and a large-screen television on the wall. In the corner of the room there was a desk with a computer. Laura had said that she often worked at home, either in this room or at the kitchen table. Mitch spent most of his time in the lab. Ella switched on the computer and checked her emails, following up on those that related to future project work.

A few hours later, she heard a noise from the back of

the kitchen and a large grey cat wandered out of the utility room. He looked at her curiously and gave a short meow in greeting.

'You're very handsome,' said Ella, walking towards him and crouching down to pat his fur. 'You're also very wet,' she said, looking beyond him into the utility room.

She spied a small towel hanging on a hook next to the sink and went to get it. The cat seemed used to being dried and it stood patiently until she'd wiped away the worst of the rain. The moment she stood up, he started purring, jumped onto a rug at the bottom of the sofa and stretched languorously.

'That's your bed, is it? I'm still hungry. I'm going to get something for lunch.' The sound of loud purring followed her to the table and she opened the fridge door.

When she'd put bread and cheese onto the table and eaten a few mouthfuls, she remembered Laura's note and turned on the television hung in the corner of the kitchen, catching the end of the Scottish news.

There was an item on a local charity and she saw the figure of Sam Renwick filling the screen.

'...We've been involved with the Social Moves charity here in the Grassmarket for over six years,' he was saying. 'It's important for local businesses to give back to the community.' There was something about his confident voice that made her immediately think that he was more interested in burnishing his reputation than in helping people. She looked behind his domineering figure and saw Robert in the background.

'He's the one doing the actual work, I'll bet,' she muttered. She clicked the television off.

Ella went back into the snug and sat in front of the computer. At least there was *something* she could do that day. The last few days had been so busy that she hadn't had time to do the basic research she usually did before any project started. She would see what she could find now.

It didn't take long – only an hour or so searching on the internet and, in that time, she hadn't been able to find anything negative about Muir Pharma, or any stories or questions that Ruth might have wanted to follow up. The company seemed to be a total success. She could find nothing except positive articles.

Sam had started the business with his childhood friend Robert, grown by successful discoveries and acquisitions, and was now a successful Scottish exporter. There was much speculation and excitement in the press about the company's future, several articles about the new laboratory in Fife and how many jobs it created in the area. She studied the pictures of the new labs and knew she'd have to get inside.

Before she switched off the computer, Ella saw a Muir Pharma icon on the desktop. Maybe she could get some more truthful background on the company. She pressed the icon but there were only draft documents in the file that were all earlier versions of what she'd already seen. After a quick check, Ella turned off the computer and left the snug. Frustrated by her lack of progress, she could be sure of only one thing: Laura was being very careful about the image of the company. Ella wasn't going to find out anything more than bland marketing statements here.

All that afternoon it still poured with rain. Cut off from the world and with only the cat's company, Ella curled up at the end of the sofa and read one of Laura's books from the snug. In the middle of the afternoon, the dullness of the sky and low cloud was taken over by the late November dusk. Ella put down her book, closed the blind and turned on more lights. Her inactivity all day suddenly prompted her into action. Laura and Mitch would be home for dinner soon and she'd just sat around in her pyjamas all day. She went into the shower, then dressed in black trousers and one of her silk shirts before going back downstairs, the sound of the shower in the ensuite of Laura and Mitch's room telling her that someone was home.

When Ella was on the last step, the back door opened and Laura came bustling in. Relieved that she'd roused herself in time, she sat down at the table and greeted her friend. Laura must have been in meetings all day. She was wearing a tight-fitting navy dress under a formal jacket. As Ella watched, she threw off the jacket, then shrugged on a mohair cardigan. She glanced at the open book on the sofa.

'You found my novels in the snug, I see. I've got lots of new ones as well as some of my favourites.'

Ella returned her smile. 'The old ones are best,' she answered. 'I haven't read *Jane Eyre* for years. I'd forgotten how good it was.' She looked around the room. 'This is a good place to relax. You've got everything here that you want.'

Laura nodded. 'When Sam suggested we could use this house, and then work was so busy, it seemed a brilliant opportunity.'

'I had a look around today,' said Ella. 'It's very smart. Are all three houses the same?'

'I think so. I've only been in the next one. I haven't been near the third one. It always seems to have workmen in it. I went next door one day because I was looking for Martin Fraser. The layout was exactly the same as in here, but his kitchen was a lighter colour, not dark blue like ours.' She stood up to get a bottle of wine from the fridge, filled three glasses and handed one to Ella. At that moment, Mitch came running down the stairs and Laura gave him the third glass.

'Thank you,' he said, sitting at the table and toasting them both.

'Have you been in the other houses yet?' Laura asked Mitch. 'What are they like?'

'I haven't been inside them,' he answered, 'but I spoke to the architect one day when he was looking around and he said they were all the same model. The first two are identical but he said something about the third one being a bit different. He also said that Sam and Robert were closely involved in the design. He was at school with them and came from the same area in Edinburgh. He said he got a lot of business from them.'

'I had a visitor today,' said Ella. 'The cat is lovely. What's his name?'

'We call him Smokey,' said Mitch. 'I'm not sure what the other people call him.'

'I was concerned when he started coming here,' said Laura, 'but spoke to the woman who owns him. She was very laid back, which was a relief. She doesn't mind that he goes walkabout. They have young children so we decided that he came here for some peace and quiet. He comes over, sleeps for a few hours then goes back home.'

Laura got up to put the oven on.

'What can I do to help?' asked Ella.

'Nothing. You just sit there. It's easy,' Laura replied. 'I'm just going to make steak, and bake some potatoes in the oven. We can have salad with it.'

In the end they all helped prepare supper. Mitch grilled the steaks and Ella mixed the salad. They talked about their lives and their shared memories of university.

When there was a lull in the conversation, Ella remembered what she'd seen on the news.

'I switched on the TV and saw a reporter talking about Sam investing in a charity in the Grassmarket. I'm sure I saw Robert doing some hard work in the background.'

Mitch chuckled. 'That's how they always operate. Sam leading the way and Robert clearing up behind him.' He sounded bitter and Laura frowned at the emotion in his voice.

To try to divert them from an argument Ella interrupted. 'I hate TV cameras, journalists and the whole press circus. They're always trying to get you to speak to them when all you want is to be left alone.'

Laura and Mitch were both looking at her, their argument forgotten. Ella knew it was her fault that she'd opened the whole subject.

'Was it very bad at the trial?' asked Laura.

Ella nodded, thinking back to that time. Outside the courtroom, they had felt like they were the ones on trial, harassed by press photographers and television cameras, and journalists bombarding them with questions as they tried to scramble into their car. She used to stare out of the car window at the people scurrying along the London streets to shelter from the rain. They were leading lives that were normal – free from the grief and guilt that now seemed to weigh on her every thought and movement.

Ella let her breath out in a deep sigh. She was grateful for some sense of justice secured for Ruth's death, but she knew that the guilty verdict wasn't the end. The fightback had already started, the horror of what Ben had done categorised and explained away by medical reports and clinical opinions.

'I'm sorry, but I can't talk about it,' said Ella. 'The more I think about it, the more difficult it is to move on.'

'Of course,' replied Laura and turned to Mitch, changing the subject smoothly. 'What are your plans for tomorrow?'

Ella listened as he talked about his day. She realised suddenly that she wouldn't find anything out from Laura, she was too influenced by Sam and too wedded to Muir Pharma. It was Mitch she had to ask. He was the one who seemed to have problems with the company. Maybe she was attaching too much importance to a note from Ruth, given everything that had happened, but she needed to find out if the note meant anything. She had to speak to Mitch alone. Without Laura there, perhaps he'd open up.

Chapter 5

The next morning, the dream started again. She was surrounded by shadows. She couldn't make out the faces of the people around her, but she knew who they were. She understood she was in a dream, but she couldn't do anything to come out of it.

'I'll never leave you alone,' came the familiar voice that echoed around her head. 'You'll never be free of me. You'll hear my voice all the time. Look over your shoulder and see my shadow. Even if it's not me, you'll think I'm there. I'm going to stay in your life. Ruth may be gone but it's your turn next.'

After what seemed like hours listening to his hypnotic voice, Ella woke up suddenly, throwing off the duvet, hot despite the coolness of the bedroom. She knew she couldn't sleep any longer so she got up to face the day.

When Laura and Mitch had gone to work, she sat in their sleek kitchen, drinking strong coffee, her nightmares fading in the normality of the kitchen, the view of the countryside out of the large picture window framed by the trees round the house. She stared at the dull green fields, replaying in her mind scenes from the last few weeks and months, when everything had begun to go wrong. She should have known at the start, she realised that now.

*

'I've invited Ben round for supper, he's been ill again,' Ruth had said.

It wasn't a question of not liking Ben Forrester, Ella thought. The problem was you could like him too much. He had a way of fascinating you that wasn't good for your peace of mind. And he knew exactly the effect he was having. She realised now that he must have planned it all along – so used to sowing discord wherever he went that his own erratic behaviour became more acceptable, more normal.

And then it became a habit. Ben knew how to be good company. He was attractive, funny and clever. If Ella thought that, mistrusting him as she did, Ruth had no chance. He introduced them to his brother Jamie, a quieter version of himself and they went out as a foursome. But that was when Ben's controlling side was kept well hidden.

Through all that time, she'd missed the signs that her sister was getting into serious trouble. Ella remembered vividly how Ruth's sweet expression had hardened when she'd tried to tell her the truth, crystallising the wedge he'd so carefully built between them. Her big sister never liked to be proved wrong. It was the same face she'd put on when Ella was ten years old and refused to play the game she had chosen.

'Ella, you're just jealous.'

'Jealous?' She wondered when he'd put that idea into her head. 'I'm only trying to help.' But her sister pulled away, refusing to look at her.

'I don't need your help. I can take care of myself.'

*

Ella looked out of the window at the grey sky, the branches of the trees buffeted in the wind. It had been raining overnight but it was dry now – not an ideal day to be outside but she knew she had to go out and walk to try to put her brooding feelings behind her, find out something more about Muir Pharma.

She put on her padded jacket and let herself out of the house, locking the door and turning to study the other two houses. The large windows in each building looked out onto the open fields, but whereas Laura and Mitch's house was set several metres away from the wood at the back, the middle house was closer to the trees and the third house was almost swallowed up by them. It was as if nature itself was trying to shroud the third one in darkness.

There were lights on in the middle house. Outside, with a muttered curse, a man was heaving a large battered suitcase into the back seat of an old Volvo. This must be Martin Fraser, she realised, Muir Pharma's medical director. During their conversations the previous evening, Laura had told her that he used the next house when he wasn't with his daughter in Edinburgh. She had been a brilliant medical student who was seriously hurt in a car accident a few years before, and now needed full-time nursing care. Ella stared at the man, his grey hair and thin build in a coat that was too large for him making him look sad and weary. She felt a pang of pity.

Walking up towards him, the cheerful greeting froze on her lips as he slammed the car door and leaned towards her.

'What are you doing nosing around my house?'

'I'm not nosing around. I'm a friend of…'

His gaze was hostile and he turned and walked to the gate, pulling it open. 'I don't care who you are. Just leave me alone.' He opened the gate wider and then got into the car, started the engine and drove past her, so close that she had to jump out of the way.

Shaken by his reaction, she turned away to walk behind the houses, hunching her shoulders against the wind and striding out to keep warm. Ella walked briskly along the path at the edge of the wood, trying to get rid of the man's boorish behaviour, and breathed in deeply as his unpleasantness began to fade. Although it was a cold day, she felt surrounded by the raw beauty of nature, the smell of wet vegetation filled her nostrils, and she caught glimpses of the fields through the trees as she skirted the small wood.

She came out on the far side of the Muir Pharma plant, a little below the main entrance to the site. She stopped and gazed at the bright white of the building and the new road leading to the entrance. On the road, just at the main gate, she saw a group of people holding placards. Even from a distance she could see the writing on their signs: 'end animal testing', 'Muir Pharma – Blood on your hands', 'Muir Pharma – No ethics just greed.'

She checked her watch, shoulders hunched against the cold wind. It was almost lunchtime, so she looked for Mitch. She wished she'd had the foresight to ask Laura for his number. After twenty minutes she started to stamp her feet to try to get the circulation going. Fifteen minutes later she was unable to feel her fingers and thought she'd have to give up. Before finally giving in and walking away, she saw Mitch emerge from the building and turn down a single-track road that led behind a nearby barn. Too good a chance to miss to talk to him alone, she hurried after him across the field. The lab was soon out of sight.

The sky had lightened as the clouds began to break up, and a beam of weak sunlight shone on the deserted barn. It looked as it was falling down, only held up by the piles of rubbish stacked on one side, its side door lying open and hanging drunkenly off its hinges. Ella studied the forlorn sight, wondering if the wrecked building was still in use, when she saw a fleeting movement next to the flimsy door. She blinked, thinking it might be Mitch, and walked towards it.

A figure appeared around the corner of the building, still a few metres away. The man was tall and wide, his shoulders huge and shapeless in a dirty, grey overcoat. It must be a farmer, she thought, but something about the man had made her heart beat faster and she felt a prickling sensation down the back of her neck. He moved out of sight and she watched the empty space, waiting for the figure to come out again, telling herself she was imagining dangers that didn't exist. He was just an ordinary man. The noise of a twig breaking behind her broke the silence and she twisted around, scanning the track and opposite field for any sign of life, but couldn't see anyone. It felt as if there was someone behind her but it must have been an animal scurrying away.

When she turned back to the barn, she gasped and took a step back when she saw the man walking purposefully towards her, his face hidden by a large hood and, under the hood, a black scarf. She flicked a glance to the side of the field and she saw two more men walking towards her. Robert had told her to be careful of activists, and of farmers driving dangerously, but these men weren't local people. They were being too threatening.

Her breath caught in her throat as she watched the men, a powerful stab of fear seized her, inchoate terrors becoming real. She turned and ran away, not looking back until she'd left the field behind. When she stopped to catch her breath, she looked behind her. No-one was following. She thought she heard the faint sound of laughter from the field behind her and anger blazed through her body. It had been so easy for them to frighten her, she thought, kicking the fence post in front of her, frustrated with herself for running away so quickly.

She leaned on the fence next to the track until her gasps gave way to even breaths. The road dropped into a dip in front of her and she saw two men facing each other. Peering closer, she was sure that one of them was Mitch, a woollen hat now pulled down over his head and his shoulders hunched against the cold. She wondered what he could be doing, meeting someone outside rather than in his heated office.

The other man was shaking his head, his dark hair blown over his face by the wind. Ella watched them closely, wondering who he was and what they were arguing about. Then Mitch turned brusquely and walked away in the opposite direction, disappearing round the next corner in the road.

The dark-haired man came towards her and this time she stayed where she was, watching his slim body approach. The droop of his shoulders made him look defeated, his head bent down as he faced the cold wind that was buffeting her back.

Suddenly a large black Range Rover came round the corner behind him. It was moving slowly and he didn't seem to hear the noise of the engine over the strengthening wind. As the car sped up and came closer, the driver was a shapeless black shadow behind the windscreen and Ella could have sworn his features were covered. Her instinct took over and she started to run towards the man walking towards her, fear catching in her throat, her voice coming out weakly as she tried to call out a warning.

The headlights of the approaching car suddenly flipped up and it rushed forward, driving directly at the dark-haired man. As the car loomed behind him, Ella clutched his jacket and pulled him off the road, through a gap in the fence into the field. They collapsed into a heap on the damp grass and she could feel the rush of air as the Range Rover hurtled past them.

After a few seconds, Ella scrambled to the fence, her breath coming out in gasps, and looked after the car, which had disappeared round the corner. She twisted round to the man who was now sitting up on the ground, wiping the mud off his knees. 'Did you get the number plate? I didn't see it.'

He shook his head.

'We should call the police,' said Ella loudly.

'No,' he said. 'I'm in enough trouble already.'

She stared at him. 'What do you mean? Who are you anyway? And was that Mitch you were meeting?'

His only response was a sneeze. Ella realised that it had started to rain again, large raindrops falling on his dark hair and rolling off his long nose. 'Come on, we need to get out of here,' she said, as she scrambled to her feet. He just sat there, so she grabbed his arm impatiently and pulled him after her across the field and away from the road, looking in all directions in case the looming Range Rover came back.

Slightly ahead, Ella ran under the nearest tree, gasping for breath. The man stopped a few feet away, gazing at her suspiciously, his dark eyes almost as black as his wet hair. He pulled the collar of his jacket more closely round his neck, shivering.

He sniffed defiantly. 'I'm not staying here, waiting around until these characters find me again. I've left my car at the café just off the motorway, so I'm just going to walk there.'

'You can't walk in this weather,' she said. 'I'll give you a lift.'

She was determined to get some of her questions answered. The more she thought about what she'd seen, the more she decided that it *had* been Mitch and she wanted to know why he'd been there.

As if he couldn't decide what to do, he glanced back across the fields and the road leading to the houses, then took out a handkerchief and dried his face.

'All right then,' he said finally. He tried to smile, but it was more like a grimace, his face lean and tense. 'Thanks for saving me back there,' he said grudgingly, following her across the field. 'I didn't hear them until it was almost too late,' he said. When they got to the car parked outside Laura and Mitch's house he turned to Ella. 'I'm Carl Davis. A journalist.'

Chapter 6

Inside the car, Carl sniffed a couple of times. 'Take the road for the motorway. There's a café just at the side. I'll tell you where to turn off.'

She drove away from the Muir Pharma plant, seeing in her rear-view mirror the group of demonstrators with placards at the main gate, until the building disappeared out of sight behind the trees and fields.

After a few moments Carl said, 'Turn right here.' And she drove onto a one-track road running down the side of the motorway. Ahead of them, she saw a low building with a small car park outside. 'My car is round the back,' he said, 'just park next to it.' She drove round the far side of the building, past a van and some other cars, stopping next to a hire car similar to the one she was driving.

'Why would someone try to run you over?' she asked. 'Was that Mitch Blake you were arguing with on the road? It looked like him.'

'Who are you then? What's your connection to Mitch?'

'My name is Ella Scott. He's a friend of mine, I'm staying at his house. What was he talking to you about?'

He studied her face. 'Don't I know you from somewhere? Have we ever met?'

She felt her heart drop. Of course, he might know who

she was if he remembered Ruth's case. He was probably one of the journalists who had been following her, throwing out questions and trying to get their story.

'It's possible,' replied Ella.

'I think I know you.'

'Then you know my story and you'll understand if I don't want to talk about it. I'm here to find out about Muir Pharma. If you can tell me anything.'

He gave a shaky sigh. He looked scared, and younger than she'd thought at first. 'You're right. It was Mitch I was speaking to.' He frowned at some memory, then shook his head and started to talk. 'I don't know him really. He called me up out of the blue. Says he's got a story for me and to come up here.'

'So, you came up to meet him,' said Ella. 'What was it about?'

'I already nearly died today for all this, why would I talk about it to you?'

'Two reasons,' Ella snapped. 'I just saved your life and also, I think we might be investigating the same thing.'

He shrugged and carried on. 'All right then. If you're a friend of his you'd better know everything. He told me he had information on Muir Pharma that the company doesn't want made public. He's alleging that they've covered up past lab results that showed serious side effects of Evexitrol and they've silenced two scientists who protested.'

'What do you mean silenced? Stopped them from speaking out?'

'No, silenced as in killed. They didn't mess around trying to enforce some kind of confidentiality agreement, they just got rid of the scientists altogether.'

Ella couldn't believe what she was hearing. Her mind was racing. Could this be what Ruth had suspected? Why she had left the note? Ella wondered whether Laura knew Mitch was a whistleblower and had such suspicions about the company she loved so much.

'So why did he go to London for a journalist? What's wrong with the people up here?'

Carl grimaced. 'He doesn't trust the Scottish press because he thinks they're in Sam Renwick's pocket and wouldn't print the story. He said it would get right back to Renwick. He thinks they'll try to kill him if they find out what he's been doing. I didn't think he was serious until today.'

Ella stared at him, wondering how much of what he said could be true. 'I can see that this could be bad publicity for the company but they're hardly going to resort to murder,' she said. The image of the car racing towards Carl flashed into Ella's mind but she pushed it away. 'And he's sure Sam Renwick is responsible?' she added.

'He says he's behind it all. Backed up by his best buddy Robert Young. They go back a long way. Came from a rundown area of Edinburgh and grew up together, before building the business up from nothing.'

'Does Mitch have proof?'

'He says he does.'

'So why didn't he go to the police?'

'He doesn't trust them either. He thinks they accepted the explanation of the deaths of the two scientists too quickly and were leaned on to drop the investigation.'

Ella frowned at the implications of what he'd said. If Mitch was right, it wasn't just the company covering up, it was the authorities as well. The conspiracy was more widespread than she could ever have suspected. If it was true. The more she heard the less believable it sounded.

'What were you arguing about?' She asked finally, aware that Carl's hand was already on the door handle.

He looked out of the car window, avoiding her stare. 'He's scared. He said he didn't want me to write the story any longer. Told me to leave.'

'What are you going to do?'

They heard the sound of another car drive into the car park and he didn't reply until the engine stopped and the café door clanged shut.

A couple of people came out from the café and stood miserably in the cold, shuffling their feet and blowing plumes of smoke into the air. Carl looked at them with a disgusted expression.

'I've never understood why people like such a filthy habit.'

'Well?'

Carl turned to look at her again. 'To be honest, he got to me a bit, with all his precautions, not wanting to meet, telling me when to phone, giving me different numbers each time because he thought they were tracking his movements. Not to go to the police if anything happened to him. It made me jumpy. And he's completely obsessed with Sam Renwick, thinks he's some kind of monster.'

'Do you believe him?'

He didn't seem to hear her question, too caught up in his own thoughts. 'Today isn't the first time I've been followed. You know what Edinburgh's like, all those dark alleys and closes – places people can hide. And even up here, I keep thinking people are following me.' He shrugged and looked away, embarrassed that he was scared.

It was what convinced Ella that he was telling the truth, that he was embarrassed about his fear.

Then the professional journalist in Carl took over. 'It could be a good story, though. I'll try to see him once more, come up tomorrow with some papers he gave me. He might have calmed down by then.'

He got out of her car with a quick wave and jumped into his own without a backward glance, driving quickly out of the car park. She moved her car round the building so she could watch him go, the sense of fear lingering around her.

She looked up when the door to the café opened. A group of men got into the van. She could see some placards inside the vehicle and realised it must be another group of demonstrators going up to the Muir Pharma plant – though this group looked intimidating, rather than the young students she expected to see. The man leading the way was wearing a denim jacket, jeans and trainers. Despite his youthful dress, a small grey ponytail peeked out from under a black baseball cap. While he was waiting for the others to climb into the van, he couldn't seem to stand still, flexing his fingers and rolling on the balls of his feet. He could have been a boxer, ready to act in an instant, unleashed to fight. She sunk further down into her car seat as they drove slowly out of the car park.

Inside the café she saw a young waitress clearing a table. Her short blond hair, dyed blue at the ends, caught the light. Ella thought she might go inside. The girl looked friendly and she suddenly felt she needed human company after Carl's tense warnings.

She stretched out her hand towards the car door when another figure came out of the café and she snatched it back. It was Robert. What a horrific coincidence that he was here. Carl's allegations about Muir Pharma still echoed in her mind.

He saw her immediately and walked towards the car smiling at her. He was holding two paper bags with the café logo. She reluctantly wound down the window and lifted her face towards him.

'Why are you sitting out here?' He looked around the small car park. 'Aren't you going inside?'

She looked beyond him to the café, torn by doubts as she remembered the group of men who had just come out. How could they have been in the same place together? Could they not know who Robert was?

'I was going to go in,' she said finally, 'but I'm not sure I'm up to company at the moment. I might just go back to the house.'

He was staring down at her, a question in his eyes, then handed her one of the paper bags. 'You shouldn't miss one of their cakes,' he said. 'It's my secret vice, but I'm not alone in that. Most of the company find their way down here. I come out here most days to buy their cakes.'

She looked inside the bag. 'Carrot cake, one of my favourites,' said Ella forcing a smile.

'My waistline will certainly thank you for taking it,' he said and then waved as he turned towards his car. It was a dark Range Rover too, reminding her of the car that had tried to run Carl down. But this one had a dog crate in the back and the windows weren't tinted. Ella wondered what kind of dog Robert had that could be so big.

Robert waited for her to start the car and he followed her along the road. She tried not to feel that she was under escort. Just before the turn off to Laura's house he blew the horn and waved again. When she went inside, she was frowning, trying to reconcile Carl's words with Robert's friendly conversation. She stood next to the coffee machine as it filled the kitchen with the strong smell of freshly ground beans. As she waited, she looked at the cake thoughtfully. Robert had seemed satisfied when he came out of the café, as if he'd just concluded a positive deal. Had he been meeting the group of men who had left just before him? She shook her head as she sat down with the coffee, realising that she hadn't even spoken to Mitch when she'd purposely gone to look for him.

Robert seemed a nice man, but was he really? She wanted to like him, but now wasn't so sure. After Ben, she couldn't trust her own judgement around the motives of others.

Chapter 7

The next morning dawned sunny and cold. Ella allowed herself a lie-in, listening to Laura get ready and leave for work, wondering what had happened to Mitch. He hadn't come home for dinner last night and Laura hadn't wanted to answer her questions. After breakfast, Ella went through to the entrance hall to pick up her jacket. The bell rung loudly next to her and she jumped. She looked through the window and saw a familiar figure hopping from one foot to another. Carl Davis's thin jacket was no protection against the Scottish weather. He was looking nervously behind him so she dropped her jacket onto the chair and opened the door.

He twisted round when he heard the door open and, before she could say anything, slid inside.

'Come in,' she said sarcastically.

'Someone's following me. I can't stand there outside so I had to come here.' He hugged his jacket around his shoulders and she shut the door behind him. 'I won't stay long,' he said. 'I'm getting out of here as soon as possible.'

She led the way to the long wooden table, sitting down on one of the chairs, to find Carl still standing at the door. She pushed a chair towards him.

'Sit down for a minute or so,' she said. 'Mitch isn't here, but you can tell me. What's the problem?'

He sat down reluctantly on the edge of the chair, his back still ramrod straight. He reached into the inside pocket of his jacket and handed her some notes, which were loosely bundled together in an elastic band. 'I was supposed to have a meeting with Mitch this morning, but he didn't turn up. I was hoping to find him here. These are the notes he gave me, the names and addresses of the scientists he wanted me to investigate – other contacts he had. I thought you could give them back to him. I don't expect to see him again.'

'That doesn't sound like Mitch.' She jumped instinctively to his defence as she flipped through the notes. 'There must have been a good reason for him not to turn up.'

'I don't care anymore,' answered Carl. 'There was one thing I wanted to do in Scotland before I left, but I'm not even sure I'm going to do that. I was trying to get a meeting with an analyst who said he would tell me about the pharmaceutical sector in Scotland, but I might just cancel it.' He relaxed in the chair. 'I don't want anything more to do with Muir Pharma and what might be going on there. I'm just going back to London.' He shuddered. 'I've had enough of the frozen north. I don't like being followed.'

She heard the fear in his voice and was suddenly filled with pity when she looked at his thin features and red nose. He leaned over and clutched her arm. She didn't pull away, gripped by the urgency in his voice and the intense look in his eyes. 'I know you only met me yesterday but I'm warning you, be careful. People who cross Sam Renwick end up dead. I'm not putting my life on the line for any story.' He gestured towards the notes. 'You'll find in there all the names and addresses that Mitch gave me.' His voice dropped. 'I gave a memory stick to Mitch with some evidence I've been working on. I don't even know whether he's looked at it, he probably hasn't, but you should ask him about it.' Carl stood up, nodded at her in farewell and let himself out of the kitchen.

Ella went to the door and watched him get into his car and drive away. She wasn't sure what she thought about him, his warnings about Muir Pharma and then her suspicions that he could have been one of the journalists who hounded her family. All she did know was that she had to see Mitch as soon as he got back.

Ella felt compelled to take advantage of the dry day, so put on her jacket and boots. Walking outside might get rid of the pervasive dread that Carl had left behind him and banish the fear of what Mitch might have got himself into.

She checked that the front door was locked and then went out of the back, making sure that it was firmly shut behind her. She knew that they were in the middle of the countryside but Robert's warning about people wandering around came back to her and she wanted to make sure that the house was secure.

She went round to the front of the house and lifted her face towards the weak sun that was flooding across the field. Although it was now the first day of December, the sun was still strong enough to dazzle. Unconsciously, she went the opposite way from the previous day, picking up a track that led away from the Muir Pharma plant. She didn't want to bump into any reckless drivers today. All she wanted was good exercise, which would justify spending the afternoon reading her book.

The countryside here was quite different from the rolling fields on the other side of the houses. She was walking into a larger forest, one that she'd seen on the map Laura had given her. This wasn't like the small patches of woodland between Muir Pharma and the motorway, among the large fields with shivering sheep cowering next to the fences trying to keep out of the wind. This was a proper forest with signs all around it, substantial fences to control the deer in the area and, twisting between the trees, larger tracks that were fit for industrial vehicles. Even the smell was different, the sweet pine of the trees filling her nostrils as she walked along one track leading into the darkness of the forest.

The sound of a large chainsaw broke the silence. The noise of a lorry up ahead made her change direction, turning to the left and avoiding the workers. She tried to get her bearings, and thought that she was walking north, but it was difficult to see beyond the trees and fields. She heard a rustle in the undergrowth and stopped. She waited, watching in the direction of the noise, and was rewarded for her patience when a small fox emerged from the forest and ran across the nearest field. She smiled. It wasn't just her who was avoiding people. All the wildlife knew it was safer to be away from human noise.

After following the track around the edges of the forest, she came upon some farm cottages next to a new building, a large modern hangar. A tractor was parked outside, its engine still running and its trailer full of hay. Leaning on a gate, she watched the farmer climb into the tractor and drive away, waving at her as he passed. Comforted by the peacefulness of the scene, she looked at the nearest farm cottage, some hens pecking the ground near the door, and saw a familiar cat sitting on the front step washing himself.

'So, this is your other house,' Ella muttered into the air. The cat didn't hear her, too engrossed in his own business, and she turned to go back.

She knew the right direction to get back to Laura's house but misjudged the distance and came through the trees next to the third house. She stood and caught her breath, looking at all three houses from the other direction. Although the third one was set back more into the trees than the others, the road did go right around it so it wasn't totally overshadowed. There was a black van at the back of the house and she saw a man in a large hooded jacket go inside carrying a heavy box. Robert's words came back to her about not approaching people that she saw around the research facility. But this man wasn't a demonstrator, he was unloading parcels from a van into one of the company houses. He was working for Robert rather than for anyone else.

Hurriedly walking to the front of the house, she looked into the large picture window in the living area, but the blinds must have been lowered because the interior was in total darkness. She glanced at the side of the house. What was a stunning statement window at the end of Laura's house, in this building had been replaced by a solid wall.

She felt a shiver of tension run down her back as she looked at the house. There was something sinister about the place. Telling herself not to imagine dangers when they weren't there, she shook her head and started walking up the road towards Laura's house. Cold from her walk, despite the exercise, she looked up at the sky and saw clouds gathering above, blocking out the sun. It was time to go inside.

Ella tried to unlock the back door and found that it was open. She took off her boots and padded into the living space. Laura was sitting at the table, papers laid out in front of her.

'You're back early,' said Ella.

Laura smiled. 'I've got a lot of reading to do this afternoon and Sam suggested I do it at home. He's worried about you, being here on your own every day.'

Ella tried not to react negatively to the misplaced concern from Sam, which sounded overbearing. 'I'm fine,' she said. 'You know that I like my own company.'

'I know,' Laura replied with a sigh. 'That's what I told him, but he still suggested I come home.' She stretched. 'To be honest, I welcomed the excuse to get away from work for a few hours. It's so busy these days that I feel I deserve a bit of down time. They're preparing for a big press conference and we have an anniversary party coming up, so it's a bit manic.'

Ella glanced at the end of the table and saw a paper bag with what must have been a cake from the motorway café inside it, with her name scribbled on the top in felt pen.

'Did you buy me a cake? That's sweet of you.' Ella went to open up the bag and looked inside. 'It's one of my favourites. You remembered I love carrot cake.'

'Oh, I didn't get it,' replied Laura. 'It was here on the table when I came in. Somebody else must have bought it for you.'

Ella was confused. 'Did I forget to lock the door?' she asked. 'I was so sure that I'd locked both doors before I went for my walk.'

'You did. Everything was locked when I got here. You didn't forget.' She laughed. 'That explains Robert's comment when I left the office. He said something about hoping we enjoyed the cake and I didn't know what he meant. He must have got it for you.'

'Does he have a key, then?' Ella asked, her voice sounding hollow.

'He has the master key to all of the houses. It was great when we moved in because we knew that he could leave stuff for us when we were out.'

'Don't you feel insecure, knowing someone else has the key to your house, and can come in at any time?'

'We don't mind,' said Laura calmly. 'You'll have noticed that we have locks upstairs and a bolt at the front door so we can always lock the place if we need to. Anyway, we're only talking about Robert. He's a good friend.'

Looking down at the cake, such an innocuous object, Ella felt hounded and didn't like the feeling of being watched. Too many people were invading her space. She didn't like Sam, with his high-handed attitude, sending Laura to look after her. Robert was probably intending to be kind, but it made her feel on edge to know that he could come into the house whenever. She wanted to like him but she was beginning to think that he and Sam had to control everything around them.

She wondered what Mitch thought about Sam and Robert's intrusive behaviour. She couldn't believe that he was happy with it. Both she and Mitch needed to be on their own as much as with other people, that's why they got on so well. It reminded her forcefully that she wanted to see him to ask about Carl's allegations, why he'd failed to meet Carl and if he really mistrusted the company Laura liked so much.

'What time will Mitch be home?' asked Ella.

'He's not coming back tonight. He's gone to Edinburgh to see some friends he used to work with at the university.

'He's gone already?' Ella collapsed onto a chair. 'He went on his own? Didn't you want to go too?'

'No,' said Laura, 'it's Mitch they want to see, not me. It's his old boss at the university. He wasn't very happy when Mitch left them and came to join Muir Pharma. Mitch was one of their specialists dealing with the animals they were using for research. They were sorry to lose him, but I think he was ready for a move. He'd been there for too long and they were taking him for granted.' Her voice grew lighter. 'It's just the two of us tonight, so I thought we could have supper and then watch a film together. You said there was one you kept on missing and wanted to watch. We can have a girls' night in like we used to.'

'That would be nice,' replied Ella automatically. 'I just need a shower first.' She turned and went up the stairs, trying not to feel too frustrated that she'd have to wait another day to speak to Mitch. She was over-reacting, something that was getting more usual these days. Once she'd spoken to Mitch she could relax.

Chapter 8

The next day, Ella was sitting at the table leafing through the bundle of notes Carl had given her, wondering when she'd be able to give it back to Mitch. She knew she was supposed to be here to recuperate but the mystery of Ruth's note was nagging at her conscience, and Carl's allegations had only deepened the mystery.

The door burst open and Laura came rushing in.

'Ella, I need to speak to you.' Her voice seemed to crack. She sank down on the sofa and drew in a shaky breath.

This wasn't like her light hearted and confident friend. She sounded distracted and angry.

'Laura, what's the matter?'

Her friend shivered and pulled her jacket more tightly round her shoulders.

'What's happened?' Ella tried again.

She waited but Laura didn't answer. Ella ignored the inner voice still telling her not to get involved, knowing that it was far too late to pull back. 'What's wrong?'

Laura sighed deeply, then her words tumbled out. 'Mitch has left,' she wailed. 'He came into the office and we had a row. Now I don't know where he's gone. I don't know what to do. I'm so busy at work, I don't have time for this.'

'Do you have any idea where he went?'

'No,' she sobbed. 'I've been calling his mobile but it's switched off. He had some stupid idea that he had to change his phone and he promised to give me the new number, but he didn't and now he's just gone.'

'When did he go?'

'I don't know exactly. We had a big argument, then he left and I came here trying to find him.'

So, a day after he'd failed to meet Carl, thought Ella. What must have been going on in his mind? She had to find him. 'What did you argue about?' asked Ella. 'Is that why he left?'

Laura hesitated for a moment before answering. 'It was just about work. We're always arguing about work. He thinks I spend too much time in the office…'

'Nothing else?'

'No, not really.' She paused and started again. 'He wanted to talk to me, said I was in danger. He's been obsessing about information he's gathered from one of our old scientists who had committed suicide. It happened years ago but Mitch seemed to think it was something to do with Muir Pharma…' She stopped and then carried on before Ella could ask what she meant. 'I was tired and didn't want to talk about it. I thought he was just jealous of Sam, but when I said that he lost his temper. Started shouting that it was me who was obsessed with Sam, not him…' She flushed at the memory. 'He's been jealous of Sam for months but he's never come up with lies about him before.'

Ella felt a chill creep over her as she watched Laura's pretty face harden. 'That doesn't sound like Mitch. Are you sure they're lies?'

Laura jumped up from the sofa and started pacing the room, the motion spurring her on, fear turning to anger. 'It's just his jealousy, it always makes him see conspiracies and problems that only exist in his imagination. He's gone too far this time. He's going to destroy everything – the company, my career, my life.'

Ella put up her hands, as if she could push back the angry words. 'But if he's missing, shouldn't you go to the police?' She hesitated as she remembered what Carl had said about Mitch not trusting the police, but she ploughed on. 'He may have had an accident. He could be injured.'

'No, I can't go to the police.' She sounded almost hysterical and then, with an effort, spoke more calmly. 'You know Mitch. He likes his own company, sometimes just needs time by himself. He would hate it if I told the police. He's just never gone off without telling me before. He may have gone to the holiday cottage. You were there once, remember? It used to belong to my parents.'

Before Ella could speak, Laura seemed to come to a decision, her voice growing firmer. 'You could try to find him for me, check the cottage for me, speak to him. You have time and I don't.'

Ella frowned. 'I am worried about him; I certainly need to speak to him.'

'That would be so helpful. I can tell you what he's been like, where else he might have gone. He can't have gone far. I just need you to find him and we can help him.'

The words echoed in Ella's brain, too close to the words Ruth had used the night they'd argued and she'd left her sister to face Ben Forrester on her own. That unwavering confidence that she could change things. *He won't hurt me,*

Ella, he's ill. I'm the only one that can help him. Despite her doubts, Ella couldn't leave Laura on her own, especially when this time she was asking for help. Ignoring the nagging voice telling her that there was a lot more going on than her best friend seemed willing to share with her, she agreed.

'All right. I'll help if I can, but you need to tell me everything.'

Laura breathed a shaky sigh of relief. She glanced at her watch and came to hug Ella. 'I'll tell you what I know, but I can't do it now. We have an important dinner with investors in Edinburgh tonight and I need to get changed.' She turned and ran up the stairs.

'When can I see you tomorrow?' Ella shouted up behind her. Helpless to stop the inevitable, Ella felt herself being drawn in as Laura's relief flooded through her voice.

'Come over in the afternoon,' Laura's reply floated down, 'I have meetings in the morning I can't get out of, but later in the afternoon is fine.' She looked over the banister. 'Ella, you've made me feel so much better already.'

'I'll go to the cottage today,' said Ella, as the door closed behind Laura.

After she had gone, Ella put on her jacket and left the house. There was no doubt that Mitch was under stress, that much she'd seen when he'd met Carl. But could his allegations about Muir Pharma possibly be true? Sam Renwick was in the public eye, running a successful company, and his reputation was very different from the image Mitch and Carl had painted.

Maybe it was all down to Laura and Mitch, Ella thought as she drove eastwards. Laura seemed happy in her boss's company, taking his side rather than believing her boyfriend. How could Laura, someone she'd known for years, one of her closest friends, work for a man responsible for what Mitch was alleging? She didn't even know if Mitch was telling the truth or was trying to find a way to punish Sam for trying to steal his girlfriend. None of it fitted with the people she knew and had known for years. And if what Mitch said was true, how much did Laura know or suspect?

Ella stopped the car beside the holiday cottage, a low stone building on a country road near the Fife coast. As she went to the back door, she was battered by the blustery wind that was whipping the dull grey sea, visible in the distance, into white ruffles. Inside she was met with silence. 'Mitch, are you here?' she said loudly and her words echoed in the empty space.

She looked around. The modern interior of the property was completely unexpected. As Ella walked through the open-plan kitchen, it became very obvious that it wasn't the cheap and cheerful holiday cottage she remembered. It was now more like a designer hideaway. She remembered Laura talking about the cottage – that it belonged to her parents and how their family all used to take turns to use it for summer holidays. It now looked like Laura had been given free rein to give it a complete overhaul.

All the surfaces were empty of possessions and there were only a few framed photographs on the mantelpiece in the living room to show that the cottage had ever been occupied. Ella picked up one of the photographs and gazed down at the smiling faces of Laura and Mitch, looking happy and relaxed. She wondered again what had happened since that photograph had been taken. It must have been fairly recently. What had gone so wrong for them?

Ella walked into every room, opening drawers and cupboards, but the cottage was deserted. Some of the drawers in the main bedroom were empty, so maybe Mitch had taken clothes from the chest before he'd left, but it was impossible to tell. All she could say was that he hadn't left anything behind and there was no trace of where he'd gone.

Ella locked up the cottage again, frustrated by the wasted journey. It had been a dead end. She drove back in the darkness, flurries of snow blowing against the car, and felt hopeless. Where could he have gone? She needed to talk to Laura before she set off on a fruitless journey again.

She let herself in to the house and had a solitary supper before going to bed early. She left a note for Laura downstairs, knowing she wouldn't be back from Edinburgh until very late. *Mitch wasn't in the holiday house. I think he might have been there, but there's no sign of where he could be now. Ella x*

Chapter 9

The next morning Ella heard Laura get up early and came downstairs before she left the house.

Laura turned a pale face towards her, the blonde hair scraped back into a ponytail, accentuating the dark shadows under her eyes. 'I'm sorry if I disturbed you last night when I got home.' Her eyes filled with tears. 'I've got no word from Mitch yet. No messages.'

Ella stared at her. She didn't know what to think: whether Mitch was really in danger or not; whether his allegations were true or not. Was it all just a figment of his imagination? She could understand, more than most, how the mind played tricks on you, inventing dangers that didn't exist, but could that explain what was happening?

'I still think you're the one to try to find him for me,' said Laura. 'Come and see me this afternoon, I can tell you what's been going on and you can see what you think.'

'Of course,' replied Ella. 'I can come any time.'

Laura gave her a quick hug and left the house. Whatever was going on in her mind, thought Ella, she was now worried about her boyfriend.

Ella poured herself a coffee and sat down at the table, the noise of the television in the background. Laura always liked watching breakfast television before she left for work.

Standing at the picture window, she looked at the dark morning sky. The other houses were both in darkness and Martin Fraser's car was nowhere to be seen. A light blinked a couple of times upstairs in the far house as if someone was shining a torch inside, only visible because it was such a dark morning. She would have to ask Laura who could be in the house. She shivered as the light flickered around and then she turned away from the window.

The sound of the news report on the television filtered into her consciousness and she looked at the screen, the announcer's voice filling the air.

'Firefighters now have the fire under control, but police have confirmed that one person has died and three people have been taken to hospital. They are asking for anyone who can provide information about the incident to contact Police Scotland.'

The camera panned out and showed a building at the back of Waverley Station, one of the windows on an upper floor blackened and still smoking. Then a picture of Carl Davis appeared on the screen.

'It is believed that the fatality in the accident is Carl Davis, a journalist who was staying at the hotel,' the announcer's voice continued.

Ella felt suddenly cold and she leaned forward, scrabbling with the remote control to turn up the volume. She'd only seen him yesterday. How could he be dead? What could have happened to him since then? Accidents seemed to affect all the people she came in contact with. And now Mitch had disappeared. Carl's death changed everything. Uneasy worries were now tangible concerns.

'Good morning, ladies and gentlemen. As you know,

there was a fire in the Old Town Hotel last night. There was one fatality and several people were taken to hospital suffering from the effects of smoke inhalation.

'The Fire & Rescue Service is still investigating the incident, but first indications are that the fire was started in one room, probably from a cigarette. A new sprinkler system installed in the hotel prevented the fire from spreading into other areas.

'It is believed that the deceased was alone when the fire started.'

Ella thought about Carl's scared face; his fear of being followed. And now he was dead. She bent her head. Violent death had come close to her again. She didn't know him very well, had only met him twice, but his life was now extinguished and it brought back the pain of her sister's death all over again.

She went over to pick up the papers he'd given her and leafed through them. A business card fell out of the pile and she stared down at it, *Gregor Munro, Investment Manager, Hodgeson Partners*. Suddenly she realised that this was the analyst Carl had planned to see. Ella groped for her mobile and called the number. Carl's death was a tragic accident and she pushed away the thought of anything more sinister. All she knew was that she had to follow up this lead because Carl had thought it was important.

The more she learned, the more desperately she had to find Mitch. She had to discover what this man could tell her.

She got through to Gregor on the first ring.

'Hello, my name is Ella Scott. I'm a friend of Carl Davis. Did he come to see you?'

'No, we were meeting at noon today. What's the problem?'

'I'm afraid…' She could feel her voice fading and cleared her throat. 'I'm sorry to tell you that he died last night in a fire in Edinburgh. You may not have heard about it.'

She heard his sharp intake of breath. 'I'm so sorry.'

'I was helping him with his story so I wanted to come and see you instead. I think it's important to finish what he started…' She could feel the tears coming and realised that she was telling the truth, that if Carl wasn't able to follow up his story, then she would instead.

After a few moments of silence he said, 'He was due with me at twelve o'clock and I said I would be free for an hour so whenever you get to my office, you can have that hour.'

'Thank you,' replied Ella. She hung up quickly and ran to get changed, pulling out her black boots, black jeans and a brightly coloured cashmere sweater. At the door she grabbed her padded jacket before heading to the car.

In the car, she lifted her eyes from the steering wheel and gazed out of the front window at the grey sky, the wind buffeting the bushes in the fields. She had left London to escape from one nightmare and find peace in Edinburgh but she felt as if she was plunged into another frightening situation.

A movement caught her attention and she saw a figure disappear round the back of the third house. Had someone been watching her? She started the car, angry with herself for letting her fears cloud her thoughts. Was she just imagining dangers where they didn't exist? Jamie Forrester couldn't have followed her up here. She would find out where Mitch could be. It must be some simple misunderstanding.

Chapter 10

By the time she reached the outskirts of Edinburgh, the grey skies had given way to sunshine. She parked near Gregor's office building at the bottom of Lothian Road and, seeing that she was a few minutes early for the meeting, slipped into the corner of Princes Street Gardens to sit quietly and marshal her thoughts. She walked quicky along the path under the trees to the first bench, her boots kicking against the dry leaves.

She sat on the bench for a few moments and gazed at the castle looming above the gardens, stark and beautiful in the sunlight. She couldn't believe that Carl was dead.

Her mobile beeped and she pulled out her phone to look at the message. It was her friend Nicole from work.

A man was asking about you outside the office. He went away when someone said you were on holiday. He was very insistent so I took these photos before he left.

Her heart pounded as she scrolled through the pictures Nicole had taken. They were from a weird angle and blurry but, to her, the figure was unmistakable. It was Jamie Forrester, Ben's brother. She shivered when she looked at the familiar face, half covered by a dark grey hoodie. He looked very like Ben, the more confident brother who had wormed his way into their lives. She knew from bitter experience that Ben could persuade anyone to do what he wanted, particularly his brother. What had he asked him to do for him this time?

At his trial, Ben Forrester stared at the ground and she only saw the top of his blond head. It was his brother Jamie who was gazing at her as she took the stand, his dark eyes almost accusing, as if he blamed her for giving evidence.

She called Nicole. When Ella asked about the man in the pictures, Nicole spoke slowly, her unease coming through her words. 'He said Ben Forrester asked him to find you, said he wanted to give you a message…'

Ella interrupted before she could carry on. 'I don't want any message from him. You know the games he plays. I don't believe he's changed.'

Ella looked over her shoulder into the group of people walking along Princes Street as if her sister's killer was going to materialise out of the crowd to torment her, manipulative as ever. He was stalking her dreams and now he was getting someone else to spy on her for him.

'I know, but he said it was important,' replied Nicole. 'There was something he needed to tell you. Something Ben Forrester wanted him to say.'

'Thanks for sending me the pictures,' Ella replied flatly. 'It's just Ben's usual lies. He's brainwashed someone else to do his dirty work.' But she kept her bitterness to herself. She didn't want to be told again she had to move on with her life. 'I want to ask you something,' Ella went on. 'It's a bit of a long-shot. In your press contact list, is a man called Carl Davis there? He's an investigative reporter.'

There was a short pause and Ella heard the sound of typing. Then Nicole replied. 'I do have his name here.

Actually, now that you mention it, do you remember that sleep-out last year that you were away for? There was one man who complained a bit at the beginning.' She fell silent, obviously trying to remember the event. 'I think it was him. Once he was involved, he seemed to get interested in the whole issue of homelessness, what causes it and so on. He went on to interview some of the service users of the charity and wrote an article a few weeks later that was remarkably good. We all thought it was very balanced. Our communications people now use it all the time.'

'I met him here. I wondered if you'd ever come across him and what you thought of him.'

'From what I know of him, and the number of pieces he wrote about homelessness, I'd say he was always aiming to get to the truth, so I think yes, he was a good journalist.'

'Thanks,' said Ella, and rang off. If it was the same man that Nicole had remembered, it made his story more believable. She could still hardly believe it. Ella hung her head when she remembered her last meeting with Carl. She felt a curl of guilt deep in her stomach. She should have helped him more, gone with him back to Edinburgh maybe, encouraged him to go back to London.

She'd lost all track of time. Glancing at her watch she saw that it was almost noon, so got up and walked briskly along to the end of the park and up Lothian Road, past the grand railway hotel at the end of the street, looking through the windows and smiling as she remembered the parties there. She knew more than anyone how people could change over the years, to deal with what life could throw at them. She just wondered what had been thrown at Laura and Mitch.

She went into the reception area of Hodgeson Partners and almost bumped into two men.

'Ella is that you?' said one of them. 'I'm Gregor Munro.' He was younger than she'd expected and looked as if he should be wearing a rugby kit rather than a smart pin-striped suit. The man next to him was wearing jeans and a woollen sweater. He handed Gregor a mobile phone.

'It should work now,' he said. 'Just call me if you have any more problems.' He turned and smiled at Ella and she returned the smile instinctively. There was a shout from reception and they all looked round to see a silver-haired man beckoning Gregor to come closer.

'Sorry, that's my boss. I need to speak to him. I won't be a moment,' said Gregor. He strode across the floor and accompanied the man to the door, deep in conversation.

Ella looked up at the man in jeans, who didn't seem to have any intention of leaving.

'Do you want to sit down?' he said. 'He might be a while, I know Gregor.' He indicated a seating area next to a flat-screen television on the wall that silently played twenty-four-hour news.

She nodded and they crossed to the chairs. When they sat down, she asked, 'I'm sorry, but who are you? Do you work here too?'

'I'm Jim Stewart. I'm just a friend. I do a bit of work round here. I haven't met you before. How well do you know Gregor?'

'I haven't met him before. I got his name from one of my contacts.' She shivered as she thought again about Carl.

He leaned forward in his chair. 'Are you all right? I'll get you some water.'

She watched him get some water from the machine and felt a pang of jealousy at how completely at ease he seemed despite how out of place he looked in his jeans and sweater.

'Thanks,' she said, as she took the water from him. 'Do you know him well?'

'Yeah, we play rugby together, go running sometimes. When he spends too much time at work, I give him something else to think about.'

She looked around. 'How long has he worked here?'

'I don't want to talk about Gregor. Tell me about you.'

She looked into his dark brown eyes and felt herself respond to his smile. There was something about him that calmed her down and she liked it.

Gregor came back. 'Sorry about that, we can start our meeting now.'

'I'm just going. I'll leave you alone.' Jim held her gaze, reached into his pocket and brought out a card. 'You can contact me on this number.'

'I'm only here on holiday, but thank you,' Ella replied, taking the card and putting it in her pocket.

'Well, if you do need anything you've got my card. Text me sometime before you go.'

'All right, get out of here,' said Gregor. 'You can stop flirting on business time.'

Jim waved at the girl at the reception desk, gave Ella a broad smile and left.

'Sorry about that,' said Gregor, as he led her through to his office, shrugging off his jacket to reveal a shirt straining to cover bulging arm muscles. 'But if you do need technology advice, he's the man to call. He's an expert on cybersecurity, that's his day job. In his spare time, he's a wizard on all kinds of tech gadgets. One of our competitors admitted that he came into their office and swept the place for bugs after one of their clients said that some of their confidential information was being leaked. Everyone thought the information was hacked, but Jim wouldn't accept the obvious answer. Then he found two bugs in the meeting room, so he was right all along.'

They both sat down.

'I'm so sorry about Carl,' said Gregor. 'I saw the news after you'd called. Did you know him well?'

She shook her head. 'Not very well, but it was still a shock.'

'What information can I help you with?'

'Some general background on pharmaceutical companies in Scotland, how drugs are developed, who the main companies are.'

'Right, well, in terms of the sector, there are some reports I dug out for Carl which will give you the background to how drugs are developed, and the profiles of some of the big companies.' He handed her a pile of documents. 'The one on the top is one of our reports on the sector in Scotland, which covers the main companies up here.'

She flicked through the reports. 'That's great.'

'In terms of the process, you know that drugs are developed through a series of clinical trials, starting with lab tests, then animal testing and finally testing on humans. It can take over a decade to go through the process, and then the compound might still fail. It's a very risky business.'

'Are there any ways a company can take shortcuts?'

He thought for a moment or two. 'Not these days. Each

stage is tightly controlled and a number of companies and regulators will be involved in the process. Some companies only do the initial discovery and testing and then contract out the larger trials to partner companies. The regulator will be looking over their shoulder all the time.'

'Can you tell me anything about Muir Pharma?' asked Ella.

'One of the rising stars of the biotech sector,' said Gregor. 'Set up by Sam Renwick, a brilliant biochemistry student. He was also a smart businessman and started taking over small research companies only a few years after university. I don't know where the initial capital came from because he didn't start with anything; comes from one of the poorest areas in Edinburgh.'

Ella thought about the confident and single-minded man she knew, as Gregor went on in his soft Edinburgh burr.

'They have lots of investors now and give generously to local charities.'

'I've also met Robert Young. Do you know anything about him?'

'I don't know so much about him. He's always been in the shadow of his friend. He and Sam have known one another since school.' He hesitated, then added. 'He's a tough character. Has always watched his friend's back. They're closer than brothers.'

'So have they had any failures along the way?'

'All pharmaceutical companies have, Ella. It's not unusual.'

'What else can you tell me?'

He paused for a few moments. 'At the top of their game,

growing fast, just moved into brand new premises, attracting a lot of interest and money from investors. They have good relationships with several of the big pharmaceutical companies, who are also investors. You see a lot of these partnerships now. The large companies have the money, and the smaller R & D firms the skills. It's how the industry has developed over the last few years.'

'Have you heard about any side effects from their drugs?'

'It's always possible that a compound could have a rare side effect not uncovered through large-scale clinical trials. But then the company would be morally bound to inform the regulator and investigate.'

'Morally or legally?'

He shrugged. 'Both. There are some well publicised stories of pharmaceutical companies not being too energetic about investigating potential side effects of successful drugs. But patients are getting much more vocal about these types of cases, so the truth does come out.'

'And have you heard anything about Muir Pharma scientists dying in mysterious circumstances?'

He sat back in his chair. 'Are you serious? Do you have someone making these allegations?'

'Yes, but all unsubstantiated at this stage. This is an important sector, doing work that is risky and expensive. At the moment, all I have are suspicions. I'd need a lot more than that.'

'I don't know anything about scientists dying in mysterious circumstances.' He paused. 'You might be better speaking to my older sister about that. She works for Police Scotland here in Edinburgh.'

'Would she be happy to meet me?'

'I would think so.' He hesitated and then went on. 'She's had a difficult time recently. Been off sick for a few months.' He sighed heavily. 'She's gone back to work in the cold cases unit at Police Scotland, or whatever it's called now, looking again at cases that have never been resolved. She might know something that could help you. I'll call her and you can set something up.'

As she was leaving, he shook her hand firmly.

'Muir Pharma has a lot of resources at its disposal and has proved itself to be litigious in the past. There was one case a couple of years ago where the CEO of a smaller competitor, a man called Andy Paige, alleged that Muir Pharma tried to put them out of business. Muir Pharma threw everything at him and he lost the case, and his company. He committed suicide. Muir Pharma, calm as you like, picked up the business from the administrators. I'm not saying they did anything illegal, but they went to great lengths to prevent their reputation being damaged and didn't seem to care that they ruined a man's life.' He went over to his desk. 'I'm sure I have the details somewhere. Wait a minute.'

He pulled a press cutting out from his drawer and held the piece of paper in his hand, frowning as he stared at it. 'I met him at a conference once and we got chatting. We had kids who were about the same age and they were all rugby mad. He said that however busy he was, and wherever he had to travel, he always tried to get back on Saturdays to watch his boys play rugby.' He handed her the piece of paper. 'If you do find out that Muir Pharma used ugly tactics to destroy him, I'd like to know. I wouldn't invest our money in a company like that and I don't think many of our competitors would.'

'Yes, of course I'd tell you.'

'Good luck. I'll send a note to Susan so you can ask her some of your questions about the scientists. I'm not sure what she might know, but she was certainly working for the police during the time you're talking about. Just be careful. Sam Renwick doesn't like to be crossed. You'll need to be very sure of your facts before going public with anything.'

Chapter 11

Ella left Gregor's office and walked towards Castle Terrace. She'd calmed down when she'd spoken to him but, on her own, she again felt thrown by the shock of hearing about Carl. She reached her car but stopped on the pavement, the bright sunlight and cold air tempting her to linger. She leaned on the car, trying to decide what to do. She was surprised about the strength of her reaction to the death of someone she hadn't known that well, or even liked that much. She thought about Nicole's description of how his morose attitude covered a principled journalist. She remembered his fears of being followed in Edinburgh. He'd been so scared that he'd reminded her of herself. She'd thought they were fantasies, but he was dead now. And, only a few days ago, a car had almost knocked him over. Maybe he'd been right to be so scared, maybe he had more reason than she had to fear the people around him.

Ella walked away from the car. She was feeling the need to go back to somewhere she knew well and so started walking towards the Grassmarket. When she was a student, they'd often come here at night. She associated it with memories of carefree times spent in a group that included Mitch and Laura. She needed to feel that comfort again.

The walk took her past groups of tourists, pubs, shops

and restaurants, and a strip club. Then there was the familiar wide thoroughfare of the Grassmarket, busy with traffic, bustling with people and dominated by public houses. In the sunshine, people sat on benches in the square and took in the views.

She glanced at the frontages of the old buildings and took a deep breath. She knew where she was going. Her step more definite, she dodged around the groups of people standing in front of her looking up at the castle, and headed for her favourite French bistro. From the look of it, she realised that it must have changed owners several times since her university days but it still looked authentic. She went inside and sat down at an empty table in front of the window, ordering the special of the day and pouring herself a glass of water, looking longingly at the wine glass but rejecting it when she remembered the car.

She stared out of the window. Something was nagging at her about what had happened to Carl. He'd been smoking in his room, the police had said, causing the fire in the building. There was something that didn't seem right about that. She thought back to her time with Carl, trying to remember what was bothering her. After a few seconds she remembered his reaction to the people smoking outside the café. The police had said that he was alone. If smoking had been the cause of the fire, it must have been someone other than Carl. He can't have been alone.

Did the authorities want a quick explanation for the fire, so hadn't asked too many questions? She didn't want to think about the alternative – that they would deliberately hide the real evidence.

She remembered a policeman who had helped them

when Ruth had been killed. He had been a good man, honestly trying to help them negotiate a difficult situation, but this was more complicated. Carl said he believed that the police were in Sam's pocket and that Mitch didn't trust them with his suspicions. Could they both have been right, after all?

Ella ate her food, barely noticing what was on her plate, and brooded about Mitch. She had to accept now that he was in a dangerous position and she felt scared for what might happen to him. She needed to speak to him urgently. Laura had said he was in Edinburgh, but Ella didn't know where, or whether he was even still there. She'd need to go back to Fife.

After paying the bill, Ella went outside and started to walk back, but before she had gone a few steps she heard a loud shout from behind her at the end of the Grassmarket as it turned into the tunnel-like darkness of the Cowgate. She saw a large car parked at the bottom of Candlemaker Row, in front of a door that looked familiar. Suddenly she remembered where she'd seen it before: in a television report she'd seen a few days before. It was the door of the charity that Sam supported. The report had said Sam would be there for most of the week.

She turned towards the noise and stopped at the bottom of Victoria Street, its old-fashioned shopfronts curving up the hill, and stood behind a group who had also turned to look. On the pavement next to the car, she saw a recognisable figure standing over another man who was holding a camera. Sam was gripping the photographer's collar, and the man was trying to struggle free. Ella couldn't hear what they were saying but someone else tried to pull Sam away.

Enraged, he threw off the man's arm and gave another ugly shout.

There was now a crowd forming at the end of the Grassmarket, watching the fight. Another driver had come out of his car to try to break them up, but Sam turned and threw the man down against the car. As if suddenly aware of the growing crowd of people watching, he looked up and across at the spectators, his eyes stopping on Ella's face. She could see the fury and the violence in his expression, and instinctively ducked behind someone in the crowd. When she looked up, he was no longer staring in her direction and she told herself he wouldn't have been able to focus on an individual face in the crowd.

Ella heard the clatter of footsteps running across the square and saw two uniformed police officers approach the Cowgate to investigate the disturbance. They almost reached Sam's car and then seemed to recognise him, slowed down, exchanged a quick glance, and then veered up Candlemaker Row, ignoring the disturbance on the roundabout. They disappeared from the Grassmarket the next moment and Ella shook her head. It looked as if they'd recognised Sam and decided they weren't going to get involved.

Sam was quickly pulled away from the man by an assistant and dragged into a building out of sight. The crowd around Ella began to lose interest and melted away, throwing a few curious stares behind them. She looked in the direction the police had gone. Why had they ignored what was happening? She took a few steps towards the building, unwilling to pass, but keen to reach her car as quickly as she could. She walked past the open door, her head down.

He shouldn't be allowed to get away with this, Ella thought angrily. Even the forces of law and order were ignoring what this man was doing. He was just like a playground bully, allowed to get his own way without any constraint or control.

She heard a roar, and her arm was grabbed fiercely. She looked up to see Sam's furious eyes, now focused on her, and was suddenly aware of his power and rage. She took a step back but he didn't let her go.

'What are you doing here?' he hissed. 'Are you following me? Don't poke your nose into what doesn't concern you.'

'What do you mean? You're hurting me.' Ella tried to pull away her arm, but however much she twisted and turned, she couldn't get free.

She heard the noise of footsteps behind her and Robert rushed towards them. He stood between them and tried to push them apart. 'Leave her alone,' he said quietly to Sam. 'We need to get out of here before the police come back and decide to ask questions.'

'There was someone taking photographs,' growled Sam. 'And then she decided to interfere. I tell you, Robert, I've had enough.'

'Shut up,' said Robert cutting Sam off and pulling him across the road to the car. They ignored Ella and she rubbed her sore arm, leaning on the wall and trying to keep her balance. She watched Sam being persuaded to go into his car but he wasn't going to give up so easily. As he saw the man with the camera still lurking nearby, Sam snatched away his camera and threw it onto the ground with a loud crash. It disintegrated into a shower of plastic and glass and she heard a howl from the man who scrambled to pick up his property.

In an instant, Sam was driven away. Two bystanders bent down to help the man pick up his smashed camera. Ella turned away from the scene, shaken by the anger and violence she'd witnessed; the rage and naked aggression in Sam's face as he looked towards her, imprinted in her memory.

She shook her head to try to clear the image as she walked briskly back to her car, but it remained fixed, potent enough to tear the veil from his usual charismatic manner, illuminating so much that she had always found troubling about Sam. She knew that he liked attention, but it was clearly only on his own terms. The man with the camera must have been taking pictures he hadn't authorised and he'd reacted with frustration and anger, his violence never far below the surface. Sam's façade had shattered, just like the man's camera on the hard pavement.

Chapter 12

As she drove back to Fife, Ella brooded over Sam's behaviour. His fury and aggression confirmed Gregor's warnings that Sam always wanted to get his own way. Gregor had been so insistent about her needing to be sure of her facts before going public that Ella wondered if he himself had ever had a run-in with Sam Renwick. It seemed that people either loved or hated Sam, perhaps relating to how much they stood in his way or not.

Ella found a parking space under the building easily. In reception, there were two uniformed security men at the door, and a third sitting near the lifts watching a bank of screens showing pictures from CCTV cameras positioned around the building. The men turned to stare at Ella as she came in.

Laura must have been looking out for her because she heard the familiar voice before the girl at reception could stretch out her hand to pick up the phone.

'You didn't find him,' Laura stated.

Ella shook her head and Laura gave her a quick hug.

'Thanks for looking anyway.' Her red eyes and jumpy manner were barely hidden by the assured voice. Laura pointed through the reception area towards an inner garden courtyard with tables. 'I thought we could go over to the restaurant – have a coffee. Nicer than sitting in a meeting room, being overlooked by everyone.'

Ella nodded and followed her, glancing back at the security men, who were watching them leave. Laura picked a table at the far end of the courtyard, next to the windows overlooking the grassy area outside. It always struck Ella how compact a city Edinburgh was, unlike the sprawl of London. You could get to the countryside from central Edinburgh within half an hour, and Muir Pharma was in an ideal situation, close to the city and the airport.

When Laura placed the steaming coffee on the table, Ella glanced over to the security men. 'They don't look very friendly.'

Laura laughed, but the sound jarred in the quiet area. 'They're all right. Because we do animal testing here, activists are always outside. We have expensive equipment in our labs, not to mention a lot of confidential data, so Sam likes to know everything is secure.'

The scene with Sam still fresh in her mind, Ella took a sip of the coffee and asked, 'What's Sam like to work for?'

Laura didn't hesitate. 'He's great. He knows what he wants and makes sure he takes everyone along with him. He's built a successful company. It's a good place to work.'

It sounded like a well-practised line. Ella bit her lip but decided to say nothing about Sam's behaviour in the Grassmarket. It was an odd feeling, not being sure whether the person sitting in front of her was still the old Laura that she once knew. She didn't like the feeling, but she knew she mistrusted people on principle these days. She could never forget that Ruth had been killed because of that trust. Ruth's death had changed Ella forever.

'I'm so glad you're here. There's no-one else I can talk to.' Laura looked much the same as before, just more polished. But the professional mask was very thin, and she lifted up her cup with hands shaking so much that the coffee dripped onto the table.

At that moment Ella felt so much pity for her. 'Why don't you start from the beginning, tell me what happened before Mitch left?'

Laura took a deep breath, glanced out of the window as if she didn't know where to start, then turned back with an effort. 'We had an argument about work. As I told you, we always seem to be arguing about work. Mitch didn't like the company, didn't like the people. Didn't even like this office.' She showed a flash of irritation, and took another sip of her coffee. 'Even though the equipment and resources we have here are miles better than the stuff he used at the university. I kept telling him that but he wouldn't listen.'

'Did he say why he didn't like it here?'

'He just said he didn't like the culture, the way people did things, the way everything had a commercial value. But I told him that it would be different from being in an academic environment. We have to look at how we're spending investors' money.'

'Why did he leave the university?'

She hesitated. 'Things had got a bit difficult there. He accused some of his closest colleagues of plagiarising his research. You know what it can be like. Everyone is very precious about their work and terrified that someone might steal it from them. I said that couldn't happen here. Everyone works for the company, and Muir Pharma owns all the rights to the discoveries. That's why they're so well compensated here, but it comes with less scientific freedom. The company wants to maximise the chance of developing successful treatments.'

She was lapsing into sales mode again, so Ella tried to bring the conversation back to Mitch. 'So, once he was here, what happened?'

Tears filled Laura's eyes again. 'I don't know exactly. I'm away a lot. My job means I work with our partners and collaborators, our main investors, and the contract research companies who carry out the larger clinical trials on the compounds we've developed. And anyway, I didn't want to always be looking over his shoulder. I thought he would get on better without me here all the time, checking his every movement.'

Ella didn't interrupt, hoping that she was at last going to get some concrete information.

'Mitch made some critical comment about the company and I must have snapped at him. He just lost his temper, started shouting at me, saying I only cared about my job and nothing else. I'd never seen him so angry before and I thought…' She flushed and then carried on. 'I thought he was going to hit me.'

'Not Mitch, surely?' Deeply shocked, Ella found it hard to believe that the Mitch she knew could be violent, but wondered if something had happened in the years since university.

'I've thought about it a lot since then. He walked out, as if he couldn't trust himself to stay in the same room as me.' Laura leaned forward in her chair, her eyes red and puffy. 'Ella, you have to find him. When he gets back, everything will be different. I'm going to tell him I'll leave Muir Pharma if he wants me to. We can move somewhere else and find work. I can't carry on like this. That's why I need to find him.'

She took deep breaths to try to calm down. Although she seemed genuinely upset, she had said nothing about Mitch's suspicions about the company, or about whether he'd told her he'd approached the press. Ella stared at her friend, willing her to say more about what she knew, but Laura stayed silent.

'So, do you have any idea where else I should start looking?' Ella asked finally. 'What about in his office here?'

'I've looked already,' Laura said firmly. 'There's nothing in his desk.'

She seemed to be closing off every possible avenue. Did Laura want him found or not? 'Are there any of his colleagues who might know anything?' Ella persisted.

'No. He didn't say anything to his team or to our personnel people. So, I've said that he's ill and will be off for a few days.'

'And what about his old university colleagues? Could he have gone there?'

Laura paused then said, 'He might have spoken to his old professor. He's in Edinburgh. Lives in Morningside.' She hesitated and then carried on. 'I haven't asked him. I don't think he'd help me find Mitch, even if he knows something. I don't think he likes me.'

'Well, if you give me his address, I'll speak to him.' Laura glanced at her watch and Ella tried to think of anything else she could ask to produce any leads. 'Did Mitch have any favourite places he might go to? Or any other friends he could stay with?'

'I really thought he'd have gone to our holiday cottage.' She shook her head again. 'He is quite a loner. Likes walking, reading, cooking as well.' She gave a misty smile. 'He's a better cook than me.'

'All right.' Ella tried to sound more definite than she was feeling. 'I'll try to speak to his old professor. See if I can find anything.' She glanced over at the security guards. 'But I'd like to see where he worked in case there's anything there that might give me a clue.'

Laura's wan smile faded and she frowned. 'I'm sorry, but we aren't allowed to take visitors round unannounced. It's one of our rules.'

Taken aback by her reluctance, Ella tried again. 'Maybe we could just walk over to his lab? I could have a quick look at it.'

'Ella, you don't understand, this isn't like a normal office. We aren't allowed to take people round unless it's all been approved.'

'There you are,' a voice behind them cut off her response.

Laura jumped up from her chair. 'Robert, I thought you and Sam were away today.'

'We came back earlier than expected. I need to speak to you about a couple of things. No rush.' He looked at Ella. 'Hi again.' Ella smiled weakly back. He acted like he had forgotten their behaviour in the Grassmarket, his usual calmness restored. The only sign that anything had happened was a cold stare directed at Ella. She peered behind him, but couldn't see Sam. A movement upstairs caught her eye, and she was sure she caught a glimpse of him disappearing into an office. She glanced back at Robert, his smile and jokes completely at odds with the tension she'd seen in him earlier.

Robert was handing over some glossy tickets to Laura, who leaned across to take them. She gave one to Ella. 'Come along to our party on Saturday,' she said. 'Sam and Robert are celebrating our successful move and our anniversary. It should make up for me working all weekend.'

'That's very kind of you,' replied Ella, looking at Robert uncertainly.

'You should come,' he said. 'It's at the Balmoral. It's going to be a big party.'

Ella watched him as he walked away across the open space, nodding at the security men on the door. Like Sam, he was certainly confident – a man who had everything he wanted in life. Robert might be in Sam's shadow, competent and controlled, but in his own quiet way he was just as charismatic.

She followed Laura back through reception, and Laura paused and pointed along a corridor with open-plan offices along the side, walkways linking them to the other wing. Grateful for any information, Ella hung on to her words.

'The building was purpose-built for us – offices along one wing and labs on the other, through those walkways. There are open spaces at each end for scientists to meet informally. It was modelled on some of the best European facilities.'

'You must do this a fair amount in your job,' Ella commented. 'Showing people around, I mean.'

'Yes. With enough warning, we can take visitors round the building. We just have to let the scientists know, to be sure that there isn't any confidential information left lying around. We have to protect our discoveries because it's such a competitive area.'

In the distance, Ella could see scientists working at lab benches, and other figures in white coats moving around the large machines behind the glass. It looked busy and efficient, everything accomplished silently. She moved towards the security barrier.

'Did Mitch work alone?'

'No, he was in a team of four.'

'And what was Mitch working on?'

She hesitated, then answered. 'One of our newest drugs. It's just about to start large clinical trials.'

As they turned away from the corridor, they almost collided with two young scientists walking towards the secure area. Ella glanced at their rubber-soled shoes. That was why the place was so eerily silent.

'Hey Laura,' said the young man, as he swiped his pass over the panel at the side of the door and the door slid open. 'Sorry to hear Mitch is off sick. Hope it isn't anything serious.'

'No, he's got a nasty bout of flu.' Laura lied smoothly. 'But he's probably going to be off the whole week, I'm afraid.'

The man looked at his colleague and grimaced. 'More work for us, then.'

Ella wasn't going to miss the opportunity. Ignoring Laura's gasp of surprise, she stuck out her hand, effectively stopping them in their tracks. 'Hello, I'm Ella. I'm a friend of Laura and Mitch. It's good to meet you both. Are you on Mitch's team? Have you worked here for long?'

'Yes, but only for a few months or so, since he joined

us. My name's Ed Tan,' he glanced at Laura uncertainly, as if seeking permission to reply.

'My name's Karen,' muttered the woman, blushing a deep red.

'And do you like it here?'

They mumbled something and made a hasty retreat into the lab. Ella glanced at Laura's rigid expression. 'They work with Mitch. They might know something we don't.' She watched her curiously, waiting for the reaction.

Laura breathed out a huge sigh. 'I know, I know. But I'm only trying to protect Mitch. And I suppose I don't really want everyone here knowing about our problems.'

'Have you reported him missing yet?'

'No. I thought if you could find him, then I wouldn't need to go to the police.'

'You need to tell them, Laura.'

She nodded. 'I suppose you're right.' She glanced behind her as if she expected to see her boss standing there. 'Sam will be wondering where I am.'

Another quick hug and she'd gone. Ella walked slowly down to the car, thinking about what she'd said. Laura seemed upset about Mitch, but was it genuine? Had Mitch told her all he'd suspected? Did she really want to find him to make a new start away from Edinburgh as she'd said, or to stop him from leaking information about the company? She was her best friend, but Ella still couldn't judge her motivations. She'd always been good at reading people but her instincts could now cheat her and she wasn't sure any longer whether she could rely on them.

At the car, Ella leaned against the door, looking again at the invitation to the party. She glanced up at the Muir

Pharma building and wondered who was telling the truth. She bent down to unlock the car, flicking the remote, but then realised it was already open and all she'd done was lock it again. She must have pressed the key in her pocket, or maybe she'd just forgotten to lock it. She stared at the CCTV camera at the corner of the building. At least no-one would have tried to steal the car under the security camera. Shaking off the uncomfortable feeling that her every movement was being watched, she climbed in and drove off, relieved when she got past the barrier to the car park and left the Muir Pharma building behind.

Chapter 13

Ella woke up the next morning feeling awful, unable to shake off unsettling dreams about a car that became a monster serpent with Ben Forrester's face. So much for her words to Nicole that she'd left Ben Forrester behind. He was part of her bad dream, mixing the present with the past, reducing her back into a quivering mass of hate and emotion.

Her phone beeped and she read a text from Gregor, groaning when she realised she had to go and see Susan Munro, Gregor's police officer sister, at lunchtime. Ella knew she had to pull herself together and focus on the present, not the past. She needed to remind herself why she wanted to see Susan. Why it was so important to gather the facts about the Muir Pharma scientists who had disappeared. She'd emailed Gregor with the few details to pass on to his sister, but couldn't ignore the small voice in her head that told her not to place much faith in a police officer to give any information. They were usually seeking information, if they were interested at all.

She waited for Susan where she'd suggested to meet, in the National Library of Scotland café on George IV Bridge, calmed by the quiet atmosphere and gentle chatter from researchers and visitors entering and leaving the ground floor of the imposing building. It was a seductive view of the normal lives of people who didn't spend their days questioning the reality around them.

'Ella? Is that you?' A short, fair-haired woman came to her table and Ella looked up into features so like Gregor's that it could only have been his sister. Where he looked just like a rugby player, Susan looked all the world like a capable farmer's wife. She put a cup of coffee, a plate with a large slice of chocolate cake and two forks down on the table between them before collapsing onto a chair. 'I can never resist the cakes in here. But you'll have to help me eat it.'

Before she had sat down, Ella would have said she couldn't have eaten a thing, but they demolished the cake between them, while going through the usual introductory chatter about how long Ella was in Edinburgh and how well she knew the city.

Ella felt instinctively that this woman could be trusted. A priceless quality for a police officer, she thought as Susan got out her notebook.

'Gregor passed on the names of the scientists you were interested in. What else can you tell me about them?' asked Susan.

'My friend told me that the first scientist, Trevor Fisher, committed suicide eight years ago. His colleague John Roper, an experienced climber and hillwalker, was killed in a freak fall while walking in the Pentlands a few days later.' She looked up at Susan. 'I don't know much more than that, and haven't found anything when I searched online, so can you tell me anything else about what happened to them?'

Susan frowned and leaned forward. 'Ella, what exactly is your interest here?'

'My friend works for Muir Pharma and says he has found information that these deaths were not simply a suicide and accident. I don't know why he's so sure, so I wondered if you had any information that would shed light on what happened.'

Susan stared at her without speaking, then said slowly, 'I can only tell you what's public information. We do know a little more about these two men so if your friend can tell us anything else we'd like to talk to him. Can you give me his details?'

'I'm afraid I don't know exactly where he is at the moment.' She sighed. 'I'm a bit worried about him. There's something else I have to tell you. There was someone Mitch was in touch with, a journalist, Carl Davis. You probably know about the fire in The Old Town Hotel? The only fatality was Carl. And Mitch has gone into hiding. I'm still trying to find him. Perhaps if you can tell me what you know I can reassure him that you might reopen the case. What else can you tell me?'

'I haven't found much more than the public information. Trevor Fisher was ruled as a suicide. There was no evidence that anyone else was involved or that his death was due to anything other than a single shot fired from a gun, licensed in his name.' Susan handed her the copy of a press cutting. 'This was published at the time in *The Scotsman.*'

'Thank you,' said Ella, skimming the article briefly, even though it seemed to contain the same information she already knew. She'd read it more carefully later. There might be a detail she'd missed, and she looked back up at

Susan, trying not to feel that she was clutching at straws.

Susan handed her a couple of longer press cuttings. 'There was more press coverage of John Roper's accident. He tripped over a steep incline while walking in the Pentlands and fell down a slope. He wasn't found until the next morning and he died of hypothermia. He was out walking alone, there was no-one with him when he was seen leaving his car that morning. Several walkers who were on the hill that day were interviewed, as it was fairly unusual for such an experienced walker and climber to have an accident on a low range like the Pentlands. His cuts and bruises were all consistent with his fall. There were a couple of other people seen in the vicinity where he fell, but they were never traced.'

Ella seized on her words. 'So, his death might not have been an accident? Could he have been pushed and then left somewhere not on the main routes? It was the cold that killed him, not the fall.'

Susan looked doubtful. 'It's possible, I suppose, but all the evidence at the time pointed to an accident.'

'But the other walkers on the hill might have been following him?' asked Ella quickly. It was a chink in what seemed like a solid conclusion, but it was something.

'It's possible, but we have no proof. We would need to have new evidence to reopen the case. There was no proof to indicate foul play at the scene, no evidence of anything other than accidental injury.'

'Is there anything else you found out that could help me get through to Mitch?' asked Ella.

Susan hesitated, then carried on, 'I shouldn't really tell you this… but before his death, Trevor Fisher's wife called the police a few times, claiming she was being followed. She talked about being harassed on one occasion. We had officers parked at the end of her road for a few weeks, but nothing came of it. It was after they'd split up, but before he died. I knew one of the officers who worked on the case and I remember him saying that he thought there was something going on with that family that they weren't prepared to talk about. He just didn't know what it was.'

Ella was about to speak when Susan held up her hands. 'As of now, the cases are still closed. If we were to reopen them, it would need to be because of real evidence that these deaths weren't what they seemed. That others were involved at the very least. We don't just need a theoretical motive, but evidence of someone acting on it.'

'Thanks for being so open with me,' said Ella. 'At least I know more of the facts now.'

There was really nothing left to say, so Ella gathered up her coat and Susan Munro did the same. They walked together along George IV Bridge towards Chambers Street, where Ella had parked her car, passing tinsel and Christmas decorations hanging in every restaurant and café on the way. Susan was carrying on to St Leonard's police station in Newington. Even though it was late in the year, it was a bright morning and there were still tourists in Edinburgh. A crowd was standing at the Greyfriars Bobby statue on the corner of the pavement in front of the gate leading into Greyfriars Kirk, their anoraks a patchwork of colours against the muted background.

'Can I give you a lift anywhere?' asked Ella.

'It would be great if you could drop me at St Leonard's. I'll give you directions.'

They stopped on the opposite side of the street from the modern building. Susan said goodbye and crossed over. Ella glanced beyond her at the door to the police station and her heart plummeted when she saw a familiar figure walking towards Susan. Ella was jolted back to the nightmare of the past. She gripped the steering wheel and felt her legs shake. It was Jamie Forrester. He was in Edinburgh. He had first come to her office in London and now he was here. He must be following her.

Why was he here? Ben must have sent him, but she had no idea why. All she could think of was escape. He couldn't know about Laura's house. She could get away from him there.

Ella started the car engine and swerved into the road, screeching to a halt behind a car trying to get into a parking space. She looked at Jamie in the rear-view mirror and realised with sick certainty that it had not been her imagination. Those glimpses of shadows she'd seen behind her must have always been him. It had never been Ben, who was locked up in a psychiatric hospital and convicted of murder. She had been right all along but gained no pleasure from the realisation. The truth scared her just as much as her fears.

Everyone told her that she was safe, that Ben would be locked up for years, but she knew better. They all underestimated him and how he could manipulate people. She could still hear his voice when he had been stopped by the police, saying it was Ella's fault Ruth was dead and how she would be next. He couldn't have followed her, but his brother still could. But how did he know she was here?

At the end of the street, when she looked again, she saw Jamie Forrester walk up to Susan and start speaking. She watched intently, confident that the police officer would rebuff him, but they continued talking. Only the noise of a car horn behind her forced her to turn the corner, and they disappeared from view.

All the way out of Edinburgh and across the Queensferry Bridge, Ella felt weighed down by the sight of Jamie Forrester. She thought she had left him and his brother far behind. What had Jamie been saying that was of such interest to Susan? The car felt hot, the enclosed space full of her ragged breathing.

When she turned off the motorway she slowed down and opened the window, taking large gulps of fresh air and feeling the spots of rain on her face. She parked her car in a layby and rested her head on the steering wheel. She couldn't believe he was in Edinburgh. Why was he following her so persistently? It could only be for revenge – to pay her back for giving evidence at Ben's trial. She looked up at the trees swinging over the layby and shivered, closing the window to keep out the raw wind. It was getting colder, the taste of snow in the air. At least he didn't know she was here, not yet anyway.

Looking around her, she saw the lights from the café at the side of the motorway and was drawn towards them, seeking suddenly the presence of other people, a sense of normality that could puncture the fear that surrounded her. Jamie Forrester knew she was in Edinburgh. How long would it take for him to find her here? The city may be full of dark alleys and closes, but at least there were people around and places to hide, unlike the countryside where you were all alone in empty fields, with few places to run to safety.

She turned and smiled at Ella. 'Sit anywhere you like. I'll be with you in a minute.'

As Ella went to the corner table, she stopped in front of a small case containing pieces of handmade jewellery, fine silver entwined round polished stones and shells. She bent down closer to look at the delicately crafted pieces.

'I make those.' The girl had come up to stand next to her. 'I gather the shells at a beach on the Fife coast, where I live. My boyfriend, Jake, helps me. The owner of the café says I can display them here.' She looked over at the empty tables. 'But I don't get many sales.'

'They're beautiful,' said Ella.

'I'm going up to Edinburgh with them soon. Somebody with a stall in the Christmas market said I could sell them there. It's one of the biggest Christmas markets in Europe. That should boost my sales. You must come and see me there, I'll have a bigger range. Look for my sign: Rona Cameron.'

She seemed very young, but the pride in her voice was polished and professional. She was small; her faded jeans and tight top could have belonged to a child, the ear studs and blue hair that of a rebellious teenager, but the tone of voice was assured and totally adult.

'What can I get you?' she asked.

'A sausage roll and coffee, please.'

As the coffee machine gurgled and hissed, the sweet rich smell of coffee beans filled the air. Ella heard the sound of a car engine outside. She stared at the door, then glanced around to see if there was another way out, but there was no escape. She watched the door slowly open, cursing that she'd come at all, regretting that her weakness for company had led to this.

A group of young people came in, all dressed in black, and headed towards a table at the opposite side of the café. They ignored her and she breathed a sigh of relief. The girl placed her order on the table with a large piece of shortbread tucked below her coffee cup.

'On the house,' she said with a smile. 'You look hungry.'

Ella took a bite of the sausage roll and realised that she was ravenous. It was delicious, and she munched contentedly, pulling towards her some leaflets that had been left on every table. It was from a local protest group, its title in bold letters screaming the message *Stop animal abuse.* Pictures of caged dogs and rabbits that had been used in testing covered the back of the leaflet.

She looked up at the group, aware of muttering between them. Rona went to take their order with a smile. She seemed to know them well and Ella listened to their chatter.

'How are you tonight?' asked Rona brightly, before a youth with a wispy beard and untidy long hair almost turned on her.

'We're leaving,' he complained. 'There's a new group of protesters and they don't want us around. One of them told us to leave and not come back. They got quite threatening, so we decided it wasn't worth staying.'

'But nobody can stop you coming if you want to protest,' said Rona.

'Oh, they can. They made it very clear that we were just amateurs and weren't welcome. The guy running them was short, stocky… nasty. When he started getting aggressive, we left.'

'What about the people at Muir Pharma?' she asked.

'They don't care, they just ignore us.' He lowered his voice and looked around the room. 'I think he knows the head of security up there. I've seen them talking together. Who knows what's going on?'

Rona took their order and they talked more quietly amongst themselves.

Ella finished her food after a few moments and she waved to get her bill. 'Thanks very much,' she said, when Rona came to the table. 'I will come and find your stall for some Christmas presents.' Dropping money on the table, Ella left the café, opening the door to a blast of freezing air.

In the car, as she drove to Laura's house, Ella went over what she'd seen and heard that day. Although it had been a shock to see Jamie Forrester in Edinburgh, the simple conversation with Rona had settled her and she felt better. As she stopped the car outside the house, she thought about the conversation with Susan, and about the scientists who had died – so many of her questions about their deaths still unanswered. Despite this, her suspicions about Muir Pharma were becoming even stronger. She looked at the dark house and remembered that Laura was away in Edinburgh. She would have to speak to Mitch. With everything that had happened, she was more and more worried about his safety, and she knew she couldn't rest until he was found.

Chapter 14

Ella was alone in the house. Laura would be in Edinburgh until the Muir Pharma party. Trying to think what else she could do, Ella wandered into Laura's office in the snug and sat at her desk. Feeling like a sneak, she opened the drawers but found nothing about Muir Pharma apart from press cuttings. And no sign of the new phone number Mitch had promised to give Laura.

She wandered back into the living room, hearing the wind whistling outside. Now and again, the noise of sleet showers whipped against the window, but the room was warm and sheltered, curtains drawn to keep out the December storm. She felt as jumpy as the wind outside and stared at the entranceway, remembering when Mitch had left the dinner party. He'd been fussing around Laura's ski jacket before leaving and she could picture him standing in front of it. Had she missed a crucial clue? Was the number there?

Suddenly excited, she ran to the jacket and felt in the outside pockets. They were empty. She must have been wrong. She pulled open the front of the jacket and looked for an inside pocket. There was nothing obvious but when she moved the material she heard the sound of crackling paper. When she pulled it out, she saw that it was a scrap of paper with a telephone number on it. This could be it.

She sat at the kitchen table and dialled the number, hoping that her hunch was right and that she would get through to Mitch. She was desperate to finally speak to him but nervous about what he might say. She'd thought she knew Mitch but now she wasn't so sure. His behaviour over the last few days had been unexpected, which was unlike his usual calm reliability. Ella held her breath. This was the first hurdle.

Someone answered the call. 'Who is this?' he barked. Ella let out her breath silently, thankful that at least she'd found him and that he was safe.

'It's Ella.'

'How did you get this number?' he asked, the tension crackling in his voice.

'You left it in Laura's jacket pocket, didn't you? There was a mobile number on it which I hoped was yours. What's happening, Mitch? Are you all right? When Laura said you'd left, I didn't know what to think. I was worried about you.'

He sighed deeply. 'I meant her to find it. I'd hoped she'd call me.' He seemed to remember who he was speaking to. 'Why are you calling me? You're here to recover. You don't want anything to do with my problems.'

'I needed to find you. There are so many weird things happening,' she replied. 'Have you heard about Carl and the fire?'

'Yes. You know about him?' His voice was hoarse. 'Another convenient death.'

He didn't sound like Mitch. The man she knew had a

low, quiet way of speaking and a soft Scottish burr. She made an effort to keep her voice calm and firm, terrified he would hang up.

'The fire in the hotel was an accident, wasn't it?' she said weakly. 'The police are treating it as an accident.'

'I'm afraid accidents are rarely accidents, Ella. They wanted to get Carl out of the way because he was asking too many difficult questions and they succeeded. Anyway, how do you know about Carl?'

She gulped and cleared her throat, trying to speak normally. 'I spoke to him after he met you the other day,' she said. 'He told me what you'd said. When I found that out and saw how scared he was, I had to speak to you. If Renwick and Young are really doing what you're alleging, they've got to be stopped. I need to help you before something else happens.'

'You can't get involved in this, Ella, I don't know where it's going to end.'

'But I *am* involved.' She wondered what she could say to make him confide in her and she spoke more firmly. 'You need me, Mitch. If you really want what is happening at Muir Pharma to come out into the open, and you can't do that, then I can help. I'm a free agent and can ask whatever questions I like. Carl can't do it anymore, but I can. You can't ask me to walk away from this if people are dying. If I know more about what you suspect and what evidence you have, I can do something.'

He didn't speak for a few seconds and she held her breath, expecting him to argue. But after a few moments he started his story, his voice calmer but still tense, liable to snap at the slightest interruption.

'I joined Muir Pharma a few months ago. You know that I'd worked at the university on research for a long time.' He gave a bitter laugh. 'I should have just stayed there, because from the very beginning I was concerned about the company's approach to its lab tests. You know how pharmaceutical companies trial drugs?' he shot out the question.

'Yes, I think so. The different phases of clinical trials, how companies collaborate to carry them out, the years it takes before a drug can be approved.'

'Well, I was involved in their latest project, a compound being developed to treat depression. We had compelling initial results in the lab with minimal toxicities. There were a few more safety experiments to complete – particularly, screening the molecule against other factors, to make sure that it wouldn't react badly with other types of medication. Once we'd done that, the drug would be sent to our contract company to start large clinical trials, involving hundreds of patients across the country. But I was told to rush through the last stages of animal testing and to hand over the results to one of my colleagues to check.'

He sounded much calmer now, so Ella gently prompted. 'What happened?'

'Usually, the results of the screening check are shared by the whole team so we can discuss them, and all the scientists and clinicians can satisfy themselves there are no potential side effects before it's tested on actual patients. But that's where everything started to go wrong. Only the summary results were put up on the database without any discussion, no opportunity to view the detail.'

'And was this the first time it had happened?'

'To me, yes. I asked to see the full results but was told to get on with my job and not ask questions.'

'What did you do?'

'I went round and asked the other scientists where to find the results. I'd already seen for myself that the culture was quite different from the university, less open, information kept to small groups, that type of thing. I assumed it was because it's a private company and they need to be much more careful about keeping information confidential. But it was more than that. After I spoke to them, people started avoiding me, some of them stopped talking to me altogether. It was almost as though they were scared.'

Ella waited as he faltered, but he carried on before she could prompt him.

'Then I stayed late one night to look through the project files to see if I could find anything. The files were all protected so I couldn't access them and I couldn't get onto the email servers to see old emails. But then I realised that the laptop I'd been working on was one of the old models, without the new security settings. It had belonged to another scientist called Trevor Fisher.'

'One of the scientists who died.' Ella breathed. 'What did you find on it?' She bit her lip, cursing her eagerness. Just let him talk, she told herself, but he didn't seem to object to her questions.

'That this had happened before. Emails to Martin Fraser, the medical director, asking to see details of early lab tests on previous drugs. Notes of his concerns, and then a diary, setting out exactly the same issues that I had. He was shut out of the work. People stopped talking to him and he couldn't stop the compound from going on to human trials. Exactly what was happening to me.'

'And this compound should never have been tested on patients?'

'He didn't think so. He managed to gather evidence of their leading drug under different conditions. His emails set out how the compound was rushed through lab tests to the next stage because the company was so desperate to have a success.'

'And why didn't he tell someone? Go to the press?'

'Because the press here in Edinburgh are in the pay of people like Renwick.' His voice grew harsh again, his sense of grievance against the man taking over the story. Ella tried to bring the conversation back.

'Do you have this laptop with you?'

'Yes. I realised I was being watched. They followed me home.' He sounded just like Carl when he'd talked of being followed.

'Who followed you?'

'Some of Renwick's security men. Robert Young uses them for all their dirty work. When I saw them parked near the house, I knew I had to get away.' He fell silent, clearly brooding over the memory.

Ella bit her lip. He'd told her what Sam Renwick had done but the company could deny everything. They needed evidence, something tangible. 'Do you have proof of side effects, information from patients? Carl must have told you that he needed proof of your allegations before he could publish anything. His lawyers wouldn't accept it otherwise.'

Ella flinched as he shouted down the line. 'Bloody

lawyers. The world is ruled by lawyers. I've got evidence. And I want everyone to know how Sam Renwick runs his business, gets his staff to suppress research results to make his drugs appear more effective than they are. Kills people who get in his way.'

'I know you're frustrated, Mitch, but it's our last chance to get this right. That means building up a story that has real power and conviction. That's the only way to get what you want. We're all taking risks here.' Ella held her breath, hoping that she had got through to him.

'All right. I understand we need evidence. Carl said he was going to find out more about the scientists who died. He said he would get all the evidence he needed.'

She sighed. 'I don't think he was able to do that. I can follow it up.'

'Just be careful. And remember, you can't trust anyone at Muir Pharma. And I mean anyone.'

'But I have to tell Laura that I've spoken to you – that you're safe.'

'No,' he shouted down the line. 'All the senior people are in on it, and that must include Laura. I hate to say this, but she must have some idea. I've tried to tell her what's going on but you know what she's like. She doesn't want to listen. At first, I thought she was just sticking her head in the sand, but now I really don't know what to think.'

Ella could hear the emotion in his voice and wished she could be there with him. He sounded very alone.

'The minute you say you've spoken to me they'll follow you too,' Mitch continued. He paused and then seemed to come to a decision. 'I'm fairly sure that's why Carl decided he didn't want to have any part of it. The last time I spoke to him he said he thought he was being followed.'

'Yes, he told me that too.'

Mitch's voice became bitter and accusing. 'You have to remember that Laura does everything Sam Renwick tells her. You can't trust her.'

Unwilling to get into an argument about Laura, Ella asked, 'When can we meet?'

'Give me a couple of days. I need to move on again. And there's something else I need you to do for me. I have a memory stick Carl gave me which had a lot of his evidence on it. I thought I'd taken it with me but it's not here. I don't know where I can have left it but I went back to the holiday cottage first to pack some clothes so it may be there. Could you go and try and find it for me? He told me it contains the kind of clinical evidence we need. It's a silver memory stick with a blue rubber band around it.'

'I've been there and I didn't see it, but I can go again and look,' replied Ella.

Laura had seemed concerned about her boyfriend, but Mitch had now questioned her motives and suggested that she couldn't be trusted. At one level, Ella found it difficult to believe what he was saying, but deep down she already had her own doubts about Laura's loyalties. And Mitch was in hiding, using burner phones to stay in contact with people. Carl was dead after looking into Muir Pharma. It might sound unbelievable, but she was beginning to think that it might be all too true and that Ruth suspected something all along.

'Do you know a place called Cleish, in Fife?' he asked. 'It's over the hill south of Muir Pharma.'

'I can find it. Is that where you are?'

'Not right now, but I've got somewhere there I can stay for a few days. An old farmhouse. It used to be owned by some friends of mine, but they're putting it up for sale in the New Year. They're down in London now and asked me to keep an eye on it. We could meet there.'

Ella grabbed a pencil.

'What's it called?'

'Brookhill Farm, near Cleish. You should be able to find it easily.'

'When should I come up?'

'Monday evening, 7 o'clock. Just make sure you're not followed.'

Ella hung up and started to pace around the room in an attempt to ease the tension in her body. She stood at the large picture window and gazed into the darkness, not only affected by Mitch's words, but by the strain in his voice. He sounded like a fugitive, living on the run and feeling hunted, imagining enemies round every corner.

The last thing she felt like doing was going to a Muir Pharma celebration party, but she might hear something that would add to the case she was building up.

Mitch could be exaggerating. Carl's death might have been a tragic accident and there may be a simple explanation for Mitch's suspicions, but Ella could not dismiss what he was saying. She still didn't know the full truth, but what she did know was that if Mitch needed her help, then she would give it. She'd failed to help Ruth when she'd most needed it and her sister had died. She wasn't prepared to fail someone else close to her again.

She could still picture Ruth pacing the floor, preparing

to advocate for a patient against another authority figure. She could remember her sister's defiant words when she had a cause to fight for. Ella smiled in the darkness. Ruth hadn't been a quiet diminutive figure, ready to accept a situation she didn't think was right. She would fight for her patients, turning from a caring nurse to a fierce defender and supporter, prepared to talk or write to anybody in a position of power to make a difference.

Over the last few months, Ella had lost sight of Ruth's essential character, in the fog of grief, in the helplessness of the murder, but it came back to her now even more strongly. She felt her loss more keenly than ever as she remembered her sister's strength, her voice raised in anger against thoughtless injustice. She might have been right again this time. Ruth's note had brought her here. She would not let her down.

Chapter 15

When Ella arrived at the Muir Pharma party, it was in full swing. Lingering in Fife and then being delayed by an accident on the road into Edinburgh meant she was much later than she'd planned. She'd had a brief shower at Laura's and changed into the one smart dress she'd thrown into her suitcase. After a quick detour to drop off her bag at her hotel in Edinburgh, she was relieved when she finally pulled into the car park at the back of Waverley Station. As Ella walked through the station and took the escalator up the Waverley Steps onto Princes Street, she was almost blown off her feet by the wind funnelling up from the station. Clutching her coat to try to keep out the bitter wind, she ran up the steps to the Balmoral Hotel.

The party was in a function room on one of the upper floors. Ella walked along the corridor, lingering to savour the sweeping view of the floodlit castle, before she saw the same security guards from the Muir Pharma office standing on each side of the door at the end of the corridor. Mitch was certainly telling the truth when he said that they never left Sam Renwick's side. Feeling vulnerable and unable to shake off the feeling that she was walking into some kind of trap, she ignored her worries and kept walking towards them.

After showing her invitation, they swung open the double doors and Ella walked into a room of noisy laughter and chatter. There must have been over a hundred people in the room and she searched for Laura, for any familiar face, in the crowd, picking up a glass of champagne from one of the waiters standing beside the door as she surveyed the room.

Circling the groups of people, Ella spied Laura at the far end of the room with Sam Renwick and Robert Young. Laura was looking up at Sam, laughing at something he'd said. He was staring down at her, both of them oblivious to the crowd around them. Ella ducked down behind a noisy group, watching the scene play out in front of her, feeling underhand by not immediately telling Laura she'd arrived, but knowing she had to find out where her real loyalties lay. Ella could feel some of Mitch's paranoia on her shoulder and she watched Laura's every movement, sensitive to every gesture as if she could read some hidden meaning into her actions.

Laura was teasing him about something and he was leaning in towards her, sharing the joke. Ella wondered again just how close they were. She certainly didn't look like the fragile woman of the previous day, upset by her boyfriend's sudden disappearance. She looked as if she didn't have a care in the world, and Ella heard again Mitch's warning not to trust anyone in Muir Pharma. Did this really include Laura? Which was the Laura who was telling the truth, she wondered. She knew she didn't have much time. Wherever the truth lay, she owed it to herself to find out.

Laura glanced across the room. She murmured

something to Sam Renwick and walked across, no longer smiling and looking more like the strained woman Ella had seen on the previous days.

'Hi, I thought you weren't coming.' They hugged and Laura's thin shoulders felt cold, despite the heat in the room.

'There was an accident on the M90 and it took me ages to get here.'

'Any news on Mitch?' asked Laura eagerly. 'Have you tried the university people?'

'Not yet, I'm planning to see his old boss tomorrow.' Biting her lip to stop herself from saying she'd spoken to Mitch, Ella took a sip of champagne and watched Laura replace one glass of orange juice with another.

Laura was working all the time, scanning the room to check how the party was going and then turning her gaze back as if satisfied that everything was going to plan. She was playing with her glass, not meeting Ella's glance, and Ella wondered again what had really been going on with her friends. Realising how little she knew about their life together.

As if feeling she had to break the silence, Laura went on. 'We haven't been to the cottage for a while, but Mitch spent time there on his own in the summer when he was working on it. I was so sure he must have just gone there for a little bit to cool down.' She shrugged almost petulantly.

'Laura, you need to introduce me to your friend.' Ella turned to see a plump, red-faced man gesturing towards her with a full glass of whisky, dark eyes flicking between them.

Laura hesitated and moved a step backwards before

she spoke. 'Ella, this is Ronnie Grant. He works for *The Scotsman*. He's written some good stories about us. Ronnie, this is my friend Ella. She's staying with me.'

Ella shook his clammy hand. 'Good to meet you, Ronnie. I'm here on holiday for a few days, catching up with Laura.'

Ronnie Grant drained his glass, smoothly placed it on a passing tray and replaced it with a full one before turning his unblinking gaze back to Ella. He reminded her of a crocodile, staring at its prey before going in for the kill.

'Excuse me, there are people I need to speak to.' Laura was backing away, but she gave Ella a hard stare. 'I'll see you later…'

'Staying with Laura up at Muir Pharma, are you?' said Ronnie, breathing whisky fumes over Ella. 'Brilliant company. They're doing such good work for the sector up here. Scotland can always do with successful companies.'

Ella stared at him. 'I don't suppose you know a journalist called Carl Davis?'

Ronnie hesitated, taking another swig of his drink. 'I remember him. He got me to meet him by telling me he wanted to share information. But when we met, he didn't have any information I could use. Turned out all he wanted was to get me to introduce him to sources for his own investigations. As if I would give over my contacts to somebody I hardly know; contacts I've worked years to develop.'

His look of disgust was genuine. Ella took a gulp of champagne but it tasted sour. 'What happened to him? I heard he was killed in a fire,' she persevered, trying to hide the tremor in her voice.

He didn't reply. His brow furrowed, he looked across

the room and took a deep breath. 'There's somebody over there I need to speak to,' he said and scurried across the room before slapping a man's shoulder in greeting. The man turned round and Ella recognised the policeman who had spoken to journalists after the fire in the hotel that had killed Carl. He looked pleased to see Ronnie and both men were quickly in deep conversation.

Ella turned away from them and felt a hand on her shoulder. When she looked around, her heart jumped as she saw Jim in front of her, standing next to Gregor, who was scanning the room. Jim was staring down at her with a smile in his eyes.

'I didn't know you were coming,' said Ella, returning his smile.

'Everybody in the sector got an invite,' answered Gregor. 'When this character heard about it, he demanded to come too.' He waved his glass towards Jim, who looked unrepentant.

Gregor was wearing a suit, while Jim was dressed more casually in chinos and a deep-blue open-necked shirt.

'I hoped you might be here,' he said quietly to Ella.

'I came with my friend Laura,' said Ella. 'I'm staying with her near the new Muir Pharma office in Fife. She and her boyfriend, Mitch, work there.' Her voice drifted, as she remembered her conversation with Mitch. At least she was going to meet him and check he was all right, but the difficulty of his situation swept over her again.

'I thought you said you were here on holiday,' said Jim. 'Are you enjoying it?'

Ella thought about her walks in the countryside and the view across the fields in front of the house and tried to inject some enthusiasm into her voice. 'Yes. I wanted to relax, get away from London for a while. I'm certainly doing that.' She looked up at him. He seemed to know what she was feeling – that something was bothering her.

'I've got three sisters,' he said, as if she had asked a question. 'It's made me super sensitive to their moods.' He chuckled. 'Growing up in that household it was the only way to survive.'

'Do your sisters live in Edinburgh?' asked Ella.

'No. One's married – lives in the Borders near where we grew up. The other two are working in London. When they need a break, my spare room is where they come. Where are you from?'

'I live with my parents in London at the moment. When I go back, I'll need to start looking for another flat.' Ella was surprised at her words. It was the first time she had said that to anyone. Her life had felt like it was on hold for the last few months but now, with a spark of optimism, Jim's questions had let her open up to the possibility of some kind of a future.

'Are you staying here tonight?' asked Jim.

Ella shook her head. 'I've booked somewhere along Royal Terrace. All the company people are staying here.'

'We need to find a seat,' said Jim. 'There's a free table over here.' He grabbed her hand and Ella followed him through the crowd, Gregor running behind them.

'Where are we going now?' he muttered.

She didn't reply until they reached one of the small tables dotted around the edge of the function room. 'Right here,' she answered as she perched on one of the high stools at the round table.

'I don't know about you,' Jim said over the hubbub of noise and laughter, 'but I'm ravenous.' Ella nodded. 'There must be food here somewhere.' He looked around the room.

Waiters were weaving through the crowd with plates of canapés. As a waiter passed by, Jim grabbed a whole plate. Ella laughed at the audacity but was relieved to be eating something.

'These are excellent,' she said.

Jim nodded and watched Gregor who stuffed some food into his mouth then turned away, disappearing into the crowd to answer his phone.

'You haven't phoned me yet,' Jim said to Ella in a low voice, a smile crinkling the corners of his eyes. 'I bet you've lost my number.'

'No, I still have it. I just haven't used it yet.' She returned his smile and held his gaze. This was going to get complicated, she thought, but she didn't have to back off yet. It was a long time since someone had smiled at her like that and she was surprised to find how much she liked it.

'What are you thinking?' he asked.

She felt herself blush and looked down. 'Nothing really, just that I don't know you very well.'

Jim spread his arms out. 'Ask me anything. I promise I'll give you answers.'

Ella was surprised at how earnest he sounded. When she glanced at him he looked serious. She'd taken him for a flirt, but perhaps she'd been wrong. She sought for a safer topic.

'Tell me about yourself.' she said finally, taking a snack from the plate before it was carried away. 'Gregor said that you worked in cybersecurity, but all I saw was you sorting out his mobile. What is your real job?'

'My main job is cybersecurity. I've been doing it for a few years now. It's getting busier all the time. These days, companies have to put more effort than ever into keeping their systems secure. I used to work for a consultancy that specialised in that, but these days I mostly work for myself. I'm a geek at heart, so I've got a side interest in gadgets and technology. I help out friends like Gregor with things like mobiles and internet connections. Keeps me up to date with what's new.' He looked over at the sound system being set up at the far end of the room. 'That's led me into working with some of the tech used for conferences. I dabble in that too.'

'You're kept busy then. I know what it's like being a freelancer, you need to earn money when you have a chance because inevitably there'll be downtimes when you don't earn as much.'

'So, what do you do?'

'I trained as an accountant – in one of the big firms in London. My specialism is forensic accounting. If a company suspects fraud, I check the money flows and work out how it's being done. I like being freelance. It gives me the chance to work for organisations that I like. My last job was in a homeless charity. They do really good work and I like being a part of that. They didn't pay as much as some, but if I want to, other times I can balance it with jobs that pay more.'

'Where do you get your work from?'

Ella thought for a moment, considering her last few projects. 'Mostly from people I've worked with before. In the last place, I had an interim project filling in during someone's maternity cover. They trained at the same firm as me so they know that's the kind of thing I do. What about you? Where does your work come from?'

'Companies I work for need me to come back fairly regularly to check that their systems are still up to scratch. Things are changing all the time so they need to constantly keep them under review.'

The conversations in the room were suddenly drowned out by Sam Renwick, who had started his speech. Everyone turned to look at him, their faces full of laughter and anticipation, except for Ronnie Grant, who stared broodingly into his glass of whisky.

The guests in the room shuffled round to look at Sam, and a group next to Ella and Jim moved forward to have a better view, almost pushing them off their stools in their eagerness not to miss a word of the speech. Ella wasn't quick enough to recover her balance, colliding into one of the group. Jim put his arm around her to stop her from falling. The man she'd bumped into cursed, surprised at their closeness, then took one look at Jim's face and moved away.

'Are you all right?' Jim said quietly, removing his arm.

'Yes. Thank you.' They exchanged a smile.

The room fell silent as Sam spoke – from the birth of Muir Pharma, 'our first business plan, hatched over a couple of bottles of red wine in an Edinburgh basement flat', to stories about the company in the early days. 'At that stage, it was just the two of us.' He nodded to Robert Young, who allowed himself a tight smile, the serious look he habitually wore, momentarily absent. It looked like everyone except Ella was swept up in his narrative, and she could only marvel as he cleverly wove his initial successes into funny stories, with colourful flourishes where the truth could have been prosaic.

By the end of fifteen minutes, gales of laughter greeted every remark, and everyone in the room was completely hooked. Ella watched them respond to his charm and began to understand how he would always get his own way, how he was able to dominate his company and persuade people to invest in it. Glancing at Robert, at Laura, at Ronnie Grant, who was now smirking, if not quite smiling, they were all caught up in Sam Renwick's story, all ready to play their part.

Ella's discomfort grew as she realised what it reminded her of, looking round the room of happy smiles. Years ago, as part of her job with another charity, she'd attended some meetings of a religious cult in London. She'd blended in with the other young women who were flocking to listen to the charismatic preacher. A number of the women who had got involved with the cult had ended up homeless. The people she met there behaved like the employees of Muir Pharma were behaving now. No-one was going to stand in Sam Renwick's way. He had them all exactly where he wanted them.

When he'd finished talking, with a final flourish where he paid tribute to the staff, they all cheered him as if he was their favourite pop star. Feeling as if she'd wandered into some parallel universe where she didn't know the rules, Ella looked around at the enthusiastic faces turned towards their hero and saw, coming towards her, the two scientists she'd met on her visit to Muir Pharma, the ones who worked with Mitch. It was too good an opportunity to miss.

'Hi, we met the other day.' She introduced them to Jim, but before anyone could speak, she saw Gregor wave across to him from the other side of the room, clearly wanting him to come over.

'I'll see you later,' said Jim, as he responded to the signal, and went across the room. Ella watched him go, suddenly feeling very alone. She gave herself a shake. She hardly knew the man, but she couldn't deny his open manner and strong presence left a big impression on her.

Less inhibited in the party atmosphere, the scientists smiled, though Ed glanced quickly across at Laura at the other side of the room, checking her back was turned before responding. 'I remember. You're a friend of Laura's.'

'Yes. Are you enjoying the party? Pity Mitch couldn't be here.'

They nodded in unison and the girl started to reply, but then she looked at her colleague and took a hurried sip of her drink instead.

Ella could see Laura watching them from the other side of the room and exchange a glance with Robert, before he put down his glass and started to cross over to them. There was no time. Ella knew she had to make some kind of connection with the girl, get her to open up a bit if she was going to get any information out of her.

'I was at university with Mitch. Is he still as intense about science as he was then?'

The girl smiled shyly. 'I've only known him for a few months, and he didn't talk much, but you could tell he had lots of experience, particularly with the animals… and he was so interested in the science. Always making sure we followed the correct protocols. It's why I can't understand why everyone thinks he—' She stopped abruptly, flushing a deep red.

'What does everyone think? What are they saying about him?' asked Ella.

'Karen,' her colleague said in a low voice, but she shook her head at the warning.

'She's an old friend. She deserves to know the lies going round about him.'

'We've been told not to discuss it…'

But his words fell on deaf ears. The girl glanced at her colleague and then back at Ella, before blurting out, 'There are all these rumours about him, so we don't know what to believe.'

'What rumours about him?' Out of the corner of her eye, Ella saw Robert being stopped by one of his colleagues on his way across the room. She turned back to the girl. 'Look, it's very difficult to talk here. We could meet up sometime and you could tell me what you're worried about.'

Karen looked uncertainly at her colleague, but, getting no support, turned back to Ella. 'I'm not sure. I might get into trouble. The culture in this company is toxic, but nobody apart from Mitch is prepared to talk about it.'

'Excuse me, could I have a private word please?' Robert interrupted before she could say anything else. The three of them walked away, leaving Ella sitting alone at the edge of the room, watching them go, hoping she hadn't got them into too much trouble, and cursing herself for not making more of the opportunity. She didn't have much faith in the likelihood of meeting Karen again – she'd probably never get near her – but she did need independent evidence of Mitch's suspicions. There were so many other things she could have asked her.

'Good grief,' said Gregor loudly to Jim as they walked back towards Ella. 'I didn't believe her when she said she'd come tonight.'

He looked nervously across the room as Sam and Robert were approached by Susan, his older sister. She was accompanied by two colleagues, and they walked across the function room directly towards the men, ignoring the whispers and glances of the people around them.

'She told me that Sam Renwick refused to see her the other day and she was going to speak to him tonight.'

Ella looked at Susan – at the professional way she had crossed the room and focused on her quarry. Short but determined. Although Ella hadn't been sure about her after she had seen her speaking to Jamie, she couldn't help but be impressed by the woman's chutzpah.

'Why is she trying to see him?' Ella asked Gregor.

'She wouldn't tell me,' replied Gregor. 'Part of some investigation she's working on.' He looked at the hostile glances from some of the guests and came to a decision. 'I don't think I should have anything to do with this.' He nudged Jim. 'Let's make ourselves scarce until she goes.' Ella watched Susan turn away after speaking to Sam and Robert for only a couple of minutes, and then leave the room with her colleagues. Ella looked around but couldn't see Gregor and Jim anywhere. The room seemed to be emptying, so she saw no reason to stay.

Laura caught her as she went to the cloakroom to collect her coat. 'You're leaving?'

'Yes, it's been a long day.'

Laura hesitated as if she wanted to say something, but Ella was tired and she'd had enough of Laura's mixed messages.

'I'm not sure I can help you find Mitch,' she said. 'I'm going to try tomorrow, but I don't know how far I'm going to get. Unless there is something you're not telling me that would give me a clue, I've nowhere else to look.'

Ella shrugged on her coat and Laura walked with her to the lift, looking miserable but not saying anything. Whatever kind of internal struggle her friend was fighting, Ella knew she wasn't yet on the winning side, because although Laura's eyes filled with tears, all she would say was, 'You can't give up on us yet, Ella. You need to help me find him, before it's too late.'

'What do you mean, before it's too late? What do you think could happen to him, Laura? What exactly are you afraid of?'

Her worry about Mitch sparked into a burst of anger as she challenged Laura to tell the truth, make her explain what was happening to them. She was one of her closest friends but now she almost seemed like a stranger.

But all she would do was shake her head, as if she couldn't trust herself to speak, as if once she started to confide in Ella, she might never stop. When the lift doors opened for Ella, she turned and walked back to the party.

Downstairs in reception, someone got up as Ella came out of the lift. It was Karen, the female scientist from the party, who walked towards her, before pulling her to one side.

'What is it?' asked Ella.

'I wanted to speak to you before you left. I thought we

should do it down here, so we were away from everyone else.' She shrugged and looked away from Ella. 'My colleagues think I'm over-reacting but I'm not so sure.'

'You were talking about rumours about Mitch?'

'They're saying that he claimed findings from research that belonged to somebody else, when he was at the university, before he ever came here. But Mitch is the last person who would do that kind of thing. Why would somebody want to risk his good name in that way? That's all I wanted to say, really.'

'I don't know,' replied Ella. 'Maybe there is a reason. I'm working on it.'

'Don't get me wrong. It's good for the CV because it's unusual to get such high-paying science jobs in Scotland, but I don't like the culture of secrecy and sometimes I think it's not worth the stress. I'm glad somebody's looking into it.'

They heard the lift door open and, before Ella could say anything else, Karen had rushed away. She looked around to see some people leaving and followed them out into the street.

Pulling her scarf tightly round her neck to keep out the bitter Edinburgh wind, Ella walked up Waterloo Place to the cheaper hotel she'd booked for the night. Laura had said she could stay at the Balmoral, where all the Muir Pharma senior staff were staying, but she preferred to be on her own and go where she wanted the next day without feeling she was being watched.

She stomped up the busy pavement, her footsteps echoing in the street, angry and frustrated with Laura because she knew she wasn't telling her everything, and with herself because she'd failed to persuade her to tell the truth. Although it was late in the evening, the streets were busy with partygoers and Ella, deep in her own thoughts, fell in behind a group of office workers walking in the same direction. It was a cold night, with flurries of snow blowing in the wind, and she was glad she was wearing her favourite black boots as she peeled away from the group when she reached the quieter street leading to her hotel. She walked more quickly now, suddenly feeling alone and vulnerable in the stillness of the empty street, hardly any lights shining from the windows of the terraced houses to light up the darker patches of pavement between the street lights.

Suddenly Ella heard a shout behind her and she turned round to see Jim running towards her. He stopped in front of her and had to catch his breath before he spoke, 'You didn't tell me you were leaving.'

'I didn't know where you'd gone.' Despite the cold wind, she felt herself flushing.

'I live out this way, I'll walk you to your hotel.' He took her arm and turned them both towards the hotel.

A car turned into the road in front of them and drove slowly towards them, turning its lights off as it stopped a few feet away. Ella's step faltered as the driver stopped but no-one got out of the car. The image of Jamie Forrester in Edinburgh filled her mind and she was thrown into another nightmare. Her breath came in short gasps and she felt Jim hold her arm in a stronger grip.

Without warning, the car catapulted forward and drove towards them, speeding up as it got closer, the shape of the driver hunched behind the wheel a dark looming mass.

Ella felt Jim's strong arms hold her steady and then she was lifted bodily at the side of the pavement, over the low barrier, into the trees in the park on the side of the road. The screeching sound of the car scraping along the stone wall filled the air, then the sound of the car accelerating away.

Ella instinctively looked up at Jim. 'Have they gone?' she stammered.

Jim was looking down the street after the car and didn't reply until he was satisfied that it had definitely gone.

'Who the hell?' he said angrily. Then he turned to stare at her, his voice deadly serious. 'Are you OK? What the hell did they think they were playing at? Just as well I decided to walk you home.'

Ella clung onto him, her body shaking uncontrollably. Her legs felt like jelly –they could hardly hold her up. She was trying to get her thoughts together but her mind was full of jumbled impressions and she could barely speak, only one clear thought tumbling out of her mouth.

'They've done this before,' she said. 'I've seen them trying to frighten somebody else.'

'You'll have to tell me everything,' said Jim. 'I'm not leaving you. Where's your hotel?'

'It's just up this road,' she answered.

'I'll come back with you and make sure you're all right.'

They walked across to the hotel, Jim keeping his arm around her.

'Thank you,' she said quietly as they walked. 'If you hadn't got me out of the way…' She couldn't finish her sentence and shuddered against his arm that tightened around her, thankful that she wasn't alone.

Chapter 16

They walked up to the door of the hotel. A concierge met them as they arrived, his wrinkled features full of concern.

'What was that? Are you all right, Miss?' He asked in a shaky voice and she recognised the ageing concierge from earlier that day when she'd left her bag at the hotel.

Jim looked at him and frowned. 'The lady has had a fright. Some idiot driving badly almost knocked into her. We need to get inside.'

'Of course, of course.'

The man fussed, and he led them into an elegant hall. Jim looked at the reception desk with a bank of keys behind it, and back at the old man.

'Have you any security in here?' he asked. Before the concierge could reply, another man, looking flushed and out of breath, came into reception. He stared at them, his glance moving from one to the other.

'I'm the security guard around here,' he said. 'What's going on?

'There's someone driving dangerously out there,' replied Jim. He turned to Ella, who was shivering. She felt deathly cold and her teeth were chattering. 'We need somewhere quiet to sit, maybe have a drink. Would you like some tea?'

She shook her head. 'I'm not a tea drinker.'

She heard the sound of laughter as the door opened at the side of the reception desk.

'Can we go somewhere quiet, please?' Ella asked the concierge.

'Of course,' he replied. 'We have a small sitting room at the side here. It will be quiet. And maybe you'd like something stronger than tea? We have a nice whisky I can bring through.'

'Yes please,' said Ella as she and Jim followed the man into a small Georgian sitting room with heavy dark curtains at the tall windows, and the embers of a fire in the corner of the room. There were two easy chairs in front of the dying fire. Ella sat down, still clutching her coat, and Jim bent down to the dying fire and pushed the coals around to try to get some more heat from the embers, then sat in the other chair and held Ella's hands, rubbing her fingers.

The security guard looked round the door and shook his bundle of keys. 'The concierge has alerted the police about the dangerous driving, but I don't think there's much they can do. I'll make sure these clowns have gone and then I'll come back.'

The concierge bustled in with two glasses and the bottle of whisky that still had a little amber liquid left. He pulled up a small table between the chairs, left the drinks and closed the door quietly behind him, shutting out the noise in reception of diners leaving the restaurant.

Ella lifted her glass with a shaking hand and took a sip of her drink. She felt the fiery liquid in her throat as she took the first mouthful and the warmth spread through her body.

'Tell me what's going on,' said Jim after a few moments.

Ella had stopped shaking and held out one of her hands to the fire, watching the flickering flames, and, for the first time, feeling the heat of the room. Her mind was now alert, the brisk walk after the initial shock of adrenaline helping her to think and to put the jumble of thoughts and impressions from the last few hours and days into words.

'I need to go back to the beginning,' said Ella. 'I told you I'm here on holiday. I came to stay with my friends Mitch and Laura.' She took another sip of her drink. 'But from the beginning I realised that Laura and Mitch were in a bad place; they'd only started going out earlier this year and they were having more arguments than I'd ever imagined. The first evening I was here they started to quarrel. It was to do with work. They're both at Muir Pharma. Laura has been there for a few years and Mitch joined the company a few months ago.' She looked across at Jim. 'You saw what Laura was like with Sam at the party, they were flirting like that the first night I was there. He doesn't seem to be able to dial down his desire to be the most popular man in the room and he was coming between Laura and Mitch.'

'Is that why they were arguing?' asked Jim. 'I can see what you mean.'

'It isn't just a problem with their relationship. I think there's a lot more to it.'

'So, what do you mean?' His calm voice settled her tense emotions and he waited patiently for her reply.

She took a deep breath. 'I know this might sound far-fetched, and I don't want to get you involved, but I need to talk to someone. Mitch says he's found out things about Muir Pharma that would send the directors to jail and destroy the reputation of the company. He believes they've suppressed some damning research results for some compounds that have become very successful. I don't know what to think about Laura. Either she's in on it, or is innocent but doesn't believe him. She thinks he's going to destroy her career. Whatever Laura said, Mitch was determined to gather evidence to support his allegations. He was in touch with a journalist to tell him the story.' She took a deep breath, then continued. 'The journalist was killed in a supposed accident, and Mitch has gone on the run.'

'So, suddenly Mitch's suspicions have become a lot more real,' said Jim.

'Yes,' answered Ella. 'I spoke to Mitch. He's all right, but he's in hiding. He thinks the journalist was killed because of the story and Mitch is afraid for his own life. I wasn't sure whether I believed him but…'

'Who were those people in the car? You said you'd seen them before.'

'Not exactly. I saw a similar car trying to run down the journalist Carl Davis. I think they all work for Sam Renwick. I see it now really clearly.'

'So why are they coming after you now?'

'They're trying to tell me not to get involved, to frighten me off.' Ella shrugged her shoulders. 'They may have seen me talking to Carl. They know I'm friends with Mitch. It could be anything.'

'And you think Sam Renwick is behind all this?'

'I think so. Robert just does what he's told. Sam's trying

to get new investment in the business and doesn't want any scandal to emerge. Mitch has got to be persuaded to talk to the police.'

Jim stared into the fire and then turned back to look at her. 'Why hasn't he gone to the police before now?'

She shook her head. 'You maybe didn't realise at the party, but some of the Edinburgh police were there as Renwick's guests. Mitch doesn't trust them.'

'Gregor's sister wasn't a guest,' countered Jim. 'She certainly isn't a fan.'

Ella had the vivid picture of Susan Munro speaking to Jamie outside the police station. 'Maybe not, but all I have is speculation until I can see Mitch. He says he has evidence but I need to see it.'

'What are you going to do now?'

'I'm going to help Mitch,' said Ella firmly. 'There's no-one else who can do it. I've no idea if we can trust Laura. And the other scientists who work with him either don't know enough or are too scared to get involved. I need to help Mitch get his evidence to the right people, whoever that turns out to be.'

'This is very dangerous, Ella. You're saying that people have died already. Why do you have to get so involved? You could go to the police now and then forget all about it, rely on them to investigate.'

'I know I could, but I have my reasons why it needs to be me. Besides, Mitch doesn't trust anyone apart from me. He needs a friend now and I'm the only person willing to help. I don't know what's going on in Laura's mind but I certainly know she's not going to take this seriously. I don't even know how much she's involved.' She shivered as she spoke, feeling the inability to rely on Laura any longer as a pain in the pit of her stomach.

'I still don't like it,' said Jim.

Ella leaned towards him and grabbed his hand. 'I'm sorry, but you don't have to like it,' she said. 'I made a mistake before and left someone alone to face a dangerous situation. I can't do the same again. I have to do all I can to help him.'

'All right, then,' said Jim. 'But if you need anything you must ask me. I can't just stand by and watch, now I know how crazy this situation is.'

'You're already helping me by listening. I felt so alone. I didn't know if I was making things up or if they were really happening – whether to believe Mitch or not. Over the last few days, I even wondered whether his allegations were all because he wanted to punish Sam for taking Laura away. Although I was terrified tonight, you've helped me to work through everything that's happened and I feel much clearer now about the truth of what he's saying.'

There was a knock at the door and the security guard came inside. 'Whoever tried to frighten you is long gone, but I'll check to make sure that everything stays that way.'

Ella nodded. 'Thank you,' she said, then turned to Jim. 'I think I'm all right now. It must be really late. You should go home.'

'Are you sure? I want you to know you can rely on me if you need to.'

'I know. I promise I will contact you if there's anything I need.'

They followed the security guard out of the room. At the bottom of the stairs Jim bent down and kissed her on the cheek. 'Try and get some sleep. Text me tomorrow to let me know you're okay.' Ella nodded and watched him leave, then climbed the stairs to her bedroom. She opened the door, closed it behind her and locked it. Images from the long day ran through her mind, from the gaiety of the party to Mitch's tense voice to the car racing towards her. She pulled the curtains to shut out the outside world and all its dangers. Feeling not just physically tired but emotionally drained, she unpacked her bag and got changed ready for bed.

As she got into bed and pulled the duvet over her head, the picture that stayed with her was of Jim pulling her out of the way of the car and holding her close. She ruffled the duvet impatiently. Just her luck that she'd met somebody she finally liked and had to tell him a crazy story that would make most men turn and run away. Jim wouldn't know what to believe, although the evidence of the threat tonight was undeniable. She closed her eyes against the confusing thoughts and, despite everything, felt herself drifting to sleep.

Chapter 17

When Ella woke up the next morning she went downstairs and looked out onto a winter scene, a thin covering of snow across Edinburgh. She sat over breakfast, spreading out the notes Carl had given her and trying to plan her day. She needed corroboration of Mitch's story. The only thing she could think of was to go to the addresses Carl had gathered, speak to people and see what came up. She might find nothing but she had to do something useful to take her mind off worrying about Mitch, so decided she'd follow up everyone on her list that had a link to Edinburgh before heading back to Fife.

She plotted out the route carefully, taking in the area near Leith Walk where John Roper, who was killed in the Pentlands had lived. Next she planned to pick up her car to go up to Morningside to speak to Mitch's old university professor. She desperately needed to speak to someone who knew Mitch well so that she could work out whether she could trust his judgement. Despite what she'd told Jim, she still couldn't quite believe that Laura would go along with Sam Renwick's schemes to falsify test results, wondering how much it was Mitch's jealousy of Renwick that made him accuse her of complicity. Ella sighed as she closed the heavy door behind her. Maybe it was her own blinkered attitude that was making her lurch from Laura's side to Mitch's side, because she just didn't want to accept that one of her friends could be involved. Could Laura consciously put her boyfriend's life in danger?

Carl had also given her the address of Martin Fraser's Edinburgh house on the south side of the city, so she decided to pass that way to see if he was there. He hadn't attended the Muir Pharma party, but it was Sunday, so he would probably be in town. She couldn't believe that he was ignorant of what was going on at the company, but needed to find a way to get him to talk to her.

Although the buses were running, Ella needed fresh air to clear her mind from all the questions that seemed to have no straight answers, so was going to walk to John Roper's flat on London Road, to the east of the centre and a short walk from her hotel. Edinburgh wasn't such a big city she convinced herself as she stomped through the thin covering of snow, the sky still heavy and grey.

The brisk walk gave Ella the opportunity to go through everything Mitch had said the day before. Even if only one of his allegations were true, it was enough to bring Muir Pharma down. If the whole story was right, then Ella knew she didn't have much time. She thought about the car that had driven towards her after the Muir Pharma party and shivered. It could have been an accident, someone losing control of their car, but it had felt like someone threatening her, trying to scare her off. Just like they'd scared Carl off before they killed him. Ella glanced over her shoulder but no-one was taking any notice of her. She'd just have to keep alert, look for anything out of the ordinary. Mitch had said not to trust anybody who had anything to do with Muir Pharma.

After a few minutes, Ella reached the end of London Road. The grand row of tall Georgian houses stretched in front of her and she paused at the door to the nearest block, glancing through the names on the doorbells. John Roper hadn't lived here for several years, but she might as well try to ask if one of his neighbours remembered anything about him. She pressed the bell at the first floor flat. There was no answer, so she pressed the ground-floor bell, looking through the window to see if there was any sign of life, stamping her cold feet to try to get some life into numb toes.

No-one came to the door so, admitting defeat, she turned and walked back along the street. She wasn't quite sure where else to go to follow up on John Roper, and tried not to feel too discouraged by the poor start to her day of research. She wandered back along the street towards Leith Walk and went into the nearest delicatessen, with a few tables at the back. The delicatessen counter was closed but a woman dressed in a long flowing dress and chunky boots was standing at the coffee machine, moodily flicking through an old copy of a local paper. Chilled from her walk in the biting wind, Ella asked for coffee and went to sit down.

The woman came up to Ella with her drink, then lingered at the table.

'I'm trying to find out about someone who used to live near here,' said Ella. 'I wondered if you knew them. It was a few years ago.'

'I'll help if I can.' She perched on the table opposite, earrings jingling as she moved. She was older than Ella had first thought and moved around the small space with confidence.

'How long have you had the café here?' asked Ella.

'Almost ten years now, since my friend opened the delicatessen. I can't believe it's that long.'

'Do you get a lot of local regulars?'

She shrugged. 'We get all sorts. People who live around here, tourists venturing down towards Leith, guys working on building sites…It's not normally as quiet as this. But with the snow and everything…'

Ella sipped the strong brew. 'I'm sure it isn't. A friend of mine used to live on this street, up at number eleven in the first block. He was called John Roper. I don't suppose you remember him coming in, do you?'

She tucked a stray wisp of hair behind her ear and frowned as she considered the question. 'I don't think so. What did he look like?'

'I've got a photo I can show you. He was keen on climbing, going hill walking, so you might have seen him with his climbing gear.'

'Honestly, I see so many faces, I'm not sure I can help you. If he was a keen climber you're probably better trying Alien Rock, the climbing centre.'

'Alien Rock?'

'It's at Newhaven. An old converted church with a climbing wall. It's not that far from here.'

Deciding that she had to make a quick detour, Ella finished her coffee and stood up. 'I'll try there now, thank you.' She stared round the café, wondering if John Roper had ever been there. She smiled gratefully at the woman and dropped some coins onto the table, before leaving.

The climbing centre was across the street from Newhaven harbour. The bracing wind coming off the sea hit her in the face as she got out of a taxi. She hunched her shoulders against the wind as she strode towards the converted church and began to have doubts about what she might find out. Ella's misgivings came to the fore, mingling with the jarring cries of the seagulls swirling over the street, telling her that she was risking everything by not going to the police for protection, that the more she tried to do things herself the greater the risk she would be stopped by Sam Renwick's men.

She arrived at the climbing centre before it opened and sat on a bench across the street, watching for someone to appear. Alien Rock was an old church, standing proudly on the street across from one of the enclosed harbours along the south bank of the Firth of Forth. The waitress had told her a bit about the place, how it had been turned into an indoor climbing centre some twenty years before, and had become a favourite with climbers ever since. She just hoped that there was someone left there who had known John Roper.

Finally, just as she thought she was going to have to find shelter from the icy wind, she saw a young man open the door to the church and disappear inside. As she crossed the road, a couple of other people went into the church. She went in behind another man with blonde hair tied back in a ponytail. She hesitated once inside, the darkness of the entrance hall after the daylight outside making it difficult to see. Once she'd blinked a few times, she was alone again and she saw a staircase in front of her. She climbed up the stairs and found herself in a small reception area, with posters and pictures on the walls. She looked around with interest, wondering where the staff had all gone, when a young man bounded down the stairs from the floor above and went behind the desk.

'Hi there. How can I help you?' He glanced at the clock behind her and looked apologetic. 'I'm afraid we're not really open yet. We're having a staff meeting just now.'

'That's all right. I'm not here to climb.' Thinking on her feet, she added, 'I'm a journalist researching an article about climbing venues and wanted to find out about the centre and the people who come here. Can I talk to you about that?'

'No worries. Happy to have a chat. Why don't you go upstairs and wait in the café and we'll find you in ten minutes or so. You can ask us your questions then.'

Ella turned and went up the second flight of stairs, looking at the pictures on the walls as she climbed. The small café area looked down onto the inside of the church with the climbing walls stretching to the top of the building. She watched the small group talking amongst themselves for a moment or two, then wandered around the room, trying to feel that she wasn't wasting her time being there, wondering what she expected them to be able to tell her that she didn't already know.

At the very end of the wall, there was a large frame with photographs of climbers stuck on with pins, the snaps jumbled together and layered on top of others. She went closer, looking at the grinning faces staring out from the photographs, scanning the faces for anyone she recognised. As she moved one larger print, she saw a host of smaller ones and looked straight into the eyes of Martin Fraser. She was sure it was him, younger and thinner, but the same man. She didn't know he was interested in climbing, but then she didn't really know much about him. She reached up and took off the photograph to look more closely at his companions and almost dropped it when she saw the face of John Roper standing next to him, clutching his shoulder. She pulled out the photos of the scientists Carl had given her and compared them. It was definitely John Roper. He must have been friends with Martin Fraser. She wondered how close their relationship had been.

'Hello, can we help you?'

The young man had appeared again and Ella waved the photo. 'Do you know these men? I think one of them is a friend of mine.'

He looked at the photo and shook his head. 'Before my time, I'm afraid. But Chris might remember them. He's been here longer than me.' He turned as the man with the ponytail came running up the stairs, and handed him the photo. 'The lady was asking about these two. Do you remember them?'

Ella looked at him, willing him to speak. He stared at her and frowned, seemed to hesitate, and then to decide that there was no reason not to tell her.

'Yes, I knew them. They always climbed together here. They were great friends.'

'When last did you see them?'

'A few years ago, now. You must know what happened?'

Ella nodded. 'I know that John died in an accident.'

The man shook his head. 'Odd thing to happen. He was an experienced walker and climber. And it was unusual he was alone that day. He and Martin always walked together.'

Ella held her breath, scared of interrupting the flow.

'Martin never came back after that. What with what happened to John and then his daughter's accident.'

'She was seriously injured by a car at about the same time, wasn't she?'

'Yes. Hit and run accident. They didn't think she'd live as long as she has. They never found the driver. Sad story really.'

Ella tried to take in the implications of what she was hearing. Martin Fraser had been a close friend of John Roper. Maybe he knew more than he was willing to say. She grasped Chris's hand. 'Thank you. You've helped a lot. I need to go now.'

'But don't you want to know anything about the centre?' the younger man stuttered.

'No, it's fine. Something else I need to do. I'll come back if I need to know more.'

Chapter 18

Ella collected her car from the car park behind Waverley Station and drove across the Meadows and Bruntsfield Links to Holy Corner, the four churches at the crossroads still standing proudly, offering the prayers and meeting places they always had, now updated with signs for cafés and children's activities. She sat in her car at the bottom of the hill leading up to Morningside, surrounded by people going about their business. Glancing at the sky, which was definitely looking lighter, she was relieved to see that the snow had melted as quickly as it had come, its whiteness dissolving into muddy puddles of slush.

Martin Fraser's house was on one of the back streets behind the main road in Bruntsfield. She parked her car and opened the window, the noise of traffic and people had given way to silence in the back street. It was a large detached house, looking as if it was still a single property, unlike its neighbours, which had all been split into flats or turned into nursing homes with modern wings sprouting off the old building. Although the house looked as grand as ever, the garden was like a jungle, bushes growing unchecked, trees and shrubs flowing over the tall stone wall and front gate, foliage obscuring the tall windows at the front of the house.

She sat in the car and stared at the house. She'd decided to come to see Martin Fraser in his home environment, hoping he might be more likely to talk to her there. He'd been with Muir Pharma for so long and had been friends with John Roper, so he must be able to answer her questions. So far, he hadn't even been prepared to exchange small talk.

A van turned into the street and a young woman got out, opened the back door, and pulled down a ramp. She then went to the gate to Martin Fraser's house. There must have been a key on the inside of the gate. She stuck her hand through the bars and turned it, then pushed open the gate and pressed it flat against the overgrown hedge to clear the way, and walked up to the front door. Ella could hear the jangling noise of the old-fashioned bell echo through the house, but no-one answered the door. Just like John Roper's flat, she thought with a flash of irritation, no-one was there. But she stood patiently and waited.

After a few moments, the front door opened and someone pushed a wheelchair into the path. Ella couldn't see the person in the chair and just glimpsed a pale hand waving in the cold air. Martin Fraser stood in the doorway. He and the young woman spoke for a few moments, then she took the handles of the wheelchair and started to walk away from the house. 'Wait,' she heard him call. 'She dropped her gloves.' Ella saw him lean over the wheelchair and tenderly help his daughter on with her gloves, before bending down to kiss her and then watch the young woman push her through the gate and into the van. He waved as they left and then dropped his arm once they had turned the corner, hunching his shoulders as he went back into the house, closing the door behind him.

It was an everyday scene, it should have been one of pleasure, but the man's hunched shoulders told another story, one of happiness snatched away and a life changed irrevocably. Ella decided she'd talk to him another time, started up the engine and slowly drove away.

On the main road down to Morningside she followed a number 23 bus. She hesitated, and then drove past the bus stop. It was only a few minutes to the terraced house where Mitch's university professor lived.

She rang the doorbell without much enthusiasm, deciding that if no-one answered immediately, then this time she would get her car and leave.

This time the door opened and a tall, white-haired man stood in front of her, smiling and welcoming, the smell of fresh baking wafting through the door. She wondered what line to take with him, how she could get Mitch's professor to confide in her, but instead she said the first thing that came into her head.

'That baking smells wonderful.'

The smile broadened and he replied in a strong Australian accent, 'And you are?'

'I'm sorry. I wondered if I could have a few moments of your time. My name is Ella Scott and I was at university with Mitch.' She waited for his smile to fade, for the cold shoulder. After all, how could he be sure who she was? 'I don't know Mitch that well,' she carried on, 'but I'm worried about him. I can explain what I think is happening and how I'm trying to help him.'

To her surprise, his smile didn't fade and he opened the door wider. 'Why don't you come in?'

Ella followed the professor into the hall and took off

her boots, wet from the front path. They went into a modern family room at the back of the house, weak sunlight coming through the windows where the cloud had started to thin. She sat at the table while some coffee brewed.

He placed a cup and a hot muffin in front of her. 'Call me Colin. Tell me what you're worried about.'

Ella took in a deep breath. 'I'll start with what I'm doing here. I'm on holiday for a few weeks, staying with my friend Laura in Fife. I met Mitch when I got here for the first time in years. It was good to see him but he's very worried about something and has been behaving strangely. He's asked for my help. You know him so much better than I do. I wanted to ask you what you thought about him – how reliable you found him.'

'Is he in trouble?'

'No. He's done nothing wrong, if that's what you mean. I think he's discovered things that other people want hidden and now he's made himself a target. I'm trying to help him.'

'That sounds like Mitch.' He sighed. 'You have to understand that Mitch is very clever and works hard but isn't so good at the networking side of being a scientist: looking for collaborators, promoting his research, influencing the decision makers in an organisation. He doesn't always see the need to get on with other people, particularly those he thinks aren't as bright as him. He's like most clever people, quietly arrogant that he knows best, and disparaging about others. But I've always trusted his judgement, if that's really what you're asking.'

'Yes. That's what I wanted to know.' Ella paused and

then asked, 'Why did he leave the university? I think he has regretted his move to Muir Pharma.'

He shrugged. 'When Mitch first came to work at the university, he was very quiet, got on with his work, but, latterly, there was one colleague he'd never got on with, who spent time cultivating contacts at a senior level everywhere she could. Mitch claimed that she was taking the credit for work done by the whole team.'

'And was she?'

'She said she was promoting the science, but as she was the only one prepared to go out and speak about their work, she became the one most associated with it. The team was working on molecules that several companies were interested in and they latched on to her.'

'So, what happened?'

'It all came to a head one day when Mitch accused her of lying about her contribution to the project. Said she was trying to claim all the credit for the research. They had a furious row and, in the end, he walked out, refusing to work there anymore if she was going to stay.'

'What did you do?'

'I was off at the time, getting treatment for cancer…'

'I'm sorry.'

He lifted his hand. 'It's all right. The treatment has been successful, for now. I haven't been at work for much of the last year. Maybe I could have done something to prevent Mitch leaving if I'd been there. The department was much stronger with him there.'

'Laura told me a bit about these problems. Do you think Mitch had exaggerated them?'

'I've thought about it a lot. This kind of thing happens all the time with university research, where the individuals who are more charismatic than others claim ownership of work that isn't wholly theirs. He may have overreacted, but I think he was onto something.'

'So, Mitch was right.'

Colin changed the subject. 'Do you know Laura very well?'

'She's an old friend, but I think she's changed quite a bit.' Ella cleared her throat. 'When I spoke to Mitch, he told me not to trust Laura.'

His eyebrows shot up at that comment. 'That's not what he said to me. He came to see me one night a few weeks ago and said that he had made a mistake joining Muir Pharma because he didn't like their methods, thought they were cutting corners. But he was very worried about Laura.'

Ella thought about what Mitch had said, how tormented he'd sounded when she asked about Laura. 'They'd had a row, the day he left, because she wouldn't believe him about Muir Pharma, or didn't even want to listen to him. I don't know exactly what was said, because Laura won't open up to me about that, but Mitch told me that she knew exactly what was happening in Muir Pharma and not to trust her.'

Colin considered her words. 'I don't know Laura very well. Mitch said she was very ambitious and would go to great lengths for that company.'

Ella knew that all the evidence pointed to Laura being implicated in what Mitch had discovered. With this thought Ella felt a heavy weight dragging her down. She finally had to accept that he was right not to trust her. It was one thing being ambitious and trying to be successful, but it was quite another to get involved with people prepared to murder their way to success. Laura had crossed that line. But she knew that neither she nor Mitch's old professor really understood their relationship and what exactly had been said when they had argued.

Colin looked tired. 'I need to go,' said Ella. 'I've made you talk too much.'

'No worries. I'm not sure I was very much help, though.'

Ella went to her car and drove out of Edinburgh, relieved not to see anyone following her this time. She shivered and put on the heater, the image of the car racing towards her the previous night still vivid and disturbing. When it finally faded, the sight of Martin Fraser waving goodbye to his daughter stayed with her long after she left the city behind.

Chapter 19

The snow had turned to freezing rain as Ella drove north across the Forth Bridge into Fife. In the country, the clouds were so low and heavy that they hid the tops of the hills. Swirls of grey tendrils trailed along tree branches at the side of the road like fragments of grubby cotton wool. She breathed a sigh of relief as she turned off the motorway, leaving behind the blinding spray that had strained her driving abilities and made the journey more dangerous than she'd bargained for. But her relief was short-lived as progress was just as slow on the road that wound along the Fife coast. The cars that had ventured out were travelling slowly, wary of the wet slush that stretched across the roads.

Ella parked next to Laura's cottage again and couldn't help contrasting this visit with the first time she had stopped by. This wasn't a general look to see if Mitch was there. She was much more worried about him this time, and she had something specific to look for. She had to find Mitch's memory stick. She got out of the car, breathing in the cold air that still smelt of the sea, and let herself into the cottage.

She walked past the photographs without stopping, and purposefully went through to the back of the cottage, starting methodically to look for the memory stick. She went through every room, pulling out drawers, looking on shelves and under furniture. It took several hours before she was back in the kitchen, having found nothing.

She sat at the kitchen table and ate the sandwich she'd bought before leaving Edinburgh, and tried to muster enough enthusiasm to make her last visit. She pulled the piece of paper Carl had given her out of her pocket. She hadn't found out much about John Roper, but Trevor Fisher's wife still lived at the same address south of Kirkcaldy. It was the weather that made the decision for her. As she watched the sea, it turned from grey to blue as the cloud lifted and a ray of sunlight lit up the sky. She would go on her way back.

Driving towards Kirkcaldy, a town once dominated by mining and heavy industry, Ella noticed expanses of waste ground and deserted industrial buildings on the outskirts. She turned off before she got to the centre. She parked a little way from the house and walked along the beachfront road past a row of bungalows that looked out onto the sea, a few hundred yards from the nursing home where Carl said Trevor's wife worked. Ella saw the curtain twitch as she walked up the front path. She rang the bell and waited, hearing a dog barking and then frantically scratching at the inside of the front door, before the door was unlocked. The second it swung open, a spaniel bounded out of the house and jumped around her legs, barking excitedly.

'Rex, get down!'

A woman grabbed his collar and pulled him away before she looked up to see who had rung the doorbell. She was slim and had long curly hair, framing a face that was pretty, but covered in fine lines. A sensitive face that had an air of fragility.

'I'm sorry, he's still a puppy and gets very excited when someone rings the doorbell.' Then she frowned, almost as if she had some sixth sense about why Ella was at the door. 'Can I help you?'

'Mrs Fisher? Katherine Fisher?'

'Kath. It's Kath Fisher.'

'Kath, my name is Ella Scott, I'm doing some research about Muir Pharma. I wondered if I could speak to you about your husband Trevor and his work there?'

It was the best reason she could come up with but she felt herself cringe as the clumsy words hung in the air between them. She'd half expected the door to be closed in her face, or an angry response to her question – but Kath Fisher just leaned against the door frame, a faint smile hovering over her face, shaking her head.

'Are you another journalist? Why you people keep digging around Muir Pharma I have no idea. I have nothing to say about them, not to you nor to the last person who came around asking questions. My husband and I separated before he died, so I can't shed any light on his actions.'

Ella stared at her face, wondering what was going on inside her mind, contrasting her calm words with Mitch's tense allegations of what had happened to her husband.

'I know another scientist who works for Muir Pharma now who has some of the same concerns about the company as your husband did.'

The smile didn't budge, but Ella saw that the knuckles of the hand that was holding the dog's lead were white.

There was a noise in the hall behind her and she turned round to a tall young man who had come up behind her. 'Jake, will you take the dog, she's hurting my arm.'

The young man stared at Ella for a few seconds, then averted his eyes before walking away, dragging the dog away from the door and into the kitchen. Ella could hear the barking behind the door and his raised voice trying to calm the animal.

'I think you should just leave,' said Kath. 'It doesn't make any difference to me what you think, but it bothers my son when strangers want to talk about his father. Every time someone starts asking questions, it unsettles him, brings it all back.' It was the first time she'd sounded angry since answering the door.

'My friend was threatened at Muir Pharma. He said that the same thing happened to your husband.'

'Ex-husband,' she snapped.

'I'm sorry. Ex-husband. All I wanted to ask you was whether he had ever talked about trials carried out by Muir Pharma that were suppressed or hushed up.'

'No, he never talked about that. And during those last few years of his life, we didn't exactly communicate very much. I really can't say what was on his mind.' She closed the door firmly.

Ella trudged back along the shore to the car, feeling she hadn't handled the conversation very well. It didn't make her feel any better when she looked back and saw Kath Fisher pull the curtains in the living room window. Her only link to one of the dead Muir Pharma scientists refused to say anything, either because there was nothing to say, or because she was frustrated by people asking her about her dead husband. The only time she'd shown any emotion was over her son, accusing Ella of stirring up old memories and unsettling him.

She leaned on the wall and looked out at the sea, letting the sounds and smells of nature chase away her doubts and worries for a few moments.

Ella's eyes followed the lanes running down to the beach, with the sun glinting on the water a few hundred yards away. The view was too enticing and she walked down onto the beach, breathing in the salty air, turning her face up towards the lingering warmth from the sun that was starting to sink in the sky. She could see Edinburgh across the Firth of Forth, the coastline running through East Lothian, and sat down on a large stone, gazing across the water, comforted by the ripple of the waves sliding onto the beach.

She looked up when she heard a dog barking. Rex was racing onto the beach followed by Jake Fisher. Ella watched as he threw a stick into the sea, then turned and came towards her and sat on the stone beside her. They both watched the dog frolic in the waves, retrieve the stick, and come running back across the beach, dropping it in front of Jake and standing expectantly, tail wagging furiously. He grinned and picked it up, throwing it along the beach, before breaking the silence, not looking at Ella but fixing his gaze on to the sea.

'She doesn't like talking about my dad. Especially to strangers.'

'I can understand that.'

After a few minutes' more silence, Ella ventured, 'How old were you when he died?'

'Twelve. I'd just started high school.'

'I'm sorry. It must have been very difficult.'

He shrugged. Ella wondered what he'd come to say, holding her breath for some information, any information that would mean her trip hadn't been a complete waste of time.

'I heard them arguing about his work at the company. Mum and Dad had been separated for years, but he came round late one night, when I was in bed. They thought I was sleeping.'

Ella stared at him, at the almost adult profile looking fixedly ahead. 'What were they arguing about?'

'I didn't really understand, but he was worried about one of his colleagues. Said he'd found out something the company wanted to keep secret.'

'What was it?'

He frowned, his dark fringe flopping over the wide forehead as he shook his head. 'I don't know. Just that they wanted to keep something a secret. He sounded scared, though. Scared that they'd get into trouble.'

'Did he say the colleague's name?'

'John. It was someone called John.'

Ella gasped, heart jolting in her chest and she tried to keep the excitement out of her voice. 'Your father worked with someone called John Roper. Could it have been him?'

'Might have been. I only heard him say John.'

'What else did he say?'

'Nothing. They must have closed the door, because I didn't hear anything else.'

The dog came bounding up again, dropping the stick, but this time Jake didn't throw it, but started stabbing it into the sand with his left hand, swirling it around in crazy patterns.

'And how long was that, before your father died?'

'Just a couple of months. Not long anyway.' He turned towards her, his eyes burning fiercely. 'Do you think someone killed him? Is that why you're asking all these questions?'

A wave of pity washed over her as she glimpsed the desperation behind the question, the need to find a reason that would explain why his father had left him. She glanced back towards the house, half expecting his mother to appear and tell her to leave.

'I honestly don't know, Jake. Someone has made allegations about Muir Pharma that go back to when your father and his colleague worked for the company, but I haven't found any proof to back those up.' But she knew that wasn't good enough, that she had to go further, to stop the wild hope she could see burning in his eyes. 'And I haven't found anything to suggest that your father's death wasn't suicide. I'm sorry.' His eyes dulled and Ella touched his arm, but he moved away and started stabbing at the sand again.

'It's just not having any reason. Not knowing why he did it or whether I could have done anything to stop it.'

He looked at her again and she saw her own grief mirrored in his eyes, bundled up with the terrible guilt.

'You couldn't have done anything.' Unlike me, her inner voice intoned.

'I know. Everyone tells me that. I almost accepted it, until...'

'Until someone like me comes along and starts asking questions again.'

He nodded.

'Jake, I promise you that if I find out anything about your father, I'll tell you.'

He nodded and stood up, whistled until the dog ran over and ambled back towards the housing estate. Ella got up too, feeling chilled and realising that the sun had gone down beneath the horizon and it was beginning to get dark. As she opened the car door, she glanced over again at the path, but Jake had gone. She wouldn't forget his burning look, nor his need to understand why his father had died, the pain still so close to the surface. Was it always like this, when you started asking questions and uncovering people's secrets and worries, not knowing where it was all going to lead? Hoping that there weren't too many people you were going to damage along the way. What she did know was that if she did find out anything about Jake's father, then she might at least do some good.

Chapter 20

Ella couldn't settle during the whole of the next day, trying to go through the research Gregor had given her. Laura was still in Edinburgh. Ella had been alone most of the day with the cat, and she was nervous every time she thought of her meeting with Mitch that evening.

Finally she could set off. Following Mitch's directions, she drove slowly and concentrated on the road ahead of her. The rough tarmac surface was lit up by the beams of the headlights that cut through the darkness, obscured by sharp flurries of snow sweeping across the road and brushing a thin layer of white on the trees. She followed the precise instructions Mitch had given her on how to find the farm. 'Just make sure you're not being followed,' was his final appeal at the end of the call.

At the bottom of the steep hill, Ella waited in a layby for a full five minutes to check no-one had followed her or had come down the hill ahead of her, her heart thumping in her chest. But all was darkness and she drove on into the heart of Kinross, seeing no other cars on the quiet road.

In the silence all around her, she heard again the conversations at the Muir Pharma party, couldn't get out of her mind the image of Sam Renwick holding forth in front of his adoring audience, then of the car speeding towards her as she was leaving. She glanced in the rear-view mirror, trying to concentrate on the road ahead rather than on her anxiety, but she couldn't help imagining the face of the driver of that car. The face jumped from Jamie Forrester to Sam Renwick. She realised, with a bitter taste in her mouth, that by trying to escape from one monster, she might have reawakened more deadly demons.

At a sharp corner, the road narrowed into one lane and Ella dragged her thoughts away from her fear because she was going to drive into the ditch if she didn't concentrate on getting safely to the farm. Mitch said there was a sign for Brookhill Farm on the left-hand side of the road at the top of a steep hill, so if you reached a crossroads then you'd gone too far. Ella slowed down even further when she reached a block of low outbuildings at the side of the road. Just before the driveway she saw an old wooden sign with Brookhill painted on it – white paint worn off in patches, but the name still clearly legible.

Relieved that she'd found it, Ella turned off the road into a driveway and parked, switching the lights off. She scrabbled round for a torch and got out of the car, peering into the darkness, trying to see where the entrance to the house was. The evening was now freezing cold and the snow had stopped. She felt totally alone. Everything was very still – no sounds of any living thing breaking the silence until her boots crunched loudly on the gravel. She saw a gate in the beam of torchlight and fumbled with the rusty catch. Walking through the gate, she was startled by a security light that suddenly came on and revealed buildings all around her, a two-storey farmhouse directly ahead and two outhouses on either side. Patches of snow glittered. There was a campervan parked inside one of the outhouses.

'Mitch, are you in there?'

Ella turned away from the bright light and walked towards the house, looking to right and left to see if there was anyone there, feet crunching on the frosty surface. She was definitely in the right place – so where was he? She reached the front door. The sound of a dog barking in the distance made her jump and, feeling distinctly bad tempered with the whole affair, she tried the door handle. It was unlocked. She pushed the door inwards. Taking a deep breath, she glanced behind her and stepped inside. It was as cold in the small hallway as it had been outside, and her breath formed small clouds as it came out in short shallow gasps.

This was ridiculous, Ella thought. There was no-one here. Then the door in front of her swung open and she saw a tall figure silhouetted against a dim light coming from the back of the room.

'Mitch, is that you?' she squeaked, throat constricting in fear. She took a step back as the tall, lean figure came towards her, his features, now closer, slowly coming into view. She gasped when she saw how much older and thinner he looked.

'Of course it's me,' he said gruffly, pulling her into a fierce hug. 'Come on inside. It's not warm, but it's better than it is outside.' She followed him inside the kitchen and he slammed the door behind her.

She looked around at what must once have been a welcoming room, but now the Aga was cold and the original furniture had been replaced by a large wooden crate and cheap plastic chairs. In the corner of the room, she saw a pile of blankets and a pillow on the flagstone floor. Mitch's makeshift bed looked cold and uncomfortable.

'Is that where you sleep?' asked Ella, a jolt of pity making her voice shake.

He nodded. 'I don't sleep very much anyway.'

The crate was covered in files and papers, a laptop open at one end. She saw that Mitch had information gathered to give her and she groaned faintly when she remembered that she had failed to find the memory stick he'd asked her to get.

They sat down on the chairs.

'Does Laura know you're meeting me?' he asked.

'No. You said to tell no-one. She doesn't know I'm here.'

He ran a shaking hand through his hair. 'I've made a mess of everything. And then that bloody newspaper man had to get himself killed. I should never have tried to speak to him. I should have kept quiet, like everyone else.'

Ella winced as his voice cracked and he turned away. 'I just wanted to stop Sam Renwick... and get Laura back.'

Ella watched him and thought about the people she'd met at Muir Pharma; about Jake, who still yearned to know the truth about his father; about Laura and her real motives. She knew she had to help Mitch finish what he'd started. There were too many people who needed to know the truth.

'I'm here to get your evidence about what's going on, then I can take the facts to the police. I have not told Laura anything and I don't intend to do so, unless you want me to.' Ella took a deep breath and continued. 'For what it's worth, I've been in the same room as Sam and seen the control he has in that company. People are scared to talk to outsiders and their security is very tight. If I hadn't been vouched for by Laura I'd never have got in there. I've also seen Sam's temper, how capable he is of violence if he's cornered. But that isn't a serious crime. What I need to establish is much worse than that and I can't do that without your help. As for Laura, I'd say her loyalties are mixed but she's very worried about you.'

At Ella's last comment his head jerked up. 'Worried or not, my ambitious girlfriend is deeply involved in Sam Renwick's tricks, and I'm seriously worried that she knows exactly what he's doing. When I told her what I was working on – said I was concerned about what had happened in the company – she wouldn't believe me, accused me of exaggerating, making everything seem worse than it was. But she'll soon find out that I'm right.'

Ella leaned forward. 'Then tell me now. Give me your evidence of what he's trying to cover up – how Trevor Fisher and John Roper really died. I've spoken to the police and it's going to take significant new evidence to get them to reopen their cases. They said that they want to see you – hear what you have to say.'

'You've talked to the police about me? You know I don't want anything to do with them; they might even be involved. At the very least, they won't listen to anything bad about Muir Pharma.'

'I can see why you think that,' replied Ella, 'but we'll need the police before this is all over. We might not trust them completely but they're going to have to listen to us. It's the only way.'

Finally, she got through to him and he sat down

opposite her with a sigh. 'All right. I don't seem to have any choice but to involve you more than I wanted. I didn't realise how much running away and hiding like this stops you from doing anything useful. I'm spending all my time and energy avoiding Renwick's security men and can't really speak to anybody so I'll need to rely on you to do that for me.'

Ella glanced at the mugs next to the kettle behind him. 'Do you have any coffee?'

He grinned, looking much more like the old Mitch. 'Laura always used to say you existed on coffee. I'm afraid I can only do instant.'

'Anything with caffeine will do.' Ella grinned back.

She insisted that he went through every scrap of information he had gathered: from the bare facts to what people had said to him, to his views on what had really gone on in Muir Pharma. The coffee was stone cold by the time he'd finished his story. Even though Ella had researched clinical trial protocols and read through the papers Gregor Munro provided, she still had to get Mitch to explain the full meaning behind the emails and database printouts he set out in front of her so she could understand everything.

'So, on several occasions, Sam Renwick has persuaded, bribed or forced someone in the development team to suppress some of the early results of lab tests, to clear the compound for the next stage, the larger clinical trials on healthy volunteers. All designed to speed up the process to getting approval.'

'Yes.' He laid out copies of emails. 'These emails were on Trevor Fisher's laptop, correspondence with Sam saying that he didn't think the results from one of the drugs he was working on, that was passed to be tested on humans, were correct. He said that he had duplicated the initial lab tests and the results he found under stress conditions showed a high risk of violent behaviour.'

'And they ignored him.'

'They suspended him. Said he was breaching the confidentiality clauses in his employment contract. He shared his concerns with the other scientist he knew best, John Roper, because he couldn't understand why the results were different.'

Ella read through the emails, which became shorter and more cryptic, until the final one, which was crystal clear.

I've checked and rechecked the results and realised that they must have been changed. The results you signed off can't be correct.

Ella held her breath and reread the email. 'John Roper was actually the one falsifying the results. He was the one responsible.'

'I think so, at the start anyway. But he always acted on Sam's orders.'

'How do you know that?'

He handed her a company announcement, dated from the same period: Sam Renwick announcing that Evexitrol had successfully passed all the lab tests and was going on to the next stage of the process. 'They were controlling everything to push it through.'

'What did Trevor do?'

'He got signed off for depression a couple of months later.'

'Caused by the stress of the whole situation.'

'I think so. And then a few months later he was dead.'

Ella frowned. 'So, he committed suicide?'

He shook his head. 'I don't think so. You have to understand the background. Both scientists joined Muir Pharma when Renwick acquired a smaller biotech firm, run by a man called Andy Paige.'

'Wait, I've heard that name before.' Ella flipped through her notebook. 'Gregor Munro told me about him, how Sam Renwick put him out of business and then took over the drugs his company was developing. I didn't realise he took over some of the scientists as well.'

'Yes, he did. And I think he put pressure on them to suppress, and then falsify, results once they joined him. John Roper did it and Trevor Fisher found out.'

'But there's no proof that Trevor's death was anything other than suicide. The police have nothing to suggest foul play,' Ella persisted. She dug into her bag, took out the press cuttings Susan had given her, and put the article about Trevor Fisher's suicide on the crate between them. 'All it talks about is his suicide. It's quite graphic.' She pursed her lips in disgust. 'I wasn't expecting so much detail.'

He handed her another email. 'Maybe his death was suicide, but I'm fairly sure that John's death wasn't an accident.'

The email was from John Roper to Sam Renwick, accusing him of being responsible for his friend's death and handing in his resignation. The email was dated three days before John Roper's accident.

'When John Roper refused to play their game any longer, they killed him and made it look like an accident,' she breathed.

'Exactly.'

Ella showed him the other articles Susan had given her that reported on the climbing accident. 'But these have no suggestion of foul play either.'

'All right then. There's nothing that can help us there,' replied Mitch.

'Though the police did say that there were other people on the hill that day they weren't able to trace,' said Ella slowly.

Mitch handed her a cutting. 'This one alleges side effects from the compound,' he said. Ella scanned the article. It quoted Martin Fraser as the source. Ella raised her eyebrows and Mitch nodded.

'He spoke to the press and then denied their report,' said Mitch. 'I found the journalist who wrote this article and he said Fraser had told him about the potential side effects of the compound when he was drunk one night, but retracted the story the next day and refused to speak to him anymore.' His face twisted into a bitter smile. 'He was probably bribed by Muir Pharma to keep silent. Pharmaceutical companies are good at that. They made him medical director to shut him up. I think his daughter was badly injured in a car accident at about that time, which may not have been a coincidence, so it's not surprising he didn't have the stomach for a fight.'

Ella picked up a more recent article in his file about an attack on a woman in Manchester. 'How is this connected? It doesn't mention Muir Pharma anywhere. Do you think it was someone else involved in the clinical trials?'

'I thought so, but it's hard to tell. I do know that Muir Pharma started to receive a few letters from doctors, who were worried about side effects in patients taking the drug. There were some from Manchester and others from London. No-one in Muir Pharma took any notice of the letters, just buried them in red tape.'

'Where are the letters now?' asked Ella, knowing the answer before he spoke.

'I don't know, I never got the chance to look at them,' he replied. 'They aren't here anyway. But that's less important than the memory stick. Carl told me that it contains a full list of the cases doctors have identified that show serious side effects from the Muir Pharma drug.'

'That's the memory stick you asked me to look for in the cottage, wasn't it?'

'You didn't find it,' he stated flatly.

'No, it wasn't anywhere in the cottage, I looked everywhere. Where else could it be?'

'I don't know. I thought I had it with me but I must have left it at home. It'll be there somewhere.'

'I'll find it,' said Ella, her voice more confident than she was feeling, knowing how important evidence from real patients would be.

'Muir Pharma should have taken action, but didn't because Evexitrol made them so much money,' continued Mitch. 'That's why I think they're trying to do the same thing now, hiding initial negative lab results and trying to push the new compound through clinical trials. It's their last chance to attract more investment from bigger pharma companies and investors. And when I started asking questions and digging around the files, they got very nervous.'

'Did they threaten you?'

'I told Carl, they followed me home one night, just after I'd found Trevor's laptop, and started going through the company database to find the results that would back up what I was reading in the emails. I decided that I had enough to go public, so that's why I contacted Carl.'

'And do you really think Laura knows what they're doing?'

He covered his face with his hands and didn't speak for several seconds. Then he gave a deep sigh and looked up. 'I think she knows, deep down, that they're breaking the rules, but she doesn't want the dream to end. She loves her job, the company and their success. Like the rest of them, she's half in love with Sam Renwick and won't believe any criticism of him. But he's using her like he uses everyone else. And the stakes are much higher than they were four or five years ago because none of his other drugs have gone through trials successfully. He needs this new one to be a success or his company will be just another failure, swallowed up by a big pharma company. At heart, the man is a narcissist, he believes his own publicity and he thinks he's too big to fail. He's prepared to succeed at any cost.'

Chapter 21

Ella glanced outside and saw the snow falling steadily. 'I have to go, or I'll never get back over the hill.'

'Yes.' He looked outside. 'I've told you all I know.'

Mitch thrust the laptop at her. 'Here, you'd better take this,' he said.

Ella took it and stuffed it into her backpack.

'So, I need to find out anything I can about John Roper that might shed light on exactly how he died. Who was the journalist Martin Fraser contacted? Is it worth finding him?'

'I wouldn't think so. His name is Ronnie Grant.'

'He was at the Muir Pharma party the other night, asking me about Carl.'

Mitch gave a bitter laugh. 'He's in Renwick's pocket now. He wouldn't write anything against him. It's why I went to Carl in the first place. I heard Ronnie Grant complaining about a London journalist to one of his cronies in a pub one night and it must have been him, so I figured he might be a good person to speak to.'

Ella turned to face him at the door and hugged him. 'I'll do what I can in the next couple of days and then come back up here.'

'Right. Same time, day after tomorrow. Don't try and

phone me again. They might be tracking the mobiles. It's not safe.'

'Okay. And Mitch?'

'Yes.'

'I promise I'll do my best to get to the bottom of this. You won't have to stay in hiding for long.'

The familiar grin broke through his weary expression. 'Thanks. Just having someone else on my side helps. Makes me feel like I'm not going mad.'

Before she could get into the car, they heard a bell ring inside the house.

'What's that noise?' asked Ella.

'It's my alarm. Someone's coming. You need to leave now.'

Mitch almost pushed her towards the car and she slid on the snow-covered gravel, afraid that she would be stranded and caught by whoever was coming. She started the car and glanced back at Mitch as she turned in the courtyard, but he was looking in the other direction, up the road coming down the hill. Through the snow, she could see distant headlights. Mitch abruptly turned back inside and closed the door behind him.

Ella drew in a deep breath as she accelerated onto the road, turning down the hill and concentrating on the way ahead, the grip from the tyres keeping the car steady on the snowy surface. Some tractors or larger vehicles had driven down the road since the snow had started and she kept within their tracks. She drove down the hill steadily and slowed to a crawl as she reached the corner at the bottom. She looked up at the farmhouse with the dim light shining in the window, and shivered when she thought about how lonely Mitch was. He'd so convinced her of his story that his flight now seemed the only logical course of action. If what he said about Muir Pharma and Sam Renwick was true, then they'd have no hesitation about killing again to protect their secrets, covering it up as another accident. She suspected now that she too was a target. The intention in Edinburgh might have only been to frighten her away, but the car had been close enough to hit her if she'd moved the wrong way.

Suddenly her mobile rang, piercing the silence and breaking her concentration. The car slithered to a stop as she glanced at the screen flashing on the passenger seat and recognised the number. It was the number Mitch had given her to call him, she was sure of it. But he'd told her not to use that number again because he said it wasn't safe. Why would he break his own rules? Her hand stretched across to pick up the mobile but the ringing stopped. Should she call him back? She waited to see if he'd left a message, unsure if she should go back or keep going. Was it a warning?

She looked ahead and then behind her, but she could see no lights in the darkness. Her mobile stayed stubbornly silent. There was no message and no way of knowing what Mitch wanted her to do. The snow began to fall more heavily, large flakes obscuring the trees next to her and blocking out the farm and outbuildings. She would have to go or she'd never get home. It was only a few miles to Laura and Mitch's house, but if she didn't start now, she might be cut off. And she had become convinced, despite Mitch's warnings, that she needed to confront her friend, to hear her say she wasn't capable of murder.

Then she heard the muffled noise of another car driving fast in the distance, coming from behind her, and she strained her eyes through the blizzard, staring in the direction of the farmhouse. She thought she saw car headlights in the road next to the farm and then they went out. A few seconds later she saw a small burst of flame that lit up the front of the farmhouse and, a few heartbeats later, a dull thud echoed down the hill. A cold weight settled in the pit of Ella's stomach as she stared through the gloom, desperate to go back and help Mitch but knowing she couldn't lose the information he'd spent so long protecting.

She reacted immediately. If there was a fire then there was only one thing to do. She grabbed her mobile and dialled 999.

'Fire service please,' she answered the woman on the line. 'I'm calling to report a fire at Brookhill Farm in Cleish. It's off Junction 5 of the M90. I don't know how far it is from the motorway, but it must be only a few miles.'

After a moment the woman replied, 'They're on their way. Are there any people there who could be inside?'

'Yes, I think so, one person,' said Ella. 'I'm not sure. The snow here is getting quite bad.'

'Yes, the snow is making driving difficult but we'll get a vehicle to you as soon as possible, please stay on the line. Are you in the vicinity of the fire?'

'I'm too far away to see what's happening and I'm going to have to leave or I'm not going to be able to get home.' Ella hung up and looked back up at the farmhouse, squinting through the thick snow that was now falling. The weather would make it difficult for a fire engine to get there, but at least she'd tried. She just hoped that Mitch had safely got away from the house.

Realising that she had to save herself, she sobbed as she started the car again and moved off. As her road came into view through the snow, she turned up the hill and dashed away the tears in her eyes, knowing she had to keep going. She couldn't afford to wait to see if the fire engine got through the snow.

Although she told herself not to imagine what was happening behind her, as the car ground up the hill, she couldn't stop thinking about Mitch and how vulnerable he had been alone in the middle of nowhere. She was in no doubt now of the danger he'd put himself in by turning whistleblower and of how close his pursuers were. She couldn't stop thinking that she might have led them there somehow.

Once she'd turned off the Brookhill road, heading south, a quirk of local weather meant that the snow didn't seem so heavy. The branches of the trees overhanging the uneven road gave her a clearer route that she followed slavishly, winding up the hill. After what seemed like an eternity, she reached flat ground and a few moments later she drew in next to the house and stopped the engine, laying her head on the steering wheel, waiting for her heart to stop thumping before taking the rucksack with Mitch's laptop into the house and locking the door behind her.

She couldn't get out of her mind the lights and the flash of flames she'd seen at the farm and hoped with all her heart that Mitch had managed to leave in time, knowing with appalling clarity that he had nowhere to run and no escape. She wanted to speak to Laura now, to tell her how wrong she'd been to dismiss her boyfriend and what was really going on all around her. But the house was quiet and empty. Laura wasn't there to listen to her.

Once inside, Ella bolted all the doors. She glanced into the utility room and saw a shaft of moonlight shining through the glass panel next to the back door. She looked through the tall window and saw patches of clear sky appear in the cloud cover. The snow had stopped falling. She sank down on the chair in the entrance hall and held her head in her hands, overcome by a wave of tiredness, not even reaching up to switch on the light. She was relieved to be back inside on her own. Slowly noises from outside filtered into the house. In the stillness Ella could hear the rustle of trees behind the house and the screech of a fox in the distance.

She lifted her head as she suddenly heard the sound of footsteps outside. Someone was walking around the house. The steps stopped outside the front and Ella was hardly able to breathe, waiting for them to go. She jumped as the handle in the door next to her moved, and she watched, paralysed by fear, as it glided down. Would the bolt hold the door? Whoever was outside must suspect she was in the house; her car was out there, but with no lights on they couldn't be sure.

She pressed her back against the wall, terrified that any movement might give away that she was there. Then she heard another step at the back door. She heard the door handle move down and a key rattled in the lock. Someone pushed against the door. Ella closed her eyes, waiting for it to open, but it stayed firmly shut. She breathed out a silent sigh of relief. They hadn't managed to get in, but she couldn't move until they had left. She suspected that they were just trying to frighten her, but however much her logical brain told her that was what they were doing, she still felt terrified.

Then behind her in the small window next to the front door she heard a dull squeak as someone scratched their finger over the glass trying to clear the frost. She sat quietly, unable to move until the noise stopped. A few moments later she heard the sound of footsteps walk away from the house.

Chapter 22

Ella tossed and turned all night. Images of Mitch running in the snow and being chased by Sam invaded her dreams and jolted her awake again and again. When she was awake one time she went downstairs to unbolt the door, knowing that Laura would be trying to get in. Even later, the noise of the front door opening and closing filtered through to her room, so she knew that Laura had come home. Ella decided that she would get up and see Laura before she left the next morning, but, exhausted from the hours of disturbed sleep, the noises from downstairs only woke her up when she heard the back door open and close. Immediately awake, Ella jumped out of bed, threw on a sweater and pulled on some fluffy rubber-soled boots before running on to the landing and down the stairs. She looked rapidly round the kitchen, heart plunging when she thought she might have missed her.

To her relief, she saw an empty mug in the sink and Laura's bag was still lying on one of the kitchen chairs, her purse sticking out of the top. Ella turned again to the back door. She must have gone out to get something from the car, but why was she taking so long? Ella picked up a ski jacket from the hook next to the door and looked out of the window at the cars, expecting at any moment to see Laura coming back into the house.

Instead of Laura's familiar figure Ella felt suddenly cold when she saw a man bending down over her car. There was no sign of Laura. Sensing danger, she pulled open the door and ran to the car, nearly losing her balance on the frosty gravel.

'Hey, what are you doing?' she shouted.

The man looked at her for a few seconds, his eyes blazing above a scarf tied around the bottom half of his face, then he turned and ran away from the house, disappearing into the trees in a matter of seconds. Ella hurried, hoping to catch him, but stopped when she saw someone collapsed on the ground. It was Laura. All thoughts of chasing after the man disappeared.

'Laura, are you hurt?'

She crouched down next to her friend, wondering whether it was safe to move her, before Laura gave a low groan and tried to sit up.

'Just take it easy, let me help you,' said Ella, trying to keep calm, but looking round in panic, wondering how she was going to get Laura inside, out of the biting cold.

'It's my head,' moaned Laura. 'The back of my head. Someone hit me. I think he was trying to get into your car. When you appeared so quickly and shouted, he ran off.'

'Do you hurt anywhere else?'

'No, just my head.'

'Here, have my coat. Let's sit for a minute or two and then we'll try and get you up,' said Ella, sounding calmer than she felt. Laura's face was very white and she was shaking with cold and shock. As they sat, Ella's mind was racing over what had happened. Who was the man and what could he have been trying to steal? She glanced at the car boot left open and the mats from the floor strewn around the inside of the car, realising, with a nasty jolt, that he must have been looking for something in particular. She felt as if events were running out of their control. First Mitch was hounded in his hiding place, and now Laura had been attacked in front of her own home.

'What's happened?'

Ella looked up and saw Martin Fraser's Volvo in the road, the car door flung wide open. 'Are you all right?' He strode towards them, moved Ella gently but firmly to one side and crouched down beside Laura. Ella stared at him, surprised at his gentle voice.

'Someone hit her,' Ella said. 'I didn't see who it was. He was wearing a mask.'

He glanced at Ella over Laura's head, frowned at her briefly, then bent his head back down to speak to Laura.

'Can you move your legs?' He ran his hand over her legs, then flexed her arms in turn. 'Nothing seems to be broken.'

'I think I can get up now.' Laura's voice sounded a bit stronger and the colour was coming back into her face.

'Let's get you inside, warm you up.' He supported Laura to stand up and Ella ran ahead to pull the back door wide open for them. He helped Laura over the step and towards the sofa.

'I'll just close the car door,' said Ella. She went back to the car, feeling chilled with cold, her feet like blocks of ice in the flimsy boots, but knowing she had to find out what the man was looking for. He'd taken a big risk to break into the car, had been wearing a mask to hide his identity, and Ella was gripped by a fierce need to know what could be so important.

She looked methodically through the car, under the seats and in the boot. She didn't really know what she was looking for, but there must have been some reason he wanted to search the car. Ella stretched her hand underneath the panels in the boot. Reaching further under, she slid her fingers as far as they could go and felt a small square object, about three inches wide. She bent forward, stretching her arm into the boot until she could reach it and remove it. She stood up and turned the object round in the light to try to work out what it was. It looked like some kind of receiver.

Ella gasped in shock and felt a chill that wasn't from the cold wind. They'd put a tracking device on her car and she had led Sam Renwick straight to Mitch. If his men had found him, it was her fault.

She stuck the gadget into her pocket and brushed the worst of the mud from the knees of her jogging bottoms, then went into the kitchen.

'You were a while,' said Martin Fraser, and then took a proper look at her. With a patient to help, he was a completely different man, the total medical professional rather than the haunted and melancholic figure she had always seen. 'You're chilled to the bone. Go and have a shower.' He glanced at Laura, who was sitting on the sofa with her head resting back against a cushion, a blanket tucked around her and her eyes shut. 'I'll stay with her until you get back. I think she's fine,' he said firmly.

Shaking with cold, Ella nodded and went upstairs. She

looked at her mobile, wondering whether it would be safe to text Mitch about what had happened. He had said not to contact him so she had no choice but to go back and check the farmhouse to see if he was still there.

When Ella came back down, Laura was drinking hot tea and Martin poured her a cup. 'Drink this. I need to get down to Edinburgh. My daughter has been taken ill.'

'I'm sorry…' Ella started to say, but he wasn't listening.

'Are you going to call the police about this?' he barked.

Before Ella could reply, Laura spoke, her voice no longer that of a scared child. 'I don't think so, Martin. It was just a petty thief who lashed out when I surprised him. We don't want any negative publicity about security, particularly with the big press conference coming up in a few days.'

He didn't address this, but with a few more words of advice, left them, and Ella saw him go to his car and drive off. She turned from the window and looked at Laura, who was watching her closely.

'What is it?' said Laura. 'I know that look. What have you found? What was that man trying to get out of your car?'

'This.' Ella placed the tracking device on the coffee table.

'What is it?' asked Laura.

'I think it's a tracking device. I found it in the boot. It may have been what led our burglar here.' Ella looked at Laura's surprised expression and her heart hardened. 'Have you seen it before?'

'I don't know anything about it,' Laura replied indignantly.

'Are you sure? You didn't keep me talking when I was at Muir Pharma so they could fit it?'

'No,' Laura said hotly, flushing scarlet. 'Why would I do that? You're my friend. I wanted you to help me find Mitch...'

'I think Sam might have found him now.' Ella covered her face with her hands, the enormity of what she'd done almost overwhelming her. 'He used this tracker to follow my car and I led him straight to Mitch.'

Laura didn't reply and seemed stunned by Ella's words. Her eyes widened as she took in the implications. 'You've found Mitch. You saw him and you didn't tell me.'

Ella could hear the accusing tone in her voice and bit out a reply. 'Are you surprised? Mitch tried to tell you what was going on in Muir Pharma, but you wouldn't listen. He thought you were on Sam's side and he said he couldn't trust you. He told me not to trust you.'

'He said that? He said not to trust me?' The anguish in her voice reverberated. Laura bent her head, muttering under her breath, 'Oh, Mitch, what's happening to us?"

Pity for her friend warred with Ella's anger and she stretched out her hand. 'But I want to trust you. I need you to tell me everything. I need you to convince me that you would never harm Mitch. I don't know where he is now and what's happened to him, but I do know that he's found out things about Muir Pharma that are criminal, and we're the only ones now who can take his evidence to the police. Tell me what's really been going on.'

Laura started her story, hesitantly at first and then growing more assured. 'I'm not really sure when things started to go wrong between Mitch and me. He was having problems at the university and seemed happy to leave and start somewhere new. I thought he'd love being in Muir Pharma.' Her eyes shone as she looked up at Ella and tried to explain. 'It was so exciting, what Sam was doing, how we were building the business. But Mitch just saw faults in everything and we started to argue all the time.'

'So, you spent even more time at work.'

She nodded. 'I was going on more foreign trips with Sam. Dealing with investors and our strategic partners. I loved it all.'

'And was he right to be jealous of Sam? Were you having an affair with him?'

'No. Absolutely not. I admit I could have, but I knew it would have been a mistake. I see how he treats women. And anyway, I wouldn't have done that to Mitch.' She looked at Ella, seeking some understanding. 'You know what Sam is like, how charismatic he is. Anyway, I didn't do it.' Getting no response, she stumbled on. 'I was just so shocked when Mitch started accusing me of the same thing. He said he wanted to talk to me and I thought he was going to ask me to marry him.' Laura flushed a deeper red and Ella could see the tears in her eyes.

'I thought we were in love and that he felt the same as me, but all he wanted to do was try to convince me of his suspicions.' She looked across at Ella, her eyes full of anguish. 'And then Mitch got obsessed with some emails at Muir Pharma from years ago. That's why we argued. He was just shouting about Sam and what he thought he'd done. He wouldn't listen to me. I thought marriage was important for both of us, but some ridiculous conspiracy was all he would talk about.' She hunched her shoulders.

'Then he just walked out to leave me to deal with it all on my own. It's why I wanted you to find him, Ella. You might get through to him when I can't.'

Ella could understand it now. Laura had been too wrapped up in her own world, her own desires, to listen to Mitch's warnings about what had been going on all around her. She'd always been single-minded, unwilling to be distracted from what she believed was important, but the consequences of her wilful blindness had been disastrous. Ella had to make her see that.

'Laura, didn't you listen to what he said? Mitch didn't leave because he was jealous but because he was scared for his own safety. Didn't you realise the implications of what he had found out?'

'Well, he was raging about the methods used at Muir Pharma in the past and I know he was spending hours on Trevor Fisher's old laptop. I said we would talk about it at the weekend but he wouldn't wait for that, he just walked out. I didn't know he had gone until I came to look for him. He just left without saying anything.'

'He left because he had evidence of Sam and Robert suppressing test results at Muir Pharma. But more than that, he began to suspect that John Roper didn't die in an accident and that there was more to Trevor Fisher's suicide than appeared at the time. And that means your great leader was not just behind fraud but murder.'

Laura pulled her arm away from Ella's grasp, as if she'd been hit by a blow – shock turning her pale. She stood up and walked back and forth across the room, her voice growing stronger, shaking her head to deny what Ella was suggesting. 'You have to believe that I didn't know about any of it. Hiding research results, killing people. I didn't have anything to do with that. How could you have thought I would be capable of betraying Mitch?'

'Because you looked like you were madly in love with your boss and would do anything he told you. What else was Mitch supposed to think? Or me, for that matter?'

'Well, you were wrong.'

Ella stared at her, wondering if she could believe her: whether she really hadn't been part of the hunt for Mitch; that she hadn't been involved.

'So where is Mitch now?' asked Laura, sitting back down on the sofa.

Ella sighed. 'That's the problem, I did see him but I led Sam Renwick's men right to him and he's gone. I might have his laptop but his testimony about Muir Pharma is still important. And he can't find the memory stick that has other important information on it. He said it was quite distinctive, silver with a blue elastic band around it. If we don't get it Muir Pharma can just carry on as they always have. They'll have won again.'

'But I have that memory stick,' cried Laura. 'I took it into the office but didn't even look at what was on it. It will still be there. If it's important, we can go and get it.'

Ella stared at her, shocked into silence. Then her words tumbled out. 'We need to get into Muir Pharma and find it, then take it to the police. I don't know what happened to Mitch last night, so we need to keep going and hope he's all right.'

Laura was pacing the floor again, concentration calming her down, her voice now brisk and business like. 'We shouldn't try and get it now; the place will be too busy. We should go in this evening.'

'So, you'll help me?' said Ella. 'It will mean the end of Muir Pharma.'

'Of course I'll help you,' answered Laura. 'You have to believe me that I would never do anything to harm Mitch.' Ella stood up and Laura pulled her into a fierce hug. 'I'm so glad you're here with us,' Laura muttered into her shoulder. 'I know that everything will be fine now.' She drew back and laughed shakily. 'After lying in all that muddy snow, I badly need a shower.'

Ella put the tracking device into her bag. 'Just make sure you lock the door behind me,' she said.

'Where are you going?'

'To find out more about this little black box. And to see if I can get something to even up the fight.'

Chapter 23

Ella opened the car door gingerly, then shut it again and locked and unlocked it. Everything worked smoothly. Their intruder must have been a professional lock-picker and expected to get away without them realising what he was doing. She climbed into the car and opened the rucksack, taking out the small black box and turning it over in her hands, looking for a switch to disable it. Even if she managed to turn it off now, she pushed away the thought that the damage had already been done, however innocently. Even if they had found Mitch, she reasoned, he might have had some warning, could have managed to escape and tried to call her to tell her not to come back to the farm. She tried to tell herself that he would be fine, tried to suppress the guilt that she'd done him more harm than good.

More easily than she'd expected, a slot of black plastic slid out of the device and a battery fell onto her lap. She placed the device carefully in her rucksack. Not wanting to repeat the nightmare journey of the night before, she kept away from the isolated road going over the hill and took the motorway.

As she drove deeper into the Cleish hills, the scene was more wintry than further south, where the snow had turned into patches of muddy, freezing slush. Here, winter had taken hold more firmly: banks of snow piled up at the side of the road and gleaming in the morning light; the clouds so heavy in the sky they seemed to rest on the tops of the hills and ridges. Further into the valley, below the drooping branches still laden with snow, the roads were covered with hard-packed ice, beyond the reach of the gritters that trundled up and down the motorway.

She turned up the hill towards Brookhill Farm and saw the solid farmhouse for the first time in the dull light of day. At first, the house looked the same, but, as she drove closer, it was clear that the right-hand edge of the roof was black and there was a stretch of police tape along the side of the outhouse next to the road that joined onto the farmhouse. The building had been burnt black, its roof gone, and fragments of stone walls rose into the grey sky like skeletal fingers. The police tape was stretched across the driveway, and Ella parked her car next to it and got out.

There wasn't a soul anywhere, so she ducked under the tape and walked round the outhouse to the grass area in the centre of the steading. To her horror, she saw that the fire had reached the end of the farmhouse where she had met Mitch, the wooden door to the entrance hall buckled and singed. She looked all around her, watching and waiting. All she could hear in the confined space was the sound of her own ragged breathing and she longed to turn and run away, drive off and leave all this destruction behind. She had no idea what could be waiting for her in that house but she knew that it had all been her fault. She had to try to find out what had happened to Mitch. 'Come on Ella, you can't back out now. Just go in and see what's in there,' she muttered in the oppressive silence.

Ella pushed open the gate to the steading, trying to swallow the lump in her throat, fear catching her breath as she crunched across the snow to the front door. When a bird flew off the roof of the house in a cacophony of flapping wings, dislodging a slab of snow that crashed to the ground with a heavy thud, she almost turned and ran back to the car. As if pushed by an unseen hand, the entrance door swung open in a gust of wind and hung awkwardly from its hinges.

Taking a deep breath, she walked into the narrow hall and pushed open the door to the kitchen.

The fire had reached the kitchen and the room was totally wrecked, fragments of boxes and chairs blackened and upended. She picked her way through the mess, sweeping the broken cups aside, hoping that something was left, but it was all gone and there was no sign of Mitch or what had happened to him.

The front door swung further open behind her with a low sigh and she almost fell over an upturned chair. They'd come back for her, she thought, terror of being trapped in that dark room making her run into the hall, but there was no-one there to block her escape. The strengthening wind was lifting the door and blowing over her tracks in the snow. She looked down as the toe of her boot caught the crumpled floor mat, and saw a dark stain across the stone flags. It was blood. It could even be Mitch's blood, bringing back the memory of the night when she'd gone back to find Ruth, her blood all over the floor.

She ran for the car, desperate to get out of that horrible

house, to get away from the memories. But she couldn't escape from the truth that she'd failed yet again to save someone who needed her help. Scrabbling with the ignition key, tears blurring her vision as she backed the car out into the road, wheels spinning over the packed snow, she drove down the hill towards the motorway as fast as she could, away from the destruction and the violence hanging over the house.

They'd won.

That was the thought she couldn't get away from, the dull realisation that she'd come up against too much opposition this time. She knew that the sensible thing now was to run away again, go back to London. Even Ben Forrester had left her nightmares, replaced by the real threats all around her. Her parents had lost one daughter already and she knew it would destroy then to lose the other one. She couldn't put them through that. She had to leave Edinburgh and let someone else stop Sam Renwick. She'd tell everything to the police, give Susan all Mitch's evidence he'd given her and they could decide what to do.

Her mind made up, she turned onto the motorway and put the radio on, flicking through the channels, seeking the distraction of normality with familiar voices and mundane news stories. She finally landed on a local Edinburgh news radio station. Sam Renwick's deep tones filled the car and she realised there was no respite in the familiarity of the normal world. It sounded as if he were sitting right next to her.

'Yes, we are confident of our new drug. It's just completing its final stages of testing with outstanding results.'

'And what about these rumours of some of your scientists being unhappy?' asked the journalist. 'What can you say about that?'

Sam laughed, his voice brimming with confidence. 'There are always some people who criticise what we do, but we're still growing. People still want to work for us. If they're not put off by disaffected scientists telling lies about the company, no-one else should be.'

It was the laugh that did it. As that laugh echoed round the car, it froze Ella's fear into anger and her fingers gripped the steering wheel, unable to put the radio off, to stop him from talking.

'And you'll be able to obtain regulatory approval by the date you've told your investors?' asked the interviewer.

'All of our results are positive,' replied Sam. 'We are submitting our application to the authorities and have all the data we need to take it to the approval stage. And we have more positive news to announce at the end of this week. We intend to take Muir Pharma to the next level.' He wouldn't give any more details, despite the interviewer's insistent questions.

How many more people would he push aside? Another independent scientist with an inconvenient ability to dig out past crimes? Another journalist who could be frightened away? She knew with sickening certainty that there was no-one else who was prepared to stand in his way.

'Everything is on track.' Sam ended the interview with a flourish.

Carl Davis had been killed. Ronnie Grant had been bought. And now Mitch was running for his life, if he'd managed to escape the night before and wasn't already dead. Ella shivered, although the car was warm. She didn't want to think about where he was now, what might have happened to him. There was no-one left to fight. She thought about her parents, about their fog of grief after Ruth's death, and how Ella wanted above everything else not to make things worse. But then she thought about what they'd always taught her, about the importance of helping others and the difference one person could make, if they were in a position to act. She knew she couldn't ignore that duty. She wasn't going to give up this time, walk away from Mitch like she'd walked away from Ruth. She'd just have to accept the consequences and hope that they would understand.

She knew what she had to do and pulled off the motorway to call Laura. 'Mitch has gone. I don't know where he is.' She heard Laura take a shaking breath and carried on. 'The place was destroyed, door smashed in, blood on the floor.' She swallowed the lump in her throat. The baldness of the words made it sound even worse.

'What should we do now?' asked Laura in a high-pitched voice.

'Keep to the plan. We have to find the memory stick. He said that information was crucial.'

'But shouldn't we go straight to the police? You found the place wrecked, Mitch gone. His life is in danger, it must be, based on what you've found out already. Surely you need to go to the police now?'

'Laura, we'll never get all the evidence if we do that. We need to go back to Muir Pharma. Then we go to the police.'

'It's too dangerous to keep chasing these men,' protested

Laura. 'I didn't believe it before but I know now what Sam will do when people get in his way.'

'I'm not going to stop getting in his way,' said Ella grimly. 'I heard him on the radio just now, convincing everyone his drugs are a success. He can't be allowed to bury the truth and get away with it.'

Laura moaned, but then asked, 'What can I do?'

'Pack a bag. I have a feeling that we might need to run. Sam Renwick was talking about some big announcement at a press conference tomorrow. He won't want anything to spoil that.'

'It's a big new foreign investor in the business. I don't know the details but they're announcing it at the press conference,' said Laura. 'They've kept me out of all the arrangements this time, giving me other things to do. They don't trust me anymore.'

'That's why we only have one chance to get in there,' answered Ella. 'You're sure it will be quiet tonight? We don't want to walk into anyone.'

'Yes, they're all in meetings in Edinburgh,' confirmed Laura.

'I'll be back as soon as I can,' said Ella, switching off the mobile. As she drove into Edinburgh, she felt a cold finger of fear when she thought about going into Muir Pharma with Laura, hoping that she was right to trust her. Could she be wrong about her friend? Had she really turned away from Sam Renwick? Ella had been wrong before and had trusted the wrong people. But she had to try one last time. She wasn't going to give up on her friend.

Chapter 24

Ella stopped on the outskirts of Edinburgh to get some petrol. It was already dark. One of those winter days that hardly got any light in the daytime. She scrabbled in the glove compartment to get her phone. She found Jim's card in her pocket and messaged him. *Can I come and see you? Got something to ask. Are you at Dublin Meuse?* After a couple of seconds, she saw that he was replying and the response appeared quickly. *Glad to hear from you. Yes, I am. You can park beside the office.*

She rang the doorbell on the small converted mews building, gazing up at the tall townhouse terraces surrounding the patch of open space, and waited for Jim to come to the door. She heard a noise from the other side of the street and whipped around, wondering if someone had followed her, but the door opened and she stumbled into the light space, glancing behind her to check there was no-one there. At the end of the street, she saw a solitary figure standing watching her. She gasped in shock and stared at the man, taking a step towards the door to try to see his face, but he turned away and disappeared into the darkness.

'Are you all right?' said Jim, taking her coat and closing the door firmly behind her, hugging her quickly. 'Was there someone out there? Are these people still following you?'

'I don't know.' Taking a grip on herself, Ella smiled at him. 'I'm glad to see you.' She looked around at the modern interior. 'It's nice to see where you work.'

'I share the space with a private investment firm. They were a client and I now seem to have become part of the furniture.' He waved a hand at the side of the room, with monitors and computer equipment piled up on top of a long table. 'I was doing some research. Looking at some of the new gadgets coming onto the market.' They sat down in an open-plan area with tables and chairs and he placed a steaming cup of coffee in front of her.

'You said you have something you wanted me to take a look at?'

Ella took the square device out of her pocket and placed it on the table between them. 'I want you to identify this.'

He picked it up and turned it over in his hand, sucking in the breath between his teeth as he examined it. 'What do you think it is?' he asked finally.

'I think it's a tracking device... I found it in my car this morning after someone tried to break in.' She held her breath, hoping he'd say it was something else, something to do with the hire car, but she felt sick when he confirmed her suspicions.

'You're right. It's a fairly sophisticated tracking device, used by private detectives and suspicious wives all over the country.' He cleared his throat, and handed it back. 'Someone has been tracking the journeys made in your car for probably the last two to three days... It's definitely disabled now.'

'I took the battery out,' said Ella faintly. 'After the break-in this morning.' If Laura hadn't interrupted him he would have taken it back before she'd found it, so she'd never have known it was there.

She bent her head, the confirmation of where she'd led them making her feel sick, and she swallowed to get rid of the lump in her throat. She thought again about the missed call from his mobile, the fire she'd seen and how exposed he was up there. All her worries from the previous evening came rushing back. He'd trusted her to be careful and she'd let him down, just like she'd let Ruth down. She felt the same grief and guilt well up again, as strong as ever.

'Are you all right?' asked Jim. 'Did anyone get hurt this morning? You've gone very pale.'

'It wasn't a big deal. We're fine.'

He stared at her, his brown eyes warm, and hesitated for a couple of seconds before carrying on. 'If someone put that device in the car you've been using, then they're fairly serious about wanting to know where you've been and who you've been meeting.' She nodded. 'Planting a tracking device probably isn't the only thing they've done to monitor what you're doing. You have to assume that they're tracking your mobile phone. They can see who you're calling – who's phoning you. They're probably listening to your calls too.'

Ella tried to think back over the previous few days and who she'd called. At least she had followed Mitch's instructions not to call him, but if they'd been listening to her conversations with Laura, then they would know exactly what she was doing every step of the way. She remembered Laura's comments the first time she'd been to the Muir Pharma lab and Ella had remarked on the level of security. If Sam Renwick's men could protect the site against suspected animal rights activists by following their conversations, they could easily do the same with her. She cursed herself for being so slow to appreciate how serious they were.

She picked up the tracking device and frowned. Sam Renwick and his men had been ahead of her all the time. They must have planted the device when she was at Muir Pharma, using her to get to Mitch. She remembered how the car had been unlocked when she'd gone back to the car park, but hadn't suspected what they'd done. And they got Laura to distract her while they did it. Did all this happen just because she was seen with Carl?

'Things seem to be getting worse,' said Jim. 'Is there anything else I can do?' Ella jumped, so tied up in her own thoughts that she'd almost forgotten he was there. She glanced again at the table piled high with gadgets. This fight didn't have to be so one sided. She'd just have to get smarter about the weapons she used.

'There are a couple of other things I may need,' she replied.

Half an hour later, she emerged from the office, satisfied with her haul, but accompanied by a very worried man.

Jim walked with her to the car and watched her unlock the door.

'Are you absolutely sure you want to go back there?' he asked for the tenth time as she got into the car.

'You said you'd help me,' answered Ella.

'I know what I said, but that was before I knew what you wanted to do.'

'I'm just taking precautions. Besides, they might not be

needed.' She paused before starting up the engine, suddenly unsure about the enormity of what she was asking him to do, someone she'd only met a few days before. 'You will help me, won't you? I can't do this without you.'

He blinked a couple of times, hearing the emotion in her voice, but his reply was steady and sure. 'You can rely on me.'

She smiled and kissed his cheek. 'Thank you. I'll make sure you get everything back, I promise.'

'Whatever you're planning to do, be careful.'

'I will.'

Ella started the engine and bumped along the cobbled streets through the New Town and along Queensferry Road out of the city. But as she drove fast up the motorway through Fife, she knew that being careful wouldn't help her now. She had to be the opposite of careful and hope that the precautions she'd put in place would save her if things went badly wrong. She could tell she was close to the truth, that she'd rattled Muir Pharma and Sam Renwick, but she also knew that it could all disappear in an instant if she made the wrong move.

Half an hour later, Ella stopped the car at Laura's house and got out. It was a cold clear evening and she shivered in the dark. As she locked the car door, she looked up at the other houses and paused as she saw a light flicker on in the far house. She wondered again who could be in there. It was supposed to be empty. She looked again at the moving light and curiosity made her take a few steps along the road past Martin Fraser's house. She listened for any noise but all was silent around her – no wind rustling the trees surrounding the houses.

She heard a step behind her. Martin Fraser came towards her and she looked at him warily. He seemed much older than he had that morning and was moving stiffly as if he was in pain.

'Where are you going?' he barked out in his gravelly voice.

She pointed towards the third house at the end of the road. 'There's a light on in there. I thought it was empty, so who could it be?'

'It's nothing,' he replied. 'Sometimes that house is used for storage. It's probably one of the security guards in there.'

She looked at him – at his hard expression – and pulled her coat round her shoulders. She saw a change in his face as he looked down at her and she remembered that his daughter was ill. Despite her mistrust, she felt a pang of pity as she looked at his tired face.

'I'm sorry to hear about your daughter. I hope she gets better soon.'

He looked away from her and seemed to measure his words very carefully. 'You should get out of here. Get away from this place. Things happen to people and you don't want to be the next. I don't just mean what happened this morning, I mean other things. Much worse things.'

Ella stared at him, her mind racing, realising that he could mean anything. He'd been at the company from the start – had seen it through its development. Just how involved was he?

'What do you mean, other things? What do you know about the dead scientists and what happened to them?'

'What have you heard?' he asked gruffly.

'I know that supposedly one had an accident and the other killed himself,' she replied. 'That was the official story. I'm not sure it tells the whole truth, or whether I believe it.'

'It's nothing to do with me,' he insisted, before turning away from her and walking towards his car. His last words, spoken over his shoulder, were almost lost in a gust of wind. 'I warned you. You should leave now. If you won't listen that's your decision.'

He got into the car and drove away. She watched the rear lights disappear into the darkness. He was refusing to tell her anything. She knew that he was John Roper's friend. How much did he know?

Ella turned back towards Laura's house. Martin's words echoed in her ears, but it was too late to stop now. She opened the door with a firm grip and closed it behind her carefully. Her fears had hardened into determination and she knew now what she had to do.

Chapter 25

They picked at the food Laura had prepared, looking at the map of the site Laura had spread out on the table between them. She pointed to the back of the building, the opposite side to the main reception where Ella had gone in before.

'There's a staff entrance at the back. A lot of the scientists use it because it's nearer to the labs. It's also a few yards from the Executive area, where my office is. We can use my pass to get in.'

'We need to try and avoid the security guards whenever we can,' added Ella.

'But I know them,' protested Laura. 'They can't be part of this.'

Ella shook her head, thinking of the hard group of men she'd seen at the café. 'We can't trust anyone.'

Laura shook her head, but then continued. 'All right, then. We'll need to be quick because the security guards walk around the building every twenty minutes or so. They rely a lot on CCTV, but that mostly covers the area around the research facility. If we time it after one walkaround, then we'll have a bit of leeway.'

'How will we know when that is?'

'The lights come on automatically when someone is in an area. We'll be able to see that.'

'Which also means they'll be able to see us.'

'Yes, but I'm a senior manager here, remember. They won't be surprised to see me come in. I just need to act as if I'm coming in to pick up some papers. I do it all the time.' She paused. 'Maybe I should go in on my own. You can wait for me outside.'

'No,' replied Ella. 'What if something happens to you? We need to get that memory stick. We aren't going to come back so we have to take it *now*.'

Ella felt her fragile trust in Laura start to seep away, but she had no real choice but to go along with her. She had no other options.

Laura reached behind her and handed Ella a white coat. 'You can be one of the scientists. There are always a few of them around the labs in the evening, checking their experiments. The security people don't know all of them. If we're stopped, we can just say we drove in together.'

It was as good a cover as she was going to get, and Ella knew she was running out of options and time to get the information she needed. 'All right. Let's do this.'

They tossed their overnight bags into Ella's car and she drove down to Muir Pharma. She switched off the headlights when she turned off the main road and into the staff car park behind the Muir Pharma office. The science wing was in total darkness on this side and Ella squinted through the windscreen.

'You should park at the side here,' said Laura, pointing to the right. 'The door is just round the corner. We won't be seen here from inside when the lights come on, and if we have to make a quick getaway we're right next to the car.'

She grinned at Ella in the dim light, but Ella struggled to return the smile. Laura seemed to have bounced back from the forlorn figure she'd been in her house, reinvigorated by the task in hand. They waited until the security guards did their rounds, the car windows open an inch to let in some fresh air, the silence of the fields only broken by the hoot of a distant owl, before the sound drifted away. Suddenly, the lights came on in the building and shone onto the car park. Ella breathed a sigh of relief that they remained in darkness and they waited for the guards to leave.

The more Laura was energised, the more Ella was beset by doubts over the whole plan. Mitch had said he didn't trust Laura, so why would he have left something so important in their house? It didn't make sense. Maybe that's what she wants to happen, thought Ella, maybe her plan was for them to get caught.

Ella started to open the car door.

'Wait.' Laura pulled the door closed as a light came back on in the corridor next to the car. 'That's the security guard again. Get down.'

They both ducked down below the windscreen and Ella hissed, 'But won't they realise the car just got here? Wonder who it is?'

'They're used to seeing employees coming and going at all hours, but no need to draw attention to ourselves. We don't want them to ask too many questions.'

Laura looked through the windscreen. 'Just a few more minutes…' The car park went dark again and she sat up. 'They've gone. We need to make our move now.'

They got out of the car and walked briskly across the

car park, Ella following Laura's lead. She swiped her card at the side of the door and pushed it open. Ella breathed a sigh of relief. At least they'd managed to get in.

Laura led the way through the dim corridor, turned a few corners and then swiped her pass again on an internal door before moving into a carpeted area, with sofas and opaque glass walls dividing the space into single offices.

'My office is over here,' she said. 'That's Sam's office.' She pointed across the room.

In her office, Laura went to her desk and unlocked the drawer. 'I'll take my laptop.' She grabbed the laptop bag and gathered up the power leads. Without looking up, she pointed towards the tall cupboard next to the door and instructed, 'The memory stick should be in that cupboard. I think I left it in the box on the top shelf.'

Ella obediently went across to the cabinet, opened the door and pulled out the box, scrabbling around for the memory stick. But it wasn't there. Before she could ask Laura where else it could be, she heard the sound of the office door opening. She froze behind the cupboard door. She heard Laura's voice, calm as ever.

'Hi, John.'

'I didn't see you come in, Laura. You're late tonight.'

'I had to come back to get my laptop and some papers. I'm done now.'

Ella heard her move towards the door.

'Aren't you going to shut the cupboard?' Suspicion growing in his voice, Ella held her breath, waiting for the door to crash into her, all hopes of getting away shattering in an instant.

'Don't worry about that. I think it's broken. I've logged

it with property. Someone should come and fix it tomorrow.' Laura's voice moved towards the door and Ella could sense the man's reluctance to follow.

'If you say so,' he said.

Ella heard the sound of heavy footsteps go towards the door and concentrated on keeping still, hardly breathing, giving no hint that someone else was in the room.

The office door opened. With a click, the lights went out and Ella was plunged into darkness. The door closed and she heard the noise of a key in the lock. She let her breath out in a big sigh. Surely Laura would come back for her. But as the minutes ticked by, all her doubts about Laura came flooding back.

She heard the noise of her car start up. So, Laura had left her all alone, ready to be discovered in the morning by the security guards. Her plan was a disaster. Despite everything that had happened, she was always too willing to trust others. Her legs were shaking as she stood there and she slowly pulled a chair towards her and sat down, looking around the dim office. Thankfully, it wasn't completely dark, the corridor lights from outside shone into the office, before they went out too. As Ella's eyes got used to the darkness she went to the door and rattled the handle but it was definitely locked. She went over to the windows but they were all locked too. She looked around the office to find another way out, but there was none. She was trapped and had no means of escape. Ella went over to the chair, dropped her head onto her arms and sighed deeply.

She lost all track of time; it could have been fifteen or thirty minutes later when she heard a siren blaring through another part of the building. She jumped out of her chair and went to try the door again but it was still locked. She tried to look through the glass panel in the door and could only see the edge of a red light pulsating through the corridor. She went over to the window to see what was happening, but it didn't look out onto the rest of the complex.

Suddenly the door crashed open. Laura burst through and came to grab Ella. 'Come with me now, we haven't got much time. They've all gone to the other bit of the building. I broke a window there and the alarm went off.' She pulled Ella outside into the corridor and round to the way out.

'I thought you'd gone.' Ella panted after her friend. 'You left me all alone.'

'No choice,' replied Laura. 'If that guard had seen you, we'd be finished.'

They ran outside and Ella jumped into the driving seat of her car. She started the engine. 'After all that, we didn't even find the memory stick,' she gasped.

'I got it,' said Laura, holding it up triumphantly. 'I found it on my desk just before the security guard appeared. I didn't have the chance to tell you.'

'Thank goodness,' said Ella. Before she could say anything else, they heard a shout from the door.

'They've seen us,' cried Laura.

Ella reversed the car sharply and then slammed her foot on the accelerator. Speeding towards the exit, she struggled to gain control of the car as it surged forwards, virtually across the main road. It bounced on to the pavement and the wing mirror snapped off as it sheered against the wall on the opposite side of the road. The noise was like a pistol shot and they both instinctively ducked down, Ella closing her eyes for a second as she scraped the car against the wall. But she regained control of the car and suddenly she had a clear road in front of her. She kept her foot down and glanced in the rear-view mirror, watching several vehicles screech round and come after her. 'They're following us. We have to lose them...'

Chapter 26

Ella sped towards the motorway. Careful not to drive too fast now as they started to meet some cars, they turned the last corner towards the road that led to the motorway slip road.

'Oh no,' Laura could barely get the words out.

Ella hit the brakes. A car was parked across the road, blocking their path, it's headlights full on. She looked in the rear-view mirror and saw headlights behind. The car following them had slowed down. They were trapped. Ella looked wildly around for any means of escape.

'Are there any tracks we can take to get around them?' she asked Laura. 'Anything over the field to get us to the motorway?'

'No. There are too many fences in the way. This road is the only one.'

Ella smacked her fist against the steering wheel, filled with anger and frustration. Bitter thoughts flooded her mind. They'd come so far and done so much to get away, and now this. They were going to be defeated at the very end.

'No, I don't accept it,' Ella burst out, her jaw rigid. 'I'm not losing now.' She stared at Laura. 'They're not going to get away with this.'

'What are you going to do?' Laura sounded scared.

'Just hold on and don't distract me. I might just be able to squeeze in behind it.' Ella screwed up her eyes and looked at the car ahead. Even if she hit it, she had to hope that her car was big enough to push the other one out of the way. It was their only hope.

'There isn't enough room to get past it,' Laura said in a high-pitched voice.

Before she could say anything the car behind them came closer, almost herding them into the trap.

'Just hold on,' Ella said again.

She pressed her foot hard on the accelerator and the car shot forwards. Ella's hands were sweating and she gripped the steering wheel as she drove directly towards the other car in the middle of the road.

'Oh God, no,' she heard Laura mutter, but she was committed now. At the last moment she twisted the wheel to swerve behind the car. The space looked too small, even though the jeep was already moving out of the way. She kept going, closing her eyes for a split second when she heard a sickening crunch and then opened them wide when she felt the car ricochet off the back of the Jeep. The car seemed to jump in the air and then righted itself again. She clung onto the steering wheel as they careered towards the motorway slip road and then the next moment the motorway stretched out in front of them.

'You've done it,' gasped Laura. She laughed shakily. 'I never thought you'd get through that space!'

'Are they following us?' was Ella's only reply.

'I can't see them. We must have got away with it.'

Ella glanced in the mirror and the road seemed fairly

quiet behind them. 'Can't have been that easy. They'll try and pick us up in Edinburgh. We'll have to decide where to dump the car. It's damaged now, so we'll be an obvious target.'

They saw the first car following them in the outskirts of the city. When it came up close behind them, Ella swung out onto the main road, almost colliding with a bus and nipping in front of it with inches to spare. The screeching of the bus's brakes and the yells from some nearby pedestrians followed her. The traffic was moving slowly and she could see the black jeep behind the bus. Suddenly, where the road was broader and the pavement wide, she looked back again and saw it screech past the bus, half mounting the pavement and scattering pedestrians, hitting a parked car in its way like a toy. The parked car twisted round and blocked the traffic, so that all she could see in her mirror was a large black vehicle on an empty road.

'Can't you get rid of them?' said Laura, less confident now.

'Not without killing someone,' said Ella, trying to think about where she could lose them.

Glancing in the rear-view mirror she saw the large black car only a couple of vehicles behind. She'd have to focus on getting away from them or she'd never have a chance to look through the memory stick.

She turned sharply down a side street, using every shortcut she knew to get away. She wouldn't let them stop her now. She was too close to the truth. But the black car stuck doggedly to her trail, sometimes falling behind but always managing to catch up and stay two or three cars away. Her hands were sliding on the steering wheel and her shoulders were aching. The car was steaming up and she felt sweat trickle down her body as she looked around frantically for a means of escape. But she was trapped, like a fox in a hole, the inevitable end drawing nearer and nearer.

'I'll have to lose them in town,' she muttered and put her foot down, trying to avoid red lights and drive through amber lights to put more distance between them. Ella drove through housing estates and they followed, like a cat following a mouse, always a couple of cars behind, waiting and watching for a chance to strike. She twisted and turned through narrow streets in the Old Town, through the Cowgate and up to the Royal Mile, trying to lose them at every turn.

Then, suddenly, she recognised a back street, leading down past the station. She knew it had an underground car park tucked round a corner, unseen from the road. She might be able to hide. If she was lucky, the gate would be open and she could drive straight into the underground garage. If she was unlucky, she'd have to head down into Leith to try to lose them.

'I know where we can go. Hold on,' she warned Laura.

They drove past the side of Waverley Station and bumped over the cobbles, but came up against temporary traffic lights on the road down the hill leading off the Royal Mile. Ella hunched down over the steering wheel and gritted her teeth. She'd have to take a chance that there was no-one coming, or they'd be found. Glancing in her rear-view mirror, Ella twisted the wheel round and drove through the amber light, heading down the hill towards Leith Walk. She took a deep breath when she saw that the road was clear. Turning left and looking for the gate to the car park, she saw it at the last minute, braked hard and turned sharply, switching off the headlights as she drove around and stopped in the far corner, completely hidden from the entrance.

She switched off the engine. Breathing heavily, and almost sobbing in fear, she dropped her head onto her hands. All she could do now was wait. Each time she heard a car she expected to see the black bonnet appear in the garage. But the minutes ticked by and no black jeep appeared. Neither of them moved or spoke. Ella stared at the rear-view mirror to see if her gamble had failed, expecting to see the car appear behind them at any moment.

After more than five minutes, Laura's voice broke the silence. 'They must have gone past by now. We lost them, Ella. We did it.' She laughed shakily.

Ella hardly heard her – mind focusing on where they could go now, how they could get away without being seen. 'They won't give up, Laura. They'll be driving around out there looking for us.'

'So, what do we do?'

Ella stretched round and took her rucksack from the back seat, feeling the sharp edges of Mitch's laptop digging into her fingers, clutching it close. 'We leave the car. It isn't safe now. We go on foot, pick up a taxi and get somewhere safe. We need to see what's on the memory stick.'

Chapter 27

They emerged from Waverley Station at the end of Princes Street, then walked along in front of the Balmoral Hotel. Ella glanced into the foyer. It was only a few days since they'd been at the Muir Pharma party, but Ella knew now that they'd been watching her all along. She'd been so naïve, she thought bitterly, walking right into their world and thinking she could upset it without them fighting back. She glanced at Laura and knew she was remembering the party too. Ella walked with her head down, not looking to left or right, trying not to draw attention to herself.

The lights in front of the Scott Monument were red and Ella looked behind her. She clutched Laura's arm. 'They're here. The car's coming up behind us. Don't look up, just walk with everyone else. I know someone with a stall in the Christmas market. We could try and get help there.'

The lights turned to green and they went with the crowd, walking into the Christmas market in Princes Street Gardens, the area full of wooden stalls and lights, people all around them drinking and celebrating.

'Are they following us?'

Ella stopped at one of the stalls and pretended to look at the crafts for sale, watched by the young girl behind the counter. She glanced over to the entrance to the market and saw a couple of men standing at the gate looking all around. One of them spoke into a radio and then came into the market.

'We have to move.' Grasping Laura's arm, Ella turned sharply away and walked into a group of youths coming the other way.

The force of one man's shoulder almost knocked her off her feet and she staggered against the side of a hut, 'Hey, watch where you're going,' he grunted, before the group disappeared into the crowd.

As Ella tried to regain her balance, a hand shot out and steadied her. She stared up at the dark eyes looking down at her and stammered. 'Jake, is that you?'

Jake Fisher stared at her. 'What are you doing here?' He stared at Laura's white face and then asked, 'What's wrong?'

Ella grasped his arm like a drowning man clutching onto a raft. 'Jake, can you help us?' she hissed. 'We're being followed. We need to find somewhere to hide.'

He didn't hesitate, and turned and opened a door in the side of the hut and pulled them inside before shutting it firmly behind them. In the cramped space, she saw a couple of stools next to a small table and sank down onto one of them, checking that she couldn't have been seen by anyone standing in front of the stall.

'Wait here.'

She saw Jake go to the front and whisper something to the young woman standing in front of the rows of silver jewellery and, with relief, Ella saw that it was Rona from the café near Muir Pharma. Rona glanced back before smiling at her, then turned back to her customers. Jake looked up and down at the people thronging through the market, before coming back to them, closing the doors behind the counter until there was only a thin shaft of light coming through

He sat down opposite Ella. 'What's going on?'

She wondered how much to tell him, not sure how he'd react to what Mitch had found out. The last thing she wanted him to do was to go out and confront Renwick's men himself. But she had to tell him some of what she'd found out. She'd promised him she would discover what had really happened to his father.

'I can't be sure about everything,' she began, 'but we're hoping we have evidence that Muir Pharma suppressed the results of early lab tests that would have shown a potentially dangerous molecule interaction that would have stopped the drug before it ever reached clinical trials, far less sold in quantity.' She took a deep breath.

'And what does this have to do with my father?' he interjected.

'Wait a minute,' Laura interrupted them. 'How do you know one another?' She turned to Ella. 'Who is this?'

'This is Jake Fisher. His father worked for…'

'Muir Pharma.' Laura finished the sentence.

'I asked what this has to do with my father.' Jake had a key in his left hand and was tapping it impatiently against the wooden stool, waiting for Ella's response.

The rhythmic sound echoed around her brain, bringing to life the links she had established. 'We have evidence that your father and the other scientist John Roper were the only two who had raised concerns that the company had suppressed lab results on one of its most successful drugs. They both died shortly after.'

'What are you saying? My dad didn't kill himself?' asked Jake.

'I don't think so, Jake,' answered Ella.

He started to stand up. 'So those thugs out there could have had something to do with it?'

She tried to pull him back down. 'We don't know yet for sure. And we aren't going to be able to prove anything if you don't help us get away from here and go to the police with the new evidence.' She clutched her bag. 'It's all in here. You need to help us escape so we can go to the police.'

He stared at her, dark eyes blazing as they had before.

Ella clutched his sleeve. 'Please, if you go out there, we'll never prove what really happened. You have to trust me. Help us get away.'

She held her breath, not sure what he would do, whether he was going to take the law into his own hands, but he sat down suddenly. 'All right. We'll help you get out.'

Rona closed the front of the stall, plunging them all into darkness. Jake switched on a single bulb at the back and Rona came through. 'You came to the café, didn't you?' she asked Ella. 'I recognise some of these men who are wandering around the market looking for someone. They came into the café too. My friends told me that Robert Young gave them money. I think they work for him.'

Ella remembered the day he'd come out of the café after the group of men. They must have been meeting that day.

Rona picked up some woollen hats from the corner and handed one to Laura and Ella. 'Wear these,' she said, putting another one on her head, hiding her blue hair completely. 'A group of my friends are coming past so we can leave with them. Where do you want to go?'

Ella shrugged. 'We just need to get away to a hotel somewhere, lock the door and make sure we haven't been followed.'

'There's a hotel we can go to on the other side of Princes Street, one of the chains that is always full of tourists. Nobody will take any notice of you there.'

There was a knock at the door to the stall. Ella pressed back against the wall, her heart racing. Rona opened the door a few inches and smiled. 'Come on,' she said, grabbing Ella's arm and they joined Rona's friends milling around the door. Jake locked the door behind them as Ella followed through the crowd leaving the Christmas market. She could hear giggling and laughter around her and the smell of mulled wine wafted over the stalls. She looked behind her and saw Laura walking between two youths. They were only teenagers but they were so tall that they blocked anyone from seeing her between them.

They reached the gate to the Christmas market, and at the edge of her vision Ella saw the two men staring at the crowd. They were never going to get past them, she told herself. They would be stopped before they could get away. She felt her feet start to drag and Rona pulled her forward.

Suddenly there was a shout behind them and everyone turned to look at a man chasing someone back through the market. The men at the gate started to run towards the noise. Ella didn't hesitate, walking briskly out and across Princes Street behind a tram full of people.

'Who were they chasing?' asked Ella.

'A couple of my friends,' answered Rona. 'I thought

that a little diversion might help. They were looking at us a little bit too closely.' When she saw Ella's worried look, she shook her head. 'They can look after themselves, don't worry about them.'

By the time Jake caught up with them they had walked along a lane behind Princes Street towards St Andrew Square. 'The hotel's just up here,' said Rona, and a few moments later they turned into the reception area.

Rona and Jake stayed with them until Ella had booked and paid for a room, their friends waiting on the pavement outside. They went with them to the lifts.

'Thanks,' said Ella. 'We wouldn't have got away without your help.' She turned to Jake. 'Once we've gone to the police, they'll be in touch with you.'

Chapter 28

In the hotel, Ella was hardly able to believe that they'd escaped to safety. Laura sank down on to one of the chairs and dropped her laptop bag on to the floor, watching Ella check that the door was locked and then go round making sure the windows were all firmly closed.

'No-one will know we're here,' said Laura, her shaky voice and the wide eyes following Ella around, belying the confidence of her words.

'Maybe, but I've underestimated them before. I'm not about to do that again,' replied Ella grimly opening her rucksack.

Laura yawned. 'Aren't you tired? I'm wrecked. I need to sleep. I'll get a migraine if I look at the computer now.'

'I can't sleep,' replied Ella. Her fingers shaking, she was desperate to open the memory stick. Ella took out the stick from the bag and opened Mitch's laptop. 'I need to look through everything on this. Go to sleep if you want to.' She plugged the computer in and switched it on, then looked at Laura's pale face. 'Thanks for getting us out of Muir Pharma. That security guard could have ruined everything.'

'It's okay. I said I'd help you. Maybe now you'll believe

that I didn't know what was going on.' Laura lay down on one of the beds and pulled the cover round her shoulders.

Ella put the memory stick into the laptop and opened the files, scared of what she would discover, but desperate to know what it contained. She forced herself to take a deep breath and go slowly. When she looked properly through the file names, she saw the name of Ruth's clinic on a folder. Inside were several letters about Ben Forrester, signed by the medical director of the unit, addressed to Angela Thomas.

Ella felt her heart lurch when she saw Ruth's name mentioned in print. She felt her eyes fill with tears. For a wild moment, she thought that Ruth could still be alive, that the tangible presence of the letter might change the cruel truth of the last few months. She touched Ruth's name with her fingers. But then she saw the date of the last letter and knew, with aching clarity, that it might explain what had happened, but couldn't change the awful truth.

The letters stated that Ben Forrester showed increasingly obsessional and violent behaviour. That trained nurse Ruth Scott had monitored the impact on his personality and was convinced that his deteriorating symptoms could be linked not only to his other medication but to his exercise regime. Ella remembered how obsessive he had been over the last few months about his fitness and his exercise. He was always going to the gym. Detailed dates and times showing the impact of the drugs he was taking and the times of his workouts. Ella's heart was beating faster as she looked at the list of dates and realised that they all came from the last few weeks of Ruth's life. The final sentence left her in no doubt.

> It is our professional judgement that, at its maximum prescribed dose, a combination of Evexitrol plus the environmental effect of extreme exercise can lead to aggressive or obsessive behaviour in patients and, in extreme cases, create psychosis and hallucinations. Given the history with this class of molecules, this should have been screened for in pre-clinical tests.

The conclusion in the letter was like a smack in the face. Everything Ella knew to be true was turned upside down and she felt sick. Gulping a few times, she jumped up from the table, unable to sit still, and stood against the window, leaning against the wall and drumming her foot against the ground, trying to take it in. She forced herself to think about Ben Forrester objectively, rather than seeing him as the manipulative and violent person who had dominated their lives. He was just another victim. She could see it now, the terrible pattern that she had not understood but now emerged so clearly.

Ruth's insistence that she could help Ben took on new meaning. She must have gone to the clinic director with her suspicions about Ben's medication and he had finally agreed with her. Why hadn't Ruth told her what she was doing? It might have changed everything. Ella might not have left her alone that night. But she knew why, and she groaned in the silent room. Ella had made her dislike of Ben Forrester so clear that Ruth didn't think she would listen.

Ella looked at Laura sleeping soundly. She clenched

her fingers into tight fists as she thought about what the company her friend had loved so much had done. She could feel herself shaking with anger, knowing it was too late to change anything, but unable to stop the rage flooding her body. The anger was with Laura, but was also with herself. By not listening – she to Ruth and Laura to Mitch – they had allowed events to develop that had changed their lives forever. Ella turned away from the bed, afraid of the strength of her anger. She may have been wrong about Laura actively betraying Mitch, but her friend had still refused to believe him at the crucial time. And now it was too late.

She thought about Ben Forrester, about his aggressive behaviour towards them and for the first time, questioned what had been in front of her eyes for all these months. The certainty of his guilt was blown away by the testimony in Ruth's letter. It changed everything and Ella knew that she'd have to learn to accept this new version of the truth. She stared out of the window at the dark empty street, thinking through the implications of what she'd read, raising new and unfamiliar questions about Ben's guilt and what Jamie Forrester was doing in Edinburgh. She remembered her bitter words after Ben's trial, her fears of being stalked, unable to move on from Ruth's death and filled with such hate for the man that had taken her away. But this letter showed that his defence might be true, that he hadn't been able to prevent what he had done, despite her unwillingness to believe it. She didn't dare think of the implications.

After a long time, Ella tabbed through the other folders on Mitch's memory stick and saw, carefully listed, other letters, which all said similar things about different patients across the country. The common trigger in all cases was the presence of Muir Pharma's Evexitrol, and the environmental factor of extreme exercise.

She read through letters – similar to the one Ruth had sent – about husbands, wives, brothers, sisters, sons and daughters whose behaviour had become more violent. Someone close to them, usually a family member, had started to link it to the beginning of their new medication. All those lives destroyed and others changed forever. Sometimes, they killed someone close to them, other times, the violence was turned on themselves and they committed suicide. What was clear from the letters was that people from all over the country had realised that there was a pattern to these behaviours and were trying to persuade the medical profession to take action.

Ella could see that there weren't many cases involved so far, only a few dozen out of the thousands who had taken the medication, but it was undeniable that those in the letters had suffered from the same extreme reaction as Ben. She looked at the stories on Mitch's memory stick and felt a powerful and burning anger. None of these instances should have occurred. None of these families, so like hers, should have suffered. Suddenly Ella knew that it wasn't only her fight. Not only her family had been affected. For these others, it had been the same nightmare and they'd all been ignored. For all of them, she had to stop Sam Renwick. She had to deliver Mitch's evidence to the police before she could be stopped. And, more than his evidence, she had to give as much proof as she could find that the deaths of the two scientists were neither suicide nor an accident. They had suspected the truth years ago but nobody had listened to them.

From all of the information Mitch had gathered, and what she herself had found out, for the first time she could see the pattern clearly. Only now her brain was clear, the fear of Ben Forrester and of his brother was no longer overwhelming. She realised now that this scandal was much bigger than she had thought, and she was the only one who could stop it, the only one with all the pieces of the puzzle. But was it enough? Would the police believe her?

She started to write some notes for Susan Munro, putting down everything that she suspected, the doubt about Trevor's suicide and John's accident, the discovery of Carl's body in the hotel and the police suspicion that his smoking that night had caused the fire. She had seen when she'd taken Carl to the café how he'd looked at the group of people smoking, had hated cigarettes and would never have smoked himself. She wrote about how Mitch had been hounded from Muir Pharma and how she herself had been targeted and followed in Edinburgh and her car bugged.

When she'd finished setting all this out, she collapsed onto the other single bed, exhausted but knowing she had to snatch a few hours' sleep. She glanced at her slumbering friend and felt a spurt of anger. She was still resentful that Laura had refused to listen to Mitch and had pushed away the truth, so unwilling was she to tarnish her gilded life. Ella knew it would take some time for that anger to cool down.

Chapter 29

Ella got out of bed while it was still dark, stretched her sore back and rubbed the sleep from her eyes, before glancing at Laura, who was still asleep. She turned on the shower and stood beneath the blast of hot water, trying to wash away the hours spent at the computer. The spectre of Ben Forrester telling her she was in danger no longer lingered in the air. The past no longer merging with the present, and draining away instead, leaving only a feeling of bitter anger.

When Ella got back to the bedroom Laura was sitting up in bed cradling a hot cup of coffee, watching breakfast news as she usually did. Ella was about to speak when Laura pressed her finger to her lips and put the cup down with a clatter. The news presenter's voice filled the room.

Police have found the body of a young man in the burnt-out ruin of a farm building in Fife. Police are now trying to establish his identity... There is an appeal for witnesses to come forward...

Ella and Laura exchanged a horrified glance. 'Not Mitch,' Ella breathed as she looked at her friend's stricken features.

'I thought you said he wasn't there,' said Laura.

'I didn't find him,' she answered. 'But part of the building was badly burned, so...'

Laura buried her face in her hands.

Her anger evaporating in the face of her friend's grief, Ella crouched down beside Laura and put her arms around her. 'It might not be him, Laura. It could be anybody. Whatever's happened to Mitch, it's up to us to finish what he started.'

'But who else could it be? You didn't know what happened to him. It may be him,' wailed Laura.

Ella stood up. 'Let me try to find out what else I can. There must be another report that could tell us something else.'

She went to the laptop to bring up the story but there was only a short article. It didn't say much more than the news report, so she closed it and turned back to Laura, knowing that they had to get going. She glanced at the clock. Despite the darkness outside, it was almost eight. She put the laptop back into the bag with the memory stick. 'We can go now,' said Ella.

Laura was sitting silently looking at her mobile. She looked up at Ella. 'I have a message. It's from Martin Fraser, he wants us to go up to his house in Fife. He has important information for you to give the police.'

'Let me see.' Ella held out her hand for the mobile and read the message.

> *I've decided to tell you everything I know. My daughter has died. I have no more reason to keep quiet. It's not just the scientists you've been asking about. I can tell you about others who*

were silenced. I must speak to you before it's too late.

'We can't go,' said Laura. 'We can't go back up there. They'll be waiting for us, we barely got away yesterday.'

She jumped to her feet and started to pace the floor. 'Poor man. If his daughter is really dead, then he'll be devastated. She was the most important thing in his life. But you can't trust him, Ella. If this is true, he's been protecting Sam and Robert for years. Why would he change now? Why can't he go to the police himself? This doesn't feel right.'

Ella read the message again and knew what she had to do. 'I know it's dangerous to go back there, but don't you see how much difference he could make? He was there all the time; he could see everything and he's now willing to tell us. I can't give up this chance, to pin the murders firmly onto Sam and Robert. Without his testimony, our case is much weaker.'

Before Ella put her jacket on, she pulled out some of the gadgets Jim had given her and taped them on. She would have to hope that they would stay securely and would work. That was the only way she could rely on the back-up plan she'd agreed with Jim and he would come if he was needed.

'What are you doing? You're not seriously going back there?' said Laura. 'Let's stick to the original plan, go to the police together and tell them everything. It's the best we can do. Martin Fraser can give his evidence to them.'

Ella stared at her friend and spoke slowly, 'I don't think it's the best we can do. I can't let Sam and Robert get away with murder, escape with their millions. I can't let them think they've won. I'm not about to take that chance. I know it's a risk but we should split up, you go to the police. At least you'll be safe and I can get his confession. If these gadgets work, I can even record it.'

'You've got that expression on your face again,' said Laura, 'the one you had when you drove right at their car. There's nothing I can say that will change your mind, is there?'

'I know this is difficult, but I need you to go to the police now. I've written a note for Susan Munro, who's my contact there, telling her everything I've found out. She works on cold cases. This *has* to be enough to get her to look again at Muir Pharma. With all Mitch and Carl's evidence, she'll have to.'

Laura obediently pulled the bag towards her. 'Are you sure you won't come with me?'

'I'm sure.' Ella zipped up her jacket. 'Don't speak to anyone else. Just wait for her. Tell her who you are.'

They went downstairs and were lucky to find a cab that had just dropped some passengers, so jumped in quickly. As they drove towards St Leonard's, Ella looked around the quiet streets but could see no-one following them. They stopped at the police station and Laura got out.

'I shouldn't be long,' said Ella. She gave Laura a card. 'If for some reason I don't come back, call the number on this card and speak to Jim. He should be able to find me.' It was the best she could do.

Laura grasped her hand and wouldn't let go. 'I'm not sure I can do this on my own.'

'I need you to,' said Ella. 'It's for Mitch. Do it for him.'

Laura nodded and Ella watched her go safely into the police station before telling the taxi driver to go to the car park.

Chapter 30

By the time she got to Fife, it had started to rain heavily. She parked her damaged hire car in Laura's open driveway and ran to Martin's house. She rang the front doorbell but there was no answer. She walked briskly round to the back door. The door was open a few inches as if Martin Fraser was inviting visitors rather than repelling them. Ella tried to banish the thought that she was walking into a trap he'd set.

The wind came in stronger gusts as she pushed open the door, branches from the trees catching in her hair and making her jump. As she glanced up at the window next to the door, her foot crunched on the gravel. She stopped and moved her foot against the ground and saw pieces of glass glinting in the dull light. She looked up at the window again. Her heart started thumping loudly as she saw that the glass was broken.

She didn't know what she would find, but she'd come this far. She couldn't give up now. She had to speak to him. He could confirm everything she'd pieced together. He might even have hard evidence. She had no choice.

Gritting her teeth, she walked into the house, almost identical to the one next door. The large open-plan kitchen and dining room that stretched along the whole ground floor were familiar, but the chairs different. Unlike in Laura and Mitch's house, there were no pictures on the wall and there was no clutter lying around the room. It looked unlived in, like a show home. Nothing left on the floor, not one thing out of place. She glanced back into the utility room. Laundry equipment lined the walls and there was an empty clothes basket on the top of a shelf next to the window. She stood quietly, listening to the sound of her own breathing, looking up the stairs, in case anyone appeared. All was quiet.

She certainly didn't want to go up, but there was nowhere else he could be. She narrowed her eyes when she saw a light coming from round the door of one of the rooms upstairs. She felt rooted to the spot, hardly able to breathe. Then she urged herself to go forward, forcing her feet to climb the wooden staircase, when all they wanted to do was turn and run away. There was no noise coming from the room, and Ella paused for several seconds to try to work out whether there was anyone in there. But, hearing nothing over the insistent tapping of a shower of rain on the hall window, she crept up to the door.

Very slowly, she pushed the door open and looked into the room. It had been turned into a study, with a large desk at the back turned to look out over the trees. The shutters had been pulled down over the windows and the only light in the room came from the flickering computer screen on the desk facing the door. It was partly obscured by the back of a chair. Checking that there was no-one else in any of the corners of the room, she moved forwards, looking at the image as it emerged from the side of the chair. She gasped as she saw a man's hand resting on the arm.

Gripped by a feeling of dread, and now focusing on the hand rather than on the computer, Ella took a couple of steps back and started to edge her way round the room. The figure was slumped across the desk, one hand next to a glass that had fallen over and an empty bottle of whisky. It was Martin Fraser. The flickering light of the screen shone on the top of his face, almost as if it was trying to animate it, make it alive, but she knew he was dead. His eyes were open, staring at nothing, his face fixed in an expression of surprise. Ella couldn't move, couldn't drag her gaze away from the frozen face. The rain continued to pour outside, the only noise in the dead house.

She thought she was going to faint and felt her knees start to buckle. Grasping the edge of the desk to steady herself, her hand clutched a piece of paper. She looked down at the paper and saw it was a letter. The words were stark and uncompromising.

> *I have no more reason to live now my daughter is dead... My guilt at hiding the death of my friend and the cause of my daughter's accident is unbearable... I was too scared to face up to the truth and tell the world what was happening and I now need to pay the price...*

Ella put up her hand to rub her eyes. Whatever he'd had to tell her was gone now, but maybe there was something else in the room.

Even as the thought entered her head, the sound of a car door shutting came from the front of the house. She had to get out before she was trapped. Turning away from the slumped body and the letter lying next to it, Ella ran down the stairs, pausing behind the utility room door, trying to control her breathing and her racing heart.

Hearing no other sounds from outside, she took her chance and slipped out of the utility room, then through the back door. Outside, she ran round the house and towards her car parked only a few feet away, but her way was blocked as another car screeched to a stop in front of her. She looked round frantically for a way to escape but, before she could take more than a step, a man got out of the car and lunged towards her. She recognised him, it was the man with the hard features and the grey ponytail she'd seen at the café. Ella spun away from him and was caught by another man. He grabbed her arm and a hood was thrown over her head. She tried to scream but the fabric caught in her mouth, muffling the noise. She fought against the arms that held her in a steely grip, but her legs were suddenly pulled from under her and, despite her violent twisting and turning, she felt herself being carried away, helpless to stop them.

Chapter 31

Ella wasn't taken far. She was dragged to another building – half lifted across a wooden floor and thrown down, her head crashing onto something hard. She grasped at it to try to keep herself from falling further, disorientated and blind to anything around her. She heard heavy doors slam shut, the sound of footsteps walking away and then another door closing. Then everything was silent. She was alone.

Surprised to realise they'd left her hands untied, Ella pulled herself into a seated position, then dragged off the hood and threw it on the floor, coughing as the dust and grit from the hood blew around her head. She sat still for a moment, catching her breath. Even with the hood off, everything was still pitch black, but she knew exactly where she was. There was only one place it could be. The third house – the one where she'd seen the van parked outside. Ella had been told this house was used for storage but she now realised it had a more ominous purpose. She wondered who else had sat here in the dark, afraid of what was going to happen to them.

Trying to work out where she was, she pictured Laura's house layout in her mind. They'd come in through an outside door and stayed downstairs. This was a small space so must be the utility room. She guessed that the door to the utility room should be in front of her. She stood up and walked a couple of steps forward, holding her hands out to feel her way. She touched a hard surface and stretched her arms around in front of her. She could feel the frame of a door, but it was completely flat and she could feel no handle or lock on either side. It was solid and immoveable. She felt right around the frame again, but the door fitted so snugly that she couldn't squeeze her fingers in anywhere.

Ella leaned her head on the door. In the short time since she'd dropped Laura at the police station, Sam and Robert had been waiting for her to fall for Martin's message and, despite Laura's warnings and her own misgivings, she'd walked right into their trap. Her friend had been right. She shouldn't have come back and now she was in a worse position than ever. At least one of them had gone to the police, so they would have been alerted, but she'd been so determined to get Martin Fraser's testimony about what had been going on that she had taken risks she should have known were too dangerous.

She couldn't get the image of Martin Fraser lying over his desk out of her mind. It was as if he was right in front of her. Had he committed suicide or had it just been made to look like that? Whatever the truth was, he wasn't going to be able to say anything. All he'd known was lost. His sadness and guilt over his daughter filled her mind. She let out a dry sob and turned back to sit on the bench, pulling her jacket around her tightly. As she sat down, she suddenly remembered her phone in her jacket pocket, but when she searched in every pocket, she realised it had gone. She had to hope Laura or Jim would play their part.

She pulled herself upright, her head starting to pound, and looked around, trying to see if there was any shaft of light to alleviate the oppressive darkness. She could feel the panic growing, the panic of being trapped in a small dark space with no way out. She thought for a fleeting second that they had locked her in to die. She wasn't going to despair yet – there must be a way out.

Standing up, she turned right and groped along the wall, feeling a worktop – strangely comforted by the familiarity. Her fingers ran over the smooth surface and then the metal of a sink. She reached out and found some taps, turned one on, relieved to find it worked, and drank some cold water out of her cupped fingers.

She started to explore further round the room, stumbling around in the darkness, the space familiar yet oddly strange and different. There was no back door as there was in Laura's house, no windows, no way to get out. She worked her way back round to the bench and sank down, trying to ignore the dull ache of her head.

Ella's eyes were growing accustomed to the darkness and she looked around the small room. She realised with a sickening certainty that they wouldn't have left her with hands untied if she'd been able to escape. She tried not to think about what they would do to her when they came back. She pushed down the feeling of dread but it threatened to overwhelm her. She'd disturbed a far more deadly set of people than she could ever have imagined. At least she'd passed on what she knew to the police. If she had the chance, she wasn't going to give in now without a fight.

Her stomach rumbled and she wondered how long it

had been since she'd eaten. Better to not think about that.

Through the door, she heard men come into the house, voices rising and falling in conversation. She went to the door to listen, to see if she could recognise their voices or pick up any information about what was going to happen to her.

Then she heard Sam's voice clearly. 'What did they think they were doing bringing her here? I've just got rid of one problem and you've given me another one. You know how important tomorrow's press conference is. We have the investors lined up and I won't have anything getting in the way of that.'

A lower voice replied and Ella strained to hear what he was saying. She only caught a few snatches. '…She's been a problem since she got here. We had to do something… We should have got rid of her at the very start.'

'Robert please…' It was definitely Sam, but he was no longer the charismatic leader, the strong one. What did it mean? Ella shook her head to banish her lingering headache and tried to think straight. Robert was the one in charge, the one telling everyone else what to do. It must have been Robert all along, controlling everything behind the scenes. She felt cold as she remembered Rona's words about Robert paying his own men to patrol the area.

She staggered back as she heard footsteps coming closer, then the door was pushed open and light shone into her small cell. Two men grabbed her and hustled her out, dragging her across the floor as her heavy legs refused to move as quickly as they wanted. They were the men who had brought her here. She'd only seen the one with the grey ponytail. The other must have been the one who'd carried her inside, his bulky torso and broken nose making him look like he'd be more at home in a boxing ring than a lab. These were the men who must have chased off the demonstrators. They'd been working for Robert all along.

She looked around the kitchen-diner, the mirror image of Laura and Mitch's. It had the same fixtures but there were no comfortable chairs or sofas and no personal items anywhere around the stark room. The large picture window looking out onto the fields had been blacked out so no-one could see inside or out. That must be why the third house always seemed so dark; whatever went on in here was hidden from the outside world. She glanced back at where she'd been held and saw that the utility room was being used as a prison cell with a reinforced door.

The bigger man pushed her down into a hard chair and went to stand at the door. Robert stared at her while Sam refused to meet her eyes. He was dishevelled, his expensive shirt crumpled and his face, when he finally turned towards her, pale and drawn, the old confidence drained away. His vigorous energy had sapped away and he seemed smaller, hardly recognisable as the man she'd met only a few days before.

In contrast to Sam, Robert was striding back and forth, more intense than ever, casting cold glances at Ella. She looked at the two men standing in front of the door, their hostile presence a constant reminder of their threat, guarding her means of escape. Freedom not far away but as unattainable as the moon.

'Martin Fraser's dead. Did you kill him?' Ella asked Robert, her voice loud in the bare room.

'Didn't have to,' he replied. 'He did it all by himself. We just used his cowardice to get you up here.'

'Why?' Her voice was thin and crackly, echoing in the hard empty space.

'You know why. We had to work out what to do with you. You were a problem the minute you started looking through Laura's computer,' Robert snapped.

'What do you mean?' Ella croaked.

Robert glared at his partner. There was a moan from Sam. 'Haven't we done enough? It's going to have to stop, Robert. We can't carry on.'

Ella flinched as Robert slapped Sam across the face. 'Shut up. Everything will be all right if you just keep your nerve. I'll deal with this mess myself.'

He turned back to Ella and crouched down in front of her, cold grey eyes staring at her unblinkingly.

'You should have gone back to London when you had the chance. But you wouldn't do that, would you? You were too busy interfering in my business. And now you've run out of time.'

She felt a spark of anger in response to his arrogant certainty that he was in control and stared back at him, seeing the nerve tick in his temple, knowing that she wanted him to admit to what he'd done. Even if no-one ever heard it, if she never got out alive, she wanted to hear him say it.

'The police are after you already,' she said. 'You won't be able to cover up another accident. Too many people know what I've found out. Not just how you killed your scientists, but what you did to Mitch.'

He smiled a nasty smile. 'Oh, I wouldn't be too sure

about that. It doesn't take much to persuade people to leave things alone.'

'Like you persuaded Martin Fraser to keep quiet? By almost killing his daughter.'

'Everyone has a weak spot,' he said. 'It's just a case of finding it.' He moved even closer and she turned her head to avoid the burning intensely of his stare, until he grasped her chin and made her look at him. 'You for example. You think you're so right. Why do you think everyone will believe you now? You may think you've gone to the police, but they're just pandering to the ravings of a woman in grief. You have no proof that will stand up in court.'

Ella twisted her head to escape from his words, but he tightened his grip so she couldn't move.

'There is proof. The police have it.'

He gave a bitter laugh. 'And you think that the police will do something about it? Listen to you? They're in our pockets, have been for years. Just like your friend Laura.'

She felt as if he'd struck her, shock taking her breath away. She'd trusted Laura to go to the police – had been so convinced by her change of heart. Could her friend be that good an actor? 'What do you mean? Did she talk to you?'

'Laura told me lots of things about you,' he answered. 'She told me lots of things about everything. I know a lot more than you think.'

'You're lying,' cried Ella. 'You can't get away with this. Too many people know what you've done.'

'You'd be surprised at what I can get away with,' he sneered. 'All you need is the right people in the right places.'

'But you've destroyed so many lives. Is your business worth so much?'

'You need to ask that? I've built up too much to let it all disappear now. The business is everything to me and I'll protect it from anyone who threatens it. I've spent my life working towards this moment. I deserve it to succeed. With our new investors, it's going to succeed.'

'And you'll get rid of anyone who gets in your way?' Ella spat out.

'You mean, like your sister? She was interfering too much,' said Robert. 'She was writing to the press about Evexitrol. I had to stop her.' He shook his head. 'I couldn't believe that idiot thought he'd done it.'

'What are you saying? Ben Forrester killed my sister. The police convicted him.' cried Ella, looking from Sam to Robert, her eyes widening.

Sam lifted his head, the mark of Robert's hand still visible on his face. 'You mean you didn't know?' he whispered. 'You must have realised what he did to your sister?'

'You mean what *we* did,' snapped Robert.

Ella sat back in her chair as if she'd been punched. She'd thought that Ben hadn't been in his right mind when he'd killed Ruth – she'd known since she'd read Ruth's letters – but this was even worse. Ben was completely innocent. Robert had killed her sister.

She turned to Sam. 'You could help me. You know what he's done is wrong. You could make up for it now.'

But he looked away. 'You know what to do,' he growled to the thugs. 'I don't want any mistakes.'

Robert pulled Sam out of his chair and pushed him towards the door. He grasped the arm of the ponytailed guard and whispered urgently into his ear. Ella leaned forward to try to hear what they were saying but couldn't make anything out. She looked around her prison for a way out and watched Sam go into the back lobby and open the door. Without thinking, Ella jumped out of her chair and made a dash to escape, throwing off the larger guard's outstretched hand on the way. She reached the door but Sam had closed it behind him and she twisted the handle trying to escape, her hands slipping on the cold metal. Before she could get out, she was pulled back into the room and thrown down roughly onto a chair. Her hands were pulled in front of her and the larger guard ripped off a length of duct tape and tied them tightly, muttering fiercely at her in a strong accent, 'Don't think you can escape from us.'

The other guard shook her arm. 'If you behave, we won't gag you. If you try any more of your tricks, we'll truss you up like a chicken.' He pulled her up and dragged her to the back door. Outside, the cold air hit her and she blinked in the daylight. She had no time to pull away as she was thrown into the back of a van and heard the doors slam behind her. She'd seen this van before, parked at the back of the house, but she hadn't realised it was for prisoners.

Ella pulled herself into a sitting position, awkwardly grasping onto the webbing at the side of the van. It was totally dark, not even windows looking onto the cab. She held on tightly as the van started to move, turning away from the house. Where were they taking her? What were they going to do with her? They didn't drive for more than a few moments before they lurched onto rough ground and bounced along until the van stopped abruptly and she heard the sound of heavy doors being closed. She twisted her head around but could still see nothing. They had gone no distance at all so she knew they must be in the countryside around the plant. In the silence, she heard the men get out of the cab, then nothing. Her nose twitched as a strong smell of grain and manure filtered into the van. They must be parked in a barn. Ella leaned her forehead on the cold metal. With sickening certainty, she knew that they'd taken her here to die.

Ella could feel the tears run down her cheeks. She had been so wrong; they had all been so wrong to blame the easiest person they could for Ruth's murder. And now she was stuck here, locked in their van, until they were ready to get her out of the way, just another problem. She had tried so hard to get justice for Ruth and she'd failed completely. Now they would get away.

She pulled her hands away from the webbing, unprepared to give up, and started to move her hands to try and get them apart, biting on the tape to break it. If she was going to have any hope of escape when the van doors opened, she needed to get her hands free.

Chapter 32

As she sat there, working on the tape on her wrists, she began to hear the sound of digging and some rustling noises. That was all she needed, she thought, rats in the barn. She lifted her head to listen as she heard the noise of a door opening, then a heavy thud as if something hard had hit the ground. Muffled grunts and the dull sound of solid objects hitting each other were followed by the noise of someone coming towards the van. She looked at the door, feet scrabbling as she pushed herself away, her heart pounding.

The door was thrown open and she heard a familiar voice. 'Bloody hell, Ella. I thought you said this wasn't going to be dangerous.'

It was Jim. She crawled towards him and his arms reached in and pulled her out. As soon as her feet hit the ground her knees buckled and Jim caught her and held her upright, pulling the tape off her wrists. Blinking in the light, she saw the interior of a barn. On the floor the guards were lying prone while two men she didn't recognise were tying them up. As she watched, Gregor came towards them carrying the guards' jackets.

'Got their phones,' he announced. 'Are you all right?' he asked Ella.

'I think so.' She looked beyond him and saw an abandoned spade in a half-dug hole in the barn floor. The proportions of the hole were unmistakable and she swallowed. 'Well, I think I'm all right now.' She looked up at Jim. 'Thank God you came in time,' said Ella. 'I was beginning to think you weren't going to find me.' She rested her head on his shoulder. Jim put his arm more tightly around her and Ella leaned into him.

One of the men she didn't recognise came up to them. 'What do you want us to do with them?' he asked Jim.

'You don't know my friends,' said Jim. 'Adam's a bouncer and Josh over there is a medic. We all play rugby together. They were up for it when I said I needed some muscle.' He looked down at her grimly, 'I thought I'd better bring a medic with me, just in case.'

'And he drove like a maniac to get here,' shouted Josh from the other side of the barn.

Ella stood up straighter. 'What's the time?' she asked Jim. 'There's a press conference I need to get to in Edinburgh, but I may have missed it already.'

'Just after two,' he answered with a quick glance at his watch. 'Do you have to?'

'Yes, I have to stop them. I don't know if the police will get there in time, and I have to do everything I can to get them to justice. After all of this,' she indicated the scene around them, 'they won't be able to get away now.' Ella turned back towards her rescuers. 'Can you tell the police they need to be at the press conference? I don't want Sam and Robert to get any warning of what's happened here.'

'We can stay and call the police,' replied Josh. 'You take the car and go back.'

'We parked along this way,' said Jim, starting to move towards the access door at the back of the barn.

Ella followed him and then stopped, turning to Josh and Adam. 'When the police come you need to tell them that there's a dead man upstairs in the middle house over the field. It looks like suicide but it may not be.'

'Nothing else you want to tell us is there?' said Josh, but Ella was already rushing through the door and didn't reply.

*

Ella ran behind Jim and Gregor onto the lane at the side of the barn. She glanced behind her and stared at the rundown building. It was the one she'd been chased away from when she was following Mitch, she was sure of it. Although the outside looked like it was falling apart, now she'd seen inside, she knew what it was really being used for.

Ella put out of her mind what could have happened there and looked forward. They came out of the field and onto the road that ran beside the barn. A few hundred metres along they turned a corner and she saw their car. Jim threw himself into the driver's seat, Gregor next to him, and he opened the back door for Ella.

'You'd better hide in the back until we get off the country lanes,' he said to Ella. 'We don't know if any of those guys are still around. There's a travel rug back there, hide under that.'

Ella pulled the travel rug around herself, glad of its comforting warmth. Her heart was racing as the car started up. 'Just get to the motorway as quickly as you can,' she hissed, impatient to get moving.

'I'll do my best,' replied Jim. 'Once we're away from here you'll be fine.'

After a few minutes Ella felt the car pick up speed. She sat up, feeling better, and laid her head on the back of the driver's seat at Jim's shoulder. He put up his hand and stroked her hair.

'You saved my life,' Ella said quietly. She lifted her head and turned to Gregor. 'All of you did. I can never thank you enough.'

After about twenty minutes they were crossing the bridge and heading towards Edinburgh. Ella had sat back and pulled the travel rug over her knees.

'It's coming up for three o'clock, so I'll go straight to the press conference. We should get there before it's finished,' said Jim.

Ella had to bite her lip several times as they stopped at red traffic lights on the way in. Every time they had to wait behind a bus she almost screamed with frustration, but she knew better than to say anything. Jim was doing his best and it would take at least twenty minutes to get to the city centre hotel where the press conference was taking place.

'I need to be there, but how will I get in?' asked Ella. 'They'll recognise me in a second if I try to come in the main door, and just throw me out. It would ruin everything.'

Gregor looked at Jim, prompting him to speak.

'There is one option,' said Jim, glancing in the mirror at Ella. 'I know the technical people in the hotel. There's a side door to the main conference room where we can go in. I'll lead the way...'

'Then I'll confront them,' Ella finished his sentence.

Jim shook his head. 'This is still a crazy plan. You've almost been killed already today.' He looked at her in the mirror again and she saw the worry on his face.

Touched by his concern and flushing under his gaze, Ella stuttered, 'I'm sorry, but I couldn't think of anything else.'

He swallowed as if the reality of the situation had just hit him, and Ella leaned forward between the seats. 'I'm all right, really.' Her voice dropped. 'Or, I am now. For a while there, I thought the tracking device can't have worked. You were so long I started to doubt that you were ever coming. The tracker you gave me was my insurance policy. You knew that.'

'It wasn't working to begin with,' answered Jim. 'Must have been some problem with the signal. But then it suddenly started working when we got closer.'

'Well at least the police will have to believe me now,' said Ella.

Gregor turned round. 'Oh, I think they had their suspicions already. From what Susan tells me, with your evidence, they're building a better case now.'

'I hadn't realised before,' added Ella, 'but it's Robert Young who's in charge. Sam Renwick is just doing what he's told. I saw that very clearly this morning. It's Young I need to stop because he's planning to leave the country after the press conference when he gets his hands on a big cash injection from his new investors. That's why it's so important that we get there.'

'What exactly do you want to do?' asked Jim.

Ella reached under her jacket lapel and put the tiny gadget she'd hidden there into Jim's top pocket.

'You used it? Did you catch something incriminating?' asked Jim. 'If I'm going to play it, I'll need to hear it first, but I can do that with the sound system. You'll need to give me a few minutes in there to check it out.'

Ella felt a spark of hope. 'We have to try. It could make all the difference.'

'It might not be acceptable evidence in a court of law,' said Gregor, 'but if you play it to the press, the questions will never stop and they'll be ruined.'

Chapter 33

Jim stopped the car opposite the hotel in the West End and he and Ella ran to the front door while Gregor jumped into the driver's seat. He went straight up to reception. 'I've got something for the press conference, Daniel needs it now, he's the sound guy.'

The girl looked up at him uncertainly, but before she could ask any questions, the man next to her said, 'You've been here before, haven't you? I can take you up there.' Jim nodded and grabbed Ella's hand. 'Thanks. He said he needed it now.'

They followed the concierge up the service stairs and emerged next to an access door. 'We're fine from here,' said Jim quickly and opened the discreet door that led into the back of the press conference at the side of the room. Ella stood behind Jim, hoping that no-one would recognise her, looking around the room as he slipped into the free chair in front of the sound console. He immediately started whispering to the stocky young man at the controls.

There were journalists standing at the back, and Ella slipped in behind one group who were standing with their notebooks and pens in their hands. Nobody was looking in her direction. They were all watching Sam answer a question at the front of the room.

Ella shivered when she looked at Robert, remembering the murderous glint in his eyes when she last saw him. She could only imagine what his expression would be like if she succeeded in her plan.

As he spoke, Sam was pale, but in control. He seemed to have recovered from Robert's physical attack, any bruising covered by make-up, but Ella thought he was watching Robert warily, as if he was afraid of making a mistake. Now she'd seen the change in their roles, it all made perfect sense. Robert, the protector and fixer for Sam, was actually the one in control. She wondered how that had happened. When had Sam realised that he was no longer giving the orders but taking them? And why he seemed unable to break free from Robert? What hold did the other man have on him? How had he reduced Sam to the shivering wreck she'd seen that morning?

Sam made the announcement of the new investment with a flash of his former confidence, his self-satisfied tone grating on Ella's over-sensitive nerves. You would never imagine what they'd done, listening to the professional spin cast over the audience…

'Delighted that one of the biggest pharmaceutical companies in the world has decided to make such a significant investment in Muir Pharma… will mean faster expansion, growth in jobs… a Scottish success.'

The man next to him then spoke in a drawling Texan accent. 'We've followed the fortunes of Muir Pharma since the business was formed, and there was no other biotechnology company we wanted to partner with in the UK market. This was our first choice and will be the platform for our European expansion,' declared the CEO of the pharmaceutical giant, before sitting down and beaming at the assembled press.

'Just a couple of questions please and then we can offer you some refreshments.' Ella could see that the communications man was in his element, mentally ticking off the names on the list of those he wanted to be there.

Ronnie Grant got up to ask a question that gave Sam the opportunity to press home the economic advantages of the deal. She winced as she witnessed the smug smiles on the platform in response to that gift.

'Thank you, ladies and gentlemen, if there are no more questions…'

Ella looked across urgently at Jim to ask him to play the tape, but he was turned away from her, still frantically working. At the front of the room, Sam and Robert were shaking hands with the new investors and she felt a spurt of anxiety. Where were the police? They were supposed to be here by now. She had to speak, to confront them with their crimes while she had the chance, ask her questions before it was too late. Otherwise, all their sacrifices would be wasted. She strode into the middle of the room, snatching a microphone from the staff member carrying it to the back.

'I have a question. Why is a major pharmaceutical company investing in Muir Pharma when it is guilty of falsifying laboratory tests and selling a drug that is unsafe? Getting rid of scientists who find malpractice. Could Mr Renwick give his comments please?'

Ella saw the shock in his and Robert's faces when they saw her. Robert took a step forward. Sam didn't hesitate. 'Get that woman out of here,' he gestured to security.

'She's disrupting the press conference; she has no right to be here.' He looked around for someone to remove Ella and she took advantage of the silence, aware that the men posted by the doors had started to move towards her.

'You've got rid of everyone trying to stop you,' said Ella in a loud voice. 'You tried to get rid of me today but you failed. You won't get away with it this time.'

On her left side, Ella's arm was grabbed by a member of the hotel staff who tried to pull her away, but she twisted out of his grasp. She was suddenly surrounded by journalists who had got up from their seats and were acting as a barrier to protect her. One of them spoke into the microphone she was still holding, 'You have a question to answer, Mr Renwick. What do you have to say?'

Robert Young stared at Sam Renwick but didn't try to intervene. The Americans on the platform also turned to Renwick, expecting him to flick away the question.

'I don't know what information you have there,' said Sam, 'but our products help thousands of people around the world. We followed all the clinical trial protocols required and were approved by all the regulatory authorities.'

'Do you admit that you suppressed the interaction reports and ignored families concerns that there was a serious side effect in some cases…' insisted Ella.

Everyone stared at Sam Renwick and they could see that he was beginning to sweat. She pressed on.

'Then you tried to silence one of your employees, Mitch Blake, who gathered evidence of what had happened to the scientists.'

'I'm afraid Dr Blake cannot be relied upon.'

'What about Dr Martin Fraser? You blackmailed your

medical director to keep the fraud secret. You hurt his daughter and ruined their lives.'

'This is ridiculous,' Sam Renwick started to say, but Ella could see that the surprise felt by the journalists was giving way to suspicion. The mood in the room had changed. His confident smile froze in front of the crowd of journalists moving as one, like a beast closing in on its prey.

The panel on the platform looked stunned as more security guards came running into the room. Another voice came through a microphone, cutting through the hubbub.

'My name is Angela Thomas and I work for the British Medical Journal,' said a tall woman at the front. She waved some pieces of paper. 'I have data here showing that you have repeatedly ignored appeals from some families to investigate the safety of Evexitrol, allowing it to be marketed aggressively, while knowing that it was unsafe.'

'Are these allegations true, Mr Renwick?' said one journalist at the back of the room.

'Did Muir Pharma cover up serious side effects?' asked another.

Soon the room was in chaos, other journalists ignoring the microphones and shouting out their own questions. Angela was passing around printed copies of her papers and Sam Renwick took a step back and clutched a chair, frozen from shock at the sudden change in the atmosphere of the room, and apparently unable to fight any longer. He threw his partner a pleading look.

Robert Young took control of the room, standing in front of the table on the platform. 'Ladies and gentlemen, this is baseless slander. Muir Pharma has always followed best practice in all of its operations and this is no exception.'

'We have full faith in Muir Pharma,' boomed an American voice on the platform. 'I'm sure any misunderstandings that have arisen can be sorted out.'

He'd hardly finished speaking when they all heard a click and suddenly Robert's harsh voice filled the room. Everyone fell silent as they understood the full impact of what they were hearing.

'You'd be surprised what I can get away with. All you need is the right people in the right place.'

'But you've destroyed so many lives. Is your business worth so much?'

'You need to ask that? I've built up too much to let it disappear now.'

In the silence that followed, Sam gave an audible groan, sinking on to the nearest chair covering his face with his hands.

'It's over, Robert, it's finished.'

'Shut up, you fool,' hissed Robert.

The two Americans had been talking quietly in the background and the senior one turned to Robert. 'What is this all about, Robert? Is there any truth in these allegations?'

'I knew it had gone too far… I knew we couldn't keep it secret…' Sam started to mutter, before Robert seemed to snap. He turned on Sam and grabbed his shirt, lifting him bodily up off the chair and shaking him like a dog, shouting uncontrollably.

'I've stood by you for years, protected your back and helped you every step of the way. It's because of me that Muir Pharma was a success, not you. It's because of me that we're doing the biggest deal we've ever done. We can finally make some real money. And you're going to ruin it all because you've got no spine. Everything we've worked for, everything we promised ourselves… gone.'

'Robert, I can't breathe…' croaked Sam.

In the shocked silence, police officers burst into the room. Tension broken, the room erupted, the journalists shouting questions at the men on the stage and the Americans trying to pull Robert off his partner.

Ella looked round the scene. Finally, it was working as she'd hoped. When she'd understood that Robert held the power in the relationship and would stop anyone standing in his way, she knew that all she needed to do was to get him to lose control in public, turn on his partner, and the questions wouldn't go away.

Two police officers ran down the sides of the room and pulled Robert away from Sam, who collapsed back on the chair, clutching his throat. To Ella, he was the same broken man from that morning.

'Get off me.' Robert pushed the policeman away and staggered forwards, pointing at Ella and shouting, 'You. You planned all this to ruin me. I'll stop you…'

He jumped off the platform and took another step towards her. Ella tried to move away but her way was blocked. Before Robert could get within touching distance, Ella sensed a movement behind her and then Jim had thrown himself in front of her and punched Robert full in the face. He breathed heavily as he waited for another attack. Robert staggered backwards, stunned by the blow and shaking his head, but before he could regain his balance, one police officer took advantage of his shock and handcuffed his wrists behind his back, before pulling him upright and frogmarching him out of the room.

Jim turned back to Ella. 'Are you all right?'

His knuckles were red and bleeding and she took his hand. 'Yes, but you're hurt.'

'It's nothing. I'd been waiting for a chance to do that ever since we got here.' He grinned sheepishly. 'After everything that happened to you this morning, he deserved it.'

Feeling light-headed with relief, Ella had to sit down, and, as if in a dream, she watched the journalists leave. A group of them clustered around Angela Thomas, copying down what she was saying.

On the platform, Susan Munro had a restraining hand on Sam's shoulder and turned to take control of the room.

'That's all there is to see, ladies and gentlemen. The press conference is over. Would you please leave and let the police do their job.'

Ella watched Susan Munro hand Sam over to the police officers, and then walk across to her.

'You came in time,' said Ella.

Susan gave a satisfied smile. 'Gregor's friends were rather insistent, but you seem to have held them back quite effectively.'

'Did Gregor's friends tell you about the barn? The men who held me prisoner were in there.'

'Yes, a team from the Fife police answered a call.' Susan turned to Jim. 'I want to listen to the rest of the recording you have.'

'Sure thing. It's at the back there,' said Jim.

Susan glanced at Angela Thomas, still surrounded by other journalists, and waved over one of the hotel staff who had come in to tidy up the room. 'Could you take Ella up to room 452?'

She turned to Ella. 'Your friend Laura is waiting to speak to you,' said Susan. 'I'll see you again when you've spoken with her. We need to get formal statements from you today.'

Chapter 34

Ella knocked on the door of the room. The door opened and Laura pulled her over the threshold and into a fierce hug.

'I told you not to go back there,' said Laura. 'Susan said you could have died.' She leaned back and studied Ella. 'Are you all right now? What happened in the press conference? Have they confessed?' She bombarded Ella with questions. 'Susan said we had to stay here until they were arrested. She didn't want to give Sam or Robert any warning of what might happen.'

'You were right, I shouldn't have gone back to Fife. It was all a trick.' Ella gripped Laura's arm and held her gaze. 'Martin Fraser's dead. The message you got didn't come from him; it came from Robert. It was just as well we split up and you went to the police. At least one of us was safe.' She looked past her friend. 'You said we. Who's with you?'

Laura pulled her across the room and Ella saw Mitch get up from a chair at a small table in the corner.

'Mitch, you're all right!' cried Ella, running towards him. He lifted her off the ground and hugged her tightly, before putting her back down again. They all sat down round the table and Mitch sat on a small sofa, Laura at his side.

'We thought you were dead,' said Ella, shaking her head. She looked at their tired smiles and saw that a huge weight had been lifted from their shoulders. She realised that she hadn't seen them like this since she'd come up to Scotland and only now appreciated the strain they'd been under.

Laura held onto Mitch's hand and stared at him.

'The police issued the statement that they'd found a body to protect me,' said Mitch. 'They knew that Robert Young's men would come after me if he thought I'd escaped that night from the farmhouse.'

'And how did you escape?' asked Ella. 'I thought they'd got you that night. Then when I went back and saw the damage caused by the fire in the steading, I felt even worse about leaving you all alone.' Her voice broke and she glanced at Laura, who was still holding Mitch's hand. Laura's eyes were brimming with tears, reliving their awful fear. 'When we heard the news on the TV that they'd found a body… we thought they'd got you.'

'I escaped just in time,' replied Mitch. 'When you left that night, I had to run away. When I heard the car, I knew it was them. There's another way out of the other side of the house, so I just ran. There was nothing else I could do; I had no options left. I know someone who lives just up the valley and went straight to them. I knew this man was in the police, so I went to him for help, trusting that he would know what to do. I was lucky because the Edinburgh police had already briefed a colleague in Fife that the investigation into Muir Pharma was being reactivated. He took me immediately to Edinburgh so that I could tell Susan Munro everything. When Laura came to the police station with my evidence, I could back up the whole story.'

'I haven't forgiven you yet for letting us believe we'd lost you,' said Laura, putting her head on Mitch's shoulder.

He shrugged. 'At that stage I didn't have much choice. I am sorry though. It must have been awful for you.'

Ella looked at her friends. 'What are you going to do now?' she asked. Their smiles gave away the answer even before they spoke.

Laura and Mitch exchanged a look. 'We're going travelling. There are lots of places we want to go,' said Laura. 'We're both going to resign and get away from here. Not that there'll be much of a company to resign from anymore.'

Ella hesitated, still getting used to the truth of what had happened, and then said, 'I do need to thank you. I would never have got justice for Ruth if it hadn't been for you. She'd been suspicious of them and of Muir Pharma anyway. I found a note she'd left behind that mentioned the company.' Ella felt herself flush as she looked at Laura. 'That's why I invited myself up, and then of course I started finding out about Mitch's suspicions.'

'The combination of what I'd found out in the company about suppressing early lab results plus the letters Carl had about serious side effects of Evexitrol were very damning,' agreed Mitch. 'Then I started to realise John and Trevor were involved and suddenly it wasn't just my job at risk.'

'But they tried to deny everything. Without Ella putting herself in danger, they might have left today and never been brought to justice,' added Laura.

'I'm afraid it's worse than you know.' Ella sighed deeply. 'Robert admitted it today, he arranged for Ruth's death in London.' Ella felt the tears prick her eyes and she could barely continue, swallowing down the lump in her throat. She went on in a shaky voice, hardly able to look at Laura and Mitch's shocked expressions. 'Ben didn't kill her, but the effect of Evexitrol on him made him believe he had. Robert was so confident today that he would get away with murder, he made the mistake of boasting about it. He thought I would never be able to tell anybody.'

Laura pushed a handkerchief into her hand. 'I'm so sorry, Ella,' she said, her own eyes bright with tears.

Ella felt a huge wave of relief as she clutched the handkerchief. She looked back at her friends. 'It's all right now. I feel that, between us, we've got justice for Ruth. I'll never stop missing her, but at least I now know what really happened and there was nothing I could have done to prevent it. I always felt guilty that I couldn't persuade Ruth that Ben could be dangerous, but the real danger wasn't him at all.'

Laura was looking at her thoughtfully. 'I could see that Sam and Robert were getting more careless,' she said. 'Robert in particular was desperate to attract more money into the business from new investors. Everything took second place to that. He and Sam had always done everything together but this time Sam wasn't confident enough that they could win. They'd always been stronger as a pair but, once the split started to happen, they just wanted to take the money and get out.' She shook her head. 'It all seems so clear now, but I wouldn't believe anything Mitch said about them at first. It all just seemed so outlandish. But what they've done is worse than either of us could ever have suspected.'

Ella stood up reluctantly. 'I need to give my statement to the police. Will I see you later?'

Laura and Mitch stood up and walked with her to the door. 'Yes,' said Laura. 'We're staying here tonight, then packing up the house tomorrow and going to stay with my parents for Christmas. We can pick up your stuff for you, if you like?'

'Yes please,' said Ella, hugging her friend. 'I couldn't bear to go back up there.'

Chapter 35

Ella went back into the conference room. It had been tidied and Daniel, the sound man, was packing up his briefcase at the back. Angela Thomas was speaking to Susan and was handing over a brown envelope to the police officer.

Ella heard a voice next to her. 'I'm off now,' said Daniel. 'Jim's with the police giving a statement. He said to tell you he'll come back and get you when they want you.'

'Thanks,' replied Ella.

He waved over at one of the desks at the back of the room. 'There's some fresh coffee over there. Do you want me to get you some?'

'Yes please,' she said gratefully, sitting down heavily on a chair, only now remembering how hungry she was. 'And… any chance of some biscuits?'

Daniel nodded and came back with a steaming mug and some brownies. As she wolfed down a couple, he smiled at her, 'Life certainly isn't dull with Jim around, jumping in and getting me to link up his recording to the system. He's always unpredictable, but this was a whole new level. He always assumes that I can deal with whatever he throws at me.'

Ella returned his smile. 'And you did. You made it work and I can't thank you enough. Believe me, it was worth it.'

'Certainly not boring,' he answered. 'You take care then.' He waved goodbye.

Ella sipped her coffee and ate another brownie. With the excitement now over, she was suddenly very tired but knew she'd have to give a statement to the police before being able to switch off. She saw that Susan had finished talking to Angela, for now, and had slipped outside. Angela came towards her.

'Do you want some coffee?' said Ella. 'It's fresh.'

Angela shook her head and sat down. She was older than she first appeared, a few grey hairs threaded through her blonde bob. She looked at Ella, who felt herself drowning in her gaze. Before Angela could speak, there was a shout from the door and Ella saw a few of the other journalists, the ones who had stood around her protectively.

'We're off to the pub,' said one of them loudly. 'Are you coming?'

'I'll follow you in a bit,' replied Angela.

'The usual?'

Angela nodded. They disappeared, letting the door swing shut.

'I'm glad you were there,' said Ella. 'I needed support and your journalist friends bought me some precious time. Made sure I wasn't thrown out before I could say what I'd come to say.'

'That's no problem,' replied Angela. 'I'd told them beforehand that I might start asking unwelcome questions and they were under strict orders to back me up. When you started to get the same treatment, they decided you must have been with me.' Her thin features broke into a wide smile. 'I think we got them, Ella. They won't be able to deny any longer what's been going on. All the people that have been forced to keep quiet, all the doctors they bribed to support them will be uncovered. I've given the police copies of all the letters that I've received.' She paused. 'I met Ruth a couple of times, you know. She was very determined – believed she should stand up for the rights of patients. I'm so sorry about what happened to her.'

Ella nodded. The grief was still there but it made a difference to know what her sister had fought for and what had really happened to her.

'I need to go now,' said Angela. 'I'm sure we'll meet another time.' She hugged Ella and left, bumping into Susan at the door. Susan closed the door carefully behind her before coming over, taking some coffee and sitting down opposite Ella.

'I'm sorry, but you need to give us a statement,' said Susan. 'My colleagues have spoken to Gregor and are just speaking to Jim now. I don't want to make you live through it all again but we do need to get all the information we can.'

'I know,' replied Ella. 'You're sure the police will investigate properly this time?'

'Yes, I'm sure. An internal enquiry has been started. Three officers have been suspended today pending an investigation into their activities. There had been suspicions before of police collusion, but Young's evidence on your recording has removed any doubt. We've also reopened the investigations into John Roper and Trevor Fisher's deaths. In the light of everything that's coming out, we need to check exactly what happened with both of the scientists.'

'Thank you.'

'I listened to the whole recording of Robert Young. I'd already spoken to the Metropolitan Police about Ben Forrester's case. They've now agreed to reopen it. I know it doesn't bring back your sister, but we need to make sure that we convicted the right man for her murder. There were some inconsistencies in the case which were already worrying them.' She grimaced. 'It might get Jamie Forrester to leave us alone for a while. He came up here to try to convince me that his brother was innocent.'

'That's why I saw him there,' said Ella, feeling guilty for not trusting her when she'd seen them together.

'He said he wanted to see you to convince you the police had got the wrong man. He came up to Edinburgh when he'd heard you'd come up here.'

'He *was* following me then,' burst out Ella. 'I could have sworn he was stalking me in London but no-one would believe me. I thought I was going mad. You're saying that he was stalking me to try to get me to forgive his brother?'

'That's what he said. He wanted you to work together to find the real killer. Turns out you didn't need his help.'

The door to the conference room opened and Jim came towards them. Without stopping to think, Ella stood up and walked into his arms.

'I'm all done. They want your statement now.'

Susan got up. 'Just take a bit of time. I'll go down and say you'll be there in ten minutes.'

Finally alone, Ella glanced up at Jim, his warm smile making her relax. 'You seem a lot calmer than I do,' she said.

His arms tightened around her. 'I might look calm, but I almost lost you. You were crazy to go back there.'

'But I knew you'd find me; you had the tracker.'

He rubbed his eyes. 'I wasn't sure it was going to work at first. I was terrified we'd be too late.'

'We'd better go down.'

As they walked arm in arm to the door, Jim stopped her before they went out. 'There is something else I have to say. I know we haven't met many times but I want to know you better. I'm serious about you – about us.'

Ella flushed. 'Jim, I don't know whether…'

He wasn't in the least put off by her confusion. 'It's all right. I know it's not the best time to talk about it. The words just came out.' He opened the door. 'Let's get this over with and then I'll take us out for supper. I think we deserve it.' He took her hand and they left together. It seemed a natural thing to do.

Chapter 36

It was the end of January before Ella went to see Ben. Even though he was no longer haunting her dreams and she had accepted that she couldn't blame him for Ruth's death, she was still nervous of meeting him. Jim had insisted on taking her to Ben's prison. He'd also told her that she didn't need to go at all – none of this was her fault. But she'd decided she had to see Ben. She felt like she owed him. They'd all been so wrong about him.

She walked behind the guard through the corridors towards the visiting area. She knew, logically, that Ben was better now, had been told that he was innocent and his conviction would be overturned, but she wondered if they would ever be free of the events that had destroyed all their lives.

The guard showed her into the room and she heard the door close behind her. Ben was sitting at one of the tables and he turned when she came across the room. Her heart was pounding. She was holding her breath, unable to look at him until he spoke.

'Thanks for coming,' he said as she sat down.

His voice was quieter than before, the impulse to dominate everyone around him no longer there. When he looked at her, his expression was clear and not controlling. She knew in that moment that his demons had gone.

'I wanted to see that you were all right,' he said. 'When I heard you were up in Scotland, I thought you were in danger.'

'I was,' replied Ella, 'but everything worked out in the end.'

'I wanted to say thank you properly for clearing my name. You'll know that the appeal is going through now. Sam Renwick's confession about what Robert Young had done to Ruth and the new evidence about Evexitrol meant we could file.'

'It wasn't only me,' said Ella. 'My friends had already suspected some of the truth and when the police picked the case up seriously, it was only a matter of time.' She thought briefly about Susan Munro and her determination to get justice for all the victims. This wasn't only their tragedy. Many more families had been affected by Robert Young than she had initially realised. She'd spoken to some of them and listened to their stories, each full of the same grief and pain. So like the experience that she and her parents had gone through.

'Are you better now?' asked Ella.

He nodded. 'The nightmares never leave me; I see again and again what happened to Ruth that night. I loved her, you know. I thought I'd killed her.' He looked at Ella bleakly. 'Can you forgive me for getting Ruth into such a dangerous situation? I still feel it's my fault.'

She felt her eyes fill with tears. Until that moment she hadn't known how she would reply. But now, looking at him, seeing the constant pain in his steady gaze, how could she make things even worse for him?

'Of course I forgive you,' she answered. 'I know you

weren't responsible for any of it, not just on that awful night when Ruth died, but for all the months before then. How you behaved wasn't really you.' She leaned forward. 'You have to believe that and try to move on. I know it's difficult, God knows it's been difficult for all of us, but Ruth wouldn't want you to suffer.'

'Thank you,' he said.

When she left Ben, she followed the guard outside. The heavy prison door clanged shut behind her. In the cold wind she took a deep breath and walked towards the busy South London road. Seeing Ben had finally laid to rest her fears and helped process what had really happened to her sister. She now felt that the events of the last few months were behind them.

Outside in the street, Jim saw her and got out of the car. She ran towards him. Her new life beckoned and she could grab it with both hands.

A Letter From Dianne

Thank you so much for reading *A Dose of Fear.*

If you enjoyed it, and want to keep up to date with all my latest releases, just sign up at the following link. Your email address will never be shared and you can unsubscribe at any point.

www.diannehaley.com/contact

I've been interested in the pharmaceutical sector for many years and have always thought it would provide a good background for a contemporary thriller. The more I researched about drug companies and their business the more I realised how risky it can be, making the stakes very high for the people involved if things go wrong. While this story is a work of fiction many of the pressures explored in this book are very plausible.

If you enjoyed this story, it would be great if you could leave a short review. I appreciate all feedback from readers. It also helps to persuade other readers to pick up one of my books for the first time.

Acknowledgements

Thanks to Katy Powell for her editing, ideas and moral support, helping to get the book out there and producing the cover design. Thanks also to Alice Main and Alan Main for their knowledge and expertise on drug companies and drug discoveries. Thanks to Martin for technical support and to Claire for social media help. I am also grateful to Alexander for his and Alice's comments and revisions to the text. Thanks to my writing buddies Jenny Harper and Jennifer Young for reading through my draft and to Jenny for her proofreading. Thanks to Eleanor Abraham for her copy editing and general advice. Any mistakes are my own.

Printed in Dunstable, United Kingdom

63396898R00163